Riftm

Tales of a cosmic traveller

Hope you enjoy!

Mile

Riftmaster

Tales of a cosmic traveller

Miles Nelson

Elsewhen Press

Riftmaster
First published in Great Britain by Elsewhen Press, 2021
An imprint of Alnpete Limited

Elsewhen Press, PO Box 757, Dartford, Kent DA2 7TQ
www.elsewhen.press
British Library Cataloguing in Publication Data.
A catalogue record for this book is available from the British Library.
ISBN 978-1-911409-81-6 Print edition
ISBN 978-1-911409-91-5 eBook edition

Printed and bound by CPI Group (UK) Ltd, Croydon, CR0 4YY

Contents

For those that need them, trigger warnings for this book can be found at http://milesnelsonofficial.com

To Chris, my husband, my love,
who has stood by me, loved me, and supported me
from the very beginning,
no matter who I chose to be.

Chapter 1
Stranded

It had happened so suddenly that Bailey could hardly believe it.

Not even an hour ago, the nineteen-year-old had been sitting together with his girlfriend in their favourite cafe, arguing over Bailey's (admittedly questionable) sense of formality.

Why did it matter whether he wore a black t-shirt rather than a nice polo? Sure, he'd had it for years and it was a little worn, but it was comfortable. And... sure, he'd worn this pair of ripped jeans yesterday as well. And maybe... just maybe, the jacket he was wearing was a little gaudy. But all they'd been doing was talking over a nice cup of coffee; it wasn't like they were going anywhere fancy afterwards.

The situation had escalated, and soon, Bailey had found himself storming out, alone.

He hadn't looked back; it was just another argument, after all. The sour taste would quickly fade. Soon one of them would cave and call, and it would all be water under the bridge... just like every other day.

But halfway home there had been a sound like thunder, a booming clash that left his ears ringing. A searing pain danced like fire across the surface of his skin and burned its way right to his core. A white light had filled his vision and after that he was falling through nothingness.

Bailey jerked back into lucidity as he collided with a deep

snowdrift. The fiery pain gave way to a feeling of pins and needles and for a moment he simply lay there, stunned and too afraid to move. But soon, the cold grew too much; with no other choice he staggered to his feet and saw nothing but a bleak snowy whiteness as far as the eye could see.

He was still half-convinced that it was some sort of terrible nightmare.

But the cold on his skin was real; so too the snowflakes that stung his eyes like razors, the gale tearing at the coat he hugged so tightly around him. His hair whipped at his face in the wind, dark brown eyes streaming with tears that soon froze to his skin. His coat was meant for a mild spring chill or autumn shower; there was no way in hell that it would keep him warm in this.

Suddenly, the argument didn't seem so important any more. Any sort of lingering pettiness squashed in the face of genuine fear. Where was he? How had he got here?

He had no choice but to keep trudging on; his feet soon growing numb, his trainers soaked through to the skin. His black hair was white with matted snow, his normally dark skin shimmering and pale with frost.

No breath he took felt like enough and the cold burned its way into his lungs every time he tried.

Bailey found himself slithering and sliding down a steep slope, at one point sinking waist-deep into a drift. He frantically searched the storm for something – anything – that might stand out. But all he could see was the bleak, hazy whiteness, and a faint red gleam of sunlight that just barely managed to break through the clouds.

He was draining fast. Hunched over, he stumbled on.

The numbness grew. At one point, the young man raised one quivering hand and found that it was turning grey. His eyelids kept sticking together, his lips cracking.

Bailey didn't know if he'd been here for minutes or hours. But with every step the trek became more difficult; whether it be from the weight of the drifts piling up upon his shoulders, or the snow that grew ever-deeper around him.

If he looked back even for a moment, he found with dismay that his track, a snaking gouge in a world of pristine whiteness, was already filling itself in.

And then, a shape. Bailey saw a shadow ahead of him,

falling on the snow. The blizzard was so thick that the source couldn't have been more than a stone's throw away. As Bailey struggled on he realised that there was something forcing its way through the gale. Bailey couldn't tell – his vision blurred – but he thought that the figure was heading towards him. His chest heaved, and he cried out in joy, but the sound was lost to the howling winds.

He waved his arms and felt the snowflakes striking hard and fast. The shadow grew larger; the young man could make out slow bobbing motions as whoever it was moved uphill towards him.

The figure wore some sort of heavy cloak that mostly obscured their shape – they flickered in and out of view, so well-camouflaged against the blizzard that they may well have been a mirage.

Bailey struck out towards the shape. His vision blurred from squinting, the vaguest outline of the stranger was all he could see. The glorious moment that he saw a chance of salvation was almost enough to help him forget the cold.

…Almost.

He was nearly there. Knee-deep in snow, he waded towards the figure. He hardly noticed the darkness creeping in at the edges of his vision. The stranger's shape grew blurred. His legs felt heavy as lead. Weighed down by clothes frozen solid and hardly able to feel below the knees, he stumbled, one last time, and found himself sinking to his knees.

He couldn't get back up.

Dazed, he dropped his chin onto his chest, and panted, drawing hoarse and rattling breaths.

The last thing he knew, the stranger's shadow had fallen over him, and a heavy cloak draped across his shoulders.

• • •

When he next awoke, Bailey's first thought was of the language essay that was due this morning. The young man jerked upright, and almost immediately felt his forehead strike an icy ceiling. Reeling with confusion, he clutched at the bump, grunting as he sank back down. His next thought was that everything – especially his fingers and toes – were *burning*. He quickly remembered the icy trek through the forsaken wilderness, the sheer despair and hopelessness.

His eyes flitted open and the first thing he saw, apart from a kaleidoscope of colours spinning in his vision, was a ceiling of slick, transparent ice. It was so crystalline clear that the young man could see the wooden foundations of the structure buried between him and the piled snow outside – thin, slightly curved branches bound in place presumably by straps of leather. His breath pooled in steamy clouds around his head. Slowly, and more carefully this time, he sat up.

Eyes watering, he gave the bump on his head one last rub, and peered around. The ceiling heightened towards the middle of the room – it looked almost enough for him to stand straight.

Still struggling to comprehend what was going on – where he was and why – Bailey slipped his phone from the still-damp pocket of his jeans and held it up. He tapped its screen and held down the *on* button, but it failed to light up. A rainbowy film of water gleamed between the screen and protector. Bailey felt a shudder of panic sweep over him. Without it, there was no way he'd be able to contact his girlfriend or college… or even find out where he was.

After the initial shock had passed, Bailey felt isolation set in. He was cut off from everyone he knew, in a strange place, after an even stranger turn of events.

Hand trembling slightly, he returned the dead phone to his pocket and looked around.

The surrounding room was relatively plain and yet, still quite unlike anything he'd ever seen. The icy ground was carpeted by a single, massive animal hide with bristly, wiry hairs almost as thick as blades of grass. It was a strange, pale pink… so close to being white, and yet somehow, slightly off. In the centre of the room was a small stone plinth, and as he studied it further, he realised that the very top was hollowed out. Within the shallow indentation, a few oddly-shaped flowers and leaves were burning with a pale purple flame. And Bailey saw similar leaves, plants and flowers packed into holes in the icy walls. Beside the fire was a pile of several objects, around the size of a closed fist. At first glance, he thought of ice cream cones, but the more he looked at them, the more they reminded him of sharp, pointed teeth.

Opposite the bed was a small archway – sealed perhaps, or simply snowed in, he couldn't tell. Even when he was seated, it only came level with his shoulders.

Although his lungs still ached, Bailey found breathing easier in here. He'd just begun to stand up when he realised he was still wearing the cloak, wrapped tightly around him. It too was covered in wiry hairs on the outside, if a slightly darker colour. It was heavy, trying to pull him back as he stood. It would take some getting used to. Clearly, it had come from a beast well-suited to the cold.

As he moved, he noticed a glint of light beneath his eyeline and realised that his hide covering was tied in place at his collarbone by a leather band. The band didn't look as though it were part of the cloak's original design; more like it used to be some sort of necklace, and had been added on later. Hanging from the band of leather was a silver pendant, inset with a glistening blue jewel. The knot holding it in place was messy, and looked hastily done, but secure.

After lifting the jewel in his hand and admiring it, Bailey let it drop back down onto his chest and ran a hand across the cloak itself. He found the feeling bristly and unpleasant. Similarly, as he put his feet down on the carpet, it prickled, but despite his bare feet it was slightly warm to the touch. The bed was, as he ran a hand across it, similar but softer, and almost pure white.

Where was he?

Bailey found himself drawn towards the fire. The smell up close was almost intoxicating; heady, and smoky, and yet oddly rich with a distinct aroma of freshly-cut wood. After warming his hands above it, he stooped to pick up one of the strange, tooth-like objects. On closer examination, it had a ridged, spiralling texture. It was rough, like sandpaper.

As Bailey examined the unusual object, he heard a muffled thud coming from the archway opposite. The snowy seal on the door crumbled and Bailey's eyes widened with confusion and a sharp stab of fear. Hastily he dropped the strange cone and scrambled back towards the bed, as if it could somehow protect him. A stranger entered the room, shaking off snow and icicles from a bushy and lion-like mane.

Bailey stared, taking in the sight with a mixture of disbelief and horror, though the majority of his attention was drawn to the spear that it carried.

The stranger – well… the creature… was short and squat. It was covered head-to-toe in thick, wiry fur that was pale pink, with white dapples. It had two large eyes, and two small ones perched upon the brows, half-hidden beneath a trailing forelock. It moved on two legs and with a strange, surefooted grace as it turned its back on the human and rested the spear it was carrying against the entranceway. Hands freed, it began to block up the exit once again, revealing a small rabbit-like tail which wiggled as it worked. Strange, plump, almost hoof-like hands moved with surprising dexterity and grace – clearly, they didn't feel the cold at all. And between two tiny, pointed ears were perched two short, squat horns, ridged, and rough-looking, and…

Finally it turned towards its guest, and Bailey was unsure of the expression that crossed its goat-like face, but he tensed nonetheless. Its nose wrinkled.

Although Bailey knew that he was staring, he couldn't stop. What *was* this thing?

Whatever it was, it began to make a sound; a series of sounds. It took a moment, but Bailey realised that it was trying to say something. He strained to listen.

"Yuman!" it barked excitedly, the suddenness causing Bailey to flinch back sharply. Clearly its voice was not meant to produce such sounds. "You woke!"

The words came with a startling realisation. Bailey released his breath in a sharp gasp. Grasping at all the familiarity he could, Bailey clung to the one thing in this place he knew for certain. Despite the fear, despite the strangeness of it all and the uncertainty, Bailey felt inches away from crying with relief.

"You speak… English…?"

There was a long pause, the… alien's…? ears twitching as it processed the question. Clearly, English wasn't a language it spoke often. And then…

"Yus," a frantic nod.

Bailey let out another breath, still struggling to understand. Who was this? What was it? Where had it come from? And… was he even still on Earth? He opened his mouth, about to ask, but then reconsidered, abruptly fearing the answer.

"Was it you that brought me here?"

Another pause. Then the creature shook its head.

"Riftmaster brought you. Good friend."

The short creature waddled away from the archway and further into its home, inadvertently bringing itself a little closer to Bailey, who watched it warily. It briefly checked that the fire was burning strong, and then set about removing herbs from several of the little nooks in the walls. As it worked, it spoke.

"I am only of my people that speak your tongue. Very different from ours."

Bailey slowly felt himself relaxing, his mind reeling. As strange as the creature's appearance was, it didn't *seem* hostile. In fact, it seemed to be doing its utmost to help him. But *why*?

Suspicion prickled up and down his spine.

"Your... people?" he ventured. And then another thought. "And... What's a Riftmaster? Why did he save me?"

Perhaps that was a good start. Figure out what he was dealing with. Make friendly conversation, and lead into the biggest questions when he was sure it wasn't a mistake.

"One at a time. We are mountain-dwellers, in your tongue. In ours–" the mountain-dweller let out a low and droning rumble. Any kind of variation or intonation it might be making was lost to human ears. "Riftmaster is a traveller of worlds. It has been living with us. Shares in our knowledge and teaches us. We do not know why it does the things it does; Riftmaster could easily have died in that storm. But it went out to find you anyway."

The alien's answer left him only with more questions.

Bailey sighed, lowering his gaze only to look up as the strange creature spoke again.

"You will meet it soon. Ask yourself."

"What about you? Do you... have a name?"

Another pause to process this. The mountain-dweller had pulled out some kind of container that looked like it was roughly hewn from stone. As Bailey watched he – for the young man had decided that *he* was better than *it* – scooped up some snow from the entrance, and mixed in with the herbs. Then it was placed on the fire pit.

"Seven-horn Speaker."

Bailey found himself checking over the mountain-dweller's head for any more horns – until he realised that they were lying at the base of the fire pit. But no – there were only four there. He looked at the spear that the alien had rested by the door – and realised that the spearhead was just a sharpened horn. Now that he looked closer, he realised that there were others, too – fragments of ivory pinned the carpet to the icy ground beneath.

"So as you shed your horns, you change your name."

"Yus. Experience changes us. The home mountain is cruel. Living to have horns at all is rare – so we are proud of them, even after falling."

As Seven-horn spoke, Bailey realised that he was growing to understand the creature more easily. His low, gruff voice, interspersed with chesty rumbles and growls, was otherworldly – but Bailey had no idea how he had come to be able to speak to him at all.

"How did you learn my language?" Bailey asked cautiously, fearing the answer.

"Riftmaster knows many tongues. Taught me this, I taught it mine."

A warm, herbal scent had joined the woody aroma as the snow melted and the water warmed. It reminded him faintly of spicy vanilla and lemon. It was only then that he realised just how hungry he was getting – his stomach let out a growl that jerked Seven-horn's head towards him.

After a moment of scrutiny, the mountain-dweller returned to his task.

Bailey watched, the quiet growing into an uncomfortable awkwardness. For a moment his gaze flicked to the mountain-dweller's tail wiggling with concentration, the next he was watching the expressions across his four-eyed face. Struggling to think of something to say that would break the tension, Bailey sucked in his breath and finally, warily, nudged the elephant in the room. "Do you know how I got here? Am I even still... on Earth?"

"Rift brought you here. And... no. Our world has no name, but your kind do not live here."

"The Rift? What's that?"

"All I know is what Riftmaster told me. Rift takes things from one world and puts them in another. At random."

"How do I get back?"

The bowl over the flame had begun to steam. Seven-horn transferred some to another bowl, this one slightly less charred. He offered it to Bailey.

"You don't."

Bailey's stomach lurched. Suddenly, he didn't feel so hungry anymore. His hands began to shake, threatening to drop the bowl. The smell was enticing and rich, but the herbs within had dissolved into a thick black mush. He eyed it, disappointedly, and suspiciously.

Surely it couldn't be true. There *must* be a way to get back. There *had* to be.

His vision blurred a little at its edges. If his last words to his girlfriend – his last words on Earth – were "*I'll show you goddamn formal*," he didn't think he'd ever be able to live it down. And his parents; he hadn't seen them in months. The last they'd heard of him was a half-arsed text of '*Merry Christmas!*' that he'd written hungover on Christmas morning and hadn't sent until the evening. All they would know was that he went to university up North, and never came home.

All the little things he'd done... or hadn't done... all came rushing in.

His grip on the bowl loosened – but a rumbling voice brought him back to the present.

"Drink. Makes the cold a little easier to bear."

Unperturbed by the still-scorching heat of his own bowl, the mountain-dweller began to drink, gulping down the mysterious fluid as though he'd never seen food before.

Slightly encouraged by the eagerness of his strange caretaker along with a fear of what might happen if he refused, Bailey blew on the strange goop, making a show of preparing to eat. There was no way he could eat it like this, fresh off the fire. He tried not to think about the thoroughly unappetising appearance of the stuff.

After all, what did he have to lose?

Finally, Bailey raised the bowl to his mouth and began to drink. It burned his tongue until his eyes watered but, surprisingly, it wasn't bad. It was slightly sweet, and slightly bitter, with a warming flare of spiciness. And the more he drank, the more intense the fire became. With the last few gulps, he found himself sniffling, the heat lingering, and the inside of his mouth stinging. It was thick, too; he felt it lying in his belly like a ton of rocks.

Seven-horn looked on, and although his expression was hard to read, Bailey thought that he was pleased. Unsure of what else to do, he held out the bowl.

The creature took it back, and placed the two bowls by the fire.

"The storm is almost over. When the snow has stopped, we go to the Mountain's Heart – the village. If there is any way for you to get back to your home–"

"–Riftmaster will know."

"Yes."

Chapter 2
The Mountain's Heart

It was another hour at least before the odd duo finally left the safety of Seven-horn's hollow – not that Bailey had a concrete way of telling the time.

The reason for the delay was simple: neither of them were convinced that Bailey's still-soaked trainers would be able to keep him warm. So, after cutting away a small section of hide from his own carpet, the mountain-dweller soon fashioned a makeshift pair of snow boots, secured with fragments of ivory and threaded with wiry, yet sturdy, grasses that were packed into one section of the wall.

Bailey had to hand it to Seven-horn; the squat little creature was resourceful, and his plump, pad-like hands were surprisingly dextrous.

Just as they were leaving, Seven-horn held something out to him. Turning it over in his hands, Bailey realised that it was a mask.

It was bone-coloured, resembling a stylised representation of a mountain-dweller's face, with a hide shroud to cover his head and shoulders. The hollow inside of its muzzle was stuffed with the same fragrant herbs that had been burning in the fire.

As though he caught wind of Bailey's faint confusion, Seven-horn explained briskly as he dug into the snowy seal separating them from the outside world.

"Helps with the attitude."

Bailey's jaw dropped just a little bit, as he stared in hurt confusion. But then, as he thought about it more, he perked up.

"Oh... do you mean the altitude?"

Seven-horn's small ears twitched.

"That too," he answered as the snowy barrier crumbled, leaving Bailey to ponder if the Riftmaster had also taught the mountain-dwellers about sarcasm.

· · ·

Soon, the pair were leaving the hollow behind them, with Seven-horn trotting ahead, and Bailey threading his way after through the trail the small creature left behind. They picked their way higher up the mountain stretching above them – its slopes so steep that Bailey couldn't even see the summit.

Even so, it was a struggle – the snow was deep enough to reach his knees, and at times, he found himself sinking to his waist. In times like these, he had to simply soldier on, and rarely kept up with his escort.

Despite the mountain-dweller's small size, Seven-horn didn't appear to be hindered by the thick snow – quite the contrary, in fact. Its wide, padded feet meant that it barely sank into the drifts at all, and its plump body and thick mane kept it warm.

Upon looking back, Bailey realised that the humble dwelling they'd left behind was almost completely invisible; burrowed into the snow and with its entrance sealed, it had the appearance of a simple snow pile. As they walked, Bailey glanced around, wondering if every little lump they passed hid a secret beneath... And how the mountain-dwellers themselves found their way.

With the blizzard long gone, Bailey could finally see the world around them – and he stared in wonder as he walked. The view was almost enough to take his mind off his current situation, the spectacular sight bringing with it a note of smugness. This, after all, was something no human had ever seen before, and probably never would.

It was just a shame that no-one would ever believe him when he got home.

...Well...

If he got home. But Bailey was trying his hardest not to think about that. Instead, he tried to focus on the view.

Even though it was midday, the sky was a pale pink, as though locked in a perpetual sunset. The light from a rusty-red sun tinted the snow rosy, rendering Seven-horn almost invisible up ahead of him. The mountain-dweller was easiest to spot whenever he turned back to wait; when his large, black eyes revealed themselves for just a moment.

There was a small moon in the sky, hanging like a pale bauble next to the sun. And as Bailey scanned the horizon he caught a glimpse of another – a massive one – just barely clearing the jagged peaks of distant mountains. Shrouded in fog and low-hanging clouds, this massive moon was visible only for a moment before clouds once again swept it from view.

A thick mist pooled ominously in the valley far below the mountain slopes.

Bailey paused in wonder, committing the view to his memory, before hurrying to catch up. Before he turned away, he risked one last glance down at the valley beneath, not liking the sight of the fog swirling in its depths. Was there anything down there?

Plants? Warmth? Oxygen?

Anything… *alive*?

"What's in the valley?" Bailey called to Seven-horn between gasping breaths as he struggled to catch up. His voice was muffled by the mask.

Seven-horn turned back towards him once again. He paused mid-stride to wait for Bailey to reach him.

"Danger," the mountain-dweller answered simply. "Our healers gather herbs there. Few survive."

Bailey looked back down the mountain, trying for a moment to peer into the mist and catch even the slightest glimpse of the mysterious world below.

"Come," Seven-horn's voice broke through his thoughts. "The mountain is cruel, but safe."

Bailey had no other choice but to follow.

For some time they pressed on in silence.

With the cold kept largely at bay and his imagination given the chance to roam, Bailey found his anticipation growing.

Other than the vague memory of the shape that had

materialised in the blizzard, Bailey had no idea what to expect of the mysterious Riftmaster; but his imagination painted wild pictures of decorated alien monsters and intergalactic kings… world-eating aliens and interstellar gods. With a name like Riftmaster, really, what else could it be?

As they climbed higher, anticipation bloomed into nervous excitement.

Bailey also clung to the faint hope that this mysterious being would be able to help him get home to Earth. He'd been there before, after all; how else would he know English? Surely Seven-horn was wrong; there had to be a way. The mountain-dweller wasn't, after all, a Rift*master*.

They climbed on, as the terrain finally began to even out.

At last, they reached the mountain's peak, and the two beings perched together on a narrow and precarious ridge. The path dropped away before them and the ridge formed a perfect circle around a wide, bowl-shaped valley. With a sharp gasp, Bailey realised where the village took shelter. The mountain-dwellers' village was built in the caldera of an ancient volcano, its crater long filled with snow.

But as Bailey searched, he saw no houses or even telltale bumps in the snow. So… where was the village?

He didn't have time to ponder it further as Seven-horn began to descend into the crater, with Bailey quickly slithering after.

When they had almost reached what Bailey perceived to be the bottom, the mountain-dweller began to dig, as he had when breaking through the snowy barrier to his home. The snow crumbled away to reveal the entrance to an icy corridor – shimmering coldly in the light streaming in from outside.

Seven-horn motioned for him to enter.

The mountain-dweller soon followed, rebuilding the snow seal as he went.

The young man ducked, and squeezed inside the hole that was clearly meant for a much smaller race. He walked, stooped, into the corridor. It reminded him strongly of Seven-horn's home in here: the walls built of clear ice, and supported with what looked to be wooden struts. It was dark – but enough sunlight shone through the snow that he could see easily when his eyes adjusted. The ground was blanketed in yet more wiry pink hide.

"Take off your face," Seven-horn said before pressing on.

Bailey felt a thrill of horrified shock before realising that the mountain-dweller meant the mask. He obeyed, but couldn't help glancing around warily. Wonder had given way to a distinct paranoia, as though reality had set in. He was on a strange planet, with a strange race of aliens, and he was completely and utterly at their mercy.

He tucked the mask under his arm, and together they descended deeper into the caldera.

Bailey had to hunch over to walk, and he didn't like how enclosed this corridor felt, nor how dark. He knew that if something happened here, there was no way he could escape. This crypt-like structure could very easily become his tomb if the mountain-dwellers so wished it.

After some time, Bailey began to hear a chorus of deep, rumbling humming sounds somewhere ahead of him.

It took a while for him to realise that it was the sound of mountain-dweller voices.

Even when the tunnel opened out, the claustrophobia never really left. The wooden struts became one massive structure that towered over him – and as he saw the shape, something finally clicked. The village centre of the mountain dwellers, he realised, was built inside the ribcage of some massive, long-dead beast. Presumably the one whose skin he now wore, and whose hide also carpeted the ground. And that wasn't all. He now knew the other tunnels – and even Seven-horn's own home – were all built around strange, brownish bone.

The thought was enough to make him feel even more nervous, and slightly sick.

In the very centre of the wide room was a bowl on a pedestal, crackling with that same purple flame; the city hall smelled just as strong as Seven-horn's home had. It was well-lit, the ice dancing with that eerie light.

In between some of the bones, other tunnels led off to all corners of the crater.

It was here that he finally caught a glimpse of the other mountain-dwellers.

He was staring slack-jawed at the icy walls and the fire when he felt something nudge past him. He looked down to see a small, hornless mountain-dweller hurrying away into the tunnel he'd just left, its arms overflowing with herbs of all colours and kinds.

As he had entered the room, he had ignored them in favour of the architecture and feeding his own paranoia, but now he realised that they were all around him. They simply went about their lives just beneath his eye level, blending into the rose-coloured hide at their feet.

Now that he knew they were there, though, they were suddenly difficult to ignore.

The village centre was bustling with squat bodies and low, rumbling voices. Whilst there was a range in their heights and builds, none of them stood taller than his chest. Bailey caught a few of the creatures casting long, presumably concerned looks in his direction, before turning to exchange words with a friend who kept staring. A few of them scattered from his path carrying shed horns or bundles of herbs.

But most didn't seem to care about the giant that had stepped into their midst.

At first glance, all of the mountain-dwellers looked the same to him. But as he looked closer and struggled to pick Seven-horn out from the crowds, he began to realise that all of them had subtle differences. A peachy fur tone here, a different pattern of white spots there. Some of them had very few spots, and some had very little pink. Some were wearing necklaces made of their own horns, or had woven their manes into plaits. Some had large, curved horns; others had none at all.

Seven-horn was, in comparison to many of his brethren, quite plain.

The mountain-dweller led him through the centre of the room, past the fire.

When Bailey finally caught up to him, he had stopped to talk to another of his kind. This one was a darker colour, with peachy fur that was quite spotless save for a patch across one eye and a faint white dappling across its belly. It wore a necklace consisting of one shed horn and a couple of rich red stones.

When Bailey approached them, both turned to look his way.

The stranger let out a low grunt as she (for Bailey had decided that this one looked more like a she) looked the strange human up and down, before wrinkling her nose.

Bailey glanced at Seven-horn, hoping for an explanation.

"Four-horn Keeper," Seven-horn said. "It will take us to the Riftmaster."

It...? What are these things, really?

Four-horn Keeper slightly inclined her head. She turned, and trotted away. Bailey watched it – her – and Seven-horn made to follow.

I suppose not everything out here has to work the way humans do.

After a moment's hesitation, Bailey trudged after them. They entered another side-tunnel, forcing the human to stoop low once again with an internal sigh.

Several of the mountain-dwellers in the city centre watched them go, before quickly returning to what they had been doing.

It seemed that on the mountain, life couldn't stop even for a moment.

The tunnel they walked now sloped downward and it looked, to Bailey, exactly the same as the one they'd walked earlier. The ice, though, soon gave way to stone – and they walked a path into the mountain itself. This tunnel seemed natural; like it had been carved by magma flows thousands of years earlier, but a thousand years of beings passing through had worn it completely smooth.

It was only a short tunnel leading out of the crater and back onto the slopes; Bailey was surprised to see that this one hadn't been sealed. The slope was a lot gentler on this side, as well. The two mountain-dwellers talked in low bleating murmurs as they walked, only occasionally turning back to check on his progress.

The young man pulled the mask on over his head, and left the tunnel.

Bailey wondered just how many other secret tunnels led into the belly of the mountain, and was fairly certain that Seven-horn had chosen to lead him up the hardest path into the village for a reason. Thinking about it more, Bailey considered the possibility that they were simply being cautious; he was, after all, a towering stranger who'd stumbled into their midst. Whoever the Riftmaster was had asked Seven-horn to save him, but they still didn't know him well enough to lower their guard.

He realised that calling the mountain-dwellers 'aliens' was very, very wrong. In this world, *he* was the alien.

Did they see him as an invader? It was with a heavy heart that Bailey followed the mountain-dwellers along a narrow ridge and then, finally, onto a gently-sloped plateau.

The young man could see shapes moving in the snow long before they reached their destination – but the closer they got, the further away he realised they were. There were... what could only be described as insectoid *beasts* grazing so peacefully here, and, whilst not massive, they were too big for Bailey to feel comfortable. They towered over mountain-dweller and human alike, the smallest adults the size of cars, with some noticeably larger. Even the smallest, the larvae that huddled so close to the adults were the size of large dogs; their fur paler and gait just a little quicker as they lumbered around.

The creatures didn't appear to be hostile... more like cattle than anything else, but Bailey still tried to keep his distance. They didn't appear to have eyes, or even faces, really. They were almost worm-like, bodies wrinkling as they stamped slowly forward on six stocky legs with thick tails leaving deep furrows in the snow. With trunk-like tendrils that emerged from hairy, heavily whiskered 'faces', they felt their way through the drifts, and occasionally pulled a minivan's worth of snow towards them – presumably guiding it to some sort of grotesque, hidden mouth.

They were covered in pale pink fur, and with a shudder Bailey was hit with the realisation that he was wearing a piece of one of them. Hoping they wouldn't notice, he hurried on to where Four-horn and Seven-horn watched his horror, presumably with amusement.

It was then that Bailey realised they were walking into the centre of the loosely scattered herd. He hung back, glancing at his companions – but they pressed on. Heart hammering, he followed.

As they got closer, he picked out a tiny figure moving between the largest of the beasts, clearly tending them.

At first, whoever it was didn't seem to notice their approach. But as they drew nearer, the figure started walking towards them. Bailey felt a rush of familiarity – he knew immediately that it was the Riftmaster, the one he'd seen so briefly in the storm. Without the snow falling, it was far easier to pick out the shape.

For being a traveller of worlds, Bailey's first impression was that the Riftmaster looked... remarkably *ordinary.* Whoever it was had two legs, two arms, and one head. Everything was in the right place and proportioned, well... human.

Bailey's stomach dropped with nerves and he halted, more than happy to let the Riftmaster come to him. The Riftmaster was dressed as he was – a pink hide cloak and similar boots, and a mask that obscured his face. A hide shroud covered in wiry pink hair fell from the mask down to his shoulders. Bailey could see little of the clothes beneath the except for a hint of faded purple cloth. As he approached, Bailey thought that the Riftmaster was smaller than he remembered – in fact, he was shorter than Bailey himself.

The stranger briefly stopped to speak to the mountain-dwellers. Bailey strained to listen, but all three spoke in the mountain-dwellers' tongue.

Finally the stranger looked back towards Bailey.

The Riftmaster covered the last few metres between them and stood opposite Bailey. Although the other's face was hidden in its entirety, Bailey knew in an instant that he was being judged, and he looked over the Riftmaster in turn.

Bailey watched in bewilderment as finally, after a momentary pause, the Riftmaster crossed slender hands over its chest, before dipping towards him in a shallow bow. Bailey caught a glimpse of a human hand as one palm was outstretched towards him.

Bailey could think of nothing else to do but stare; the gesture felt strange and almost ritualistic, but it must have been some sort of a greeting.

Before he even had the chance to figure out a suitable etiquette, the Riftmaster was removing the mask from his face. Bailey hesitated, and then did the same.

Chapter 3
The Riftmaster

Bailey was underwhelmed.

If there was anything that he'd been expecting of the mysterious and esteemed Riftmaster, it was definitely not this. And it was with a gut-clenching feeling of guilt the student felt all of his hopes and dreams melt. He tried his best to keep the look on his face neutral, but he knew immediately that his expression collapsed.

For standing opposite him, mask held in dainty hands, was a man.

A short, slender, and relatively shabby-looking young man. The Riftmaster's hair was a mess – wavy and red, it was cropped unevenly to the length of his chin with shorter locks falling into his face, and strays sticking out at every angle. His beaming cheeks were freckled, his eyes a stormy grey. His face was round, his nose pointy, and around his slender neck he wore several leather bands. These bands were decorated with various trinkets – Bailey could see teeth, scales, fragments of bone, and jewelled pendants among them. He looked to be in his mid or early twenties – making the Riftmaster only a few years Bailey's superior.

He didn't even have a beard to lend him a look of unruly wisdom; he was fresh-faced and youthful – effeminate, even – as he smiled Bailey's way.

A rosy grey cloud began to inch past the sun, a vast shadow gradually sweeping up the mountain slopes.

Vaguely, Bailey was aware of the mountain-dwellers leaving with a few rumbled goodbyes. Riftmaster nodded a farewell their way, and Bailey quickly copied him.

Then the two humans were suddenly left alone on the barren mountainside, surrounded by massive beasts that moved with the sounds of crunching snow.

After a silence that felt like minutes but was in actuality only a few fleeting seconds, Bailey extended his hand.

After a moment of hesitation, Riftmaster swept both hands forward to shake Bailey's. It was a dramatic motion for such a small action, and a moment later Bailey found his hand sandwiched in between two. The handshake that followed was vigorously enthusiastic, and followed by a hearty clap on the shoulder.

After a moment, Bailey let go and stepped back; the stranger's enthusiasm clashed with his own mixed emotions. The Riftmaster remained where he was, expression faltering.

"You're the... ah... Riftmaster, right?" Bailey broke the uncomfortable silence.

The Riftmaster nodded, the man's smile widening. Or at least... Bailey *thought* he was a man. When he spoke, his voice was light and high-pitched, yet slightly gravelly.

It was hard to distinguish as being either exclusively male or female.

"That's right! It seems my reputation precedes me," after puffing himself up a little proudly, the Riftmaster let out a breath, noticeably relieved that Bailey had been the one to speak first. His gaze flitted away for a moment before he clasped his hands over his chest and swiftly moved on. "Goodness... You have no idea how pleased I am to see you're okay! That blizzard almost had you."

Bailey chuckled, a trifle awkwardly. "You could say that."

"...I expected it to have cost you a few toes, at least. But here you are! Still in one piece, right? No frostbite?"

"Yeah, still in one piece."

"Good, good! Fantastic! You have no idea how long it's been. I never expected to ever meet another human, let alone one so fighting fit! Look at you! Seven-horn treated you well, I hope? Do you have a name, young Rifthopper?"

Bailey feared that if he didn't interrupt, he'd never get a word in edgeways.

"Y-yeah. He – uh – it took good care of me. And my name's Bailey. Bailey Jones." A pause. Despite having so many questions, Bailey was suddenly stumped on what to say. "Rifthopper?"

"A Rifthopper is what we-... well... what I call new Rifters. They're in the early stages of their journey and they've only seen a few worlds. No offense, but you don't strike me as being..." he looked Bailey up and down. "...Well-versed in survival."

"I... see. What makes you a Riftmaster, then?"

"Uh..." the Riftmaster looked at him with a sheepish smile. "That would be my name."

"Your name? So you're self-proclaimed?" Bailey asked, unimpressed.

"You... could say that."

"What about your real name?"

"My Earth-name doesn't matter anymore. The thing is, 'Riftmaster' is easier to speak between different languages, because it usually has a solid translation. When you start learning intergalactic tongues, you'll probably pick one like that for yourself as well –"

"Hold on, hold on. Stop –" Bailey held up his hands for a moment and broke in. He sucked in his breath, gathered his nerves and squashed the spark of guilt, and spoke. "Enough of all this... space stuff. I need to know how to get back to Earth. Seven-horn said if there was a way, you'd know."

He looked at the man with pleading eyes, waiting with bated breath. But by the Riftmaster's shocked, rapidly-falling expression he knew that the answer wasn't the one he had hoped for. He noticed then with the loss of his smile that the man's eyes were tired – far more tired than could be expected of a man his age.

"...No. If there was, I'd have found it by now," the Riftmaster murmured hesitantly, his expression sympathetic. "Have you... been to many other worlds before this one?"

Bailey shook his head.

"Have you been to *any* other worlds?"

He shook his head again, only vaguely aware of the Riftmaster suddenly glancing away.

"...Ah."

His heart sank as the little light of hope went out. Suddenly he couldn't pretend it was all going to be fine. He felt the cold creeping in like he hadn't before. The young man turned his face away and instead looked at the mask he held in his hands. His eyes prickled and ached as he struggled to hold back the tears. His vision blurred.

Vaguely he was aware of the Riftmaster's voice.

"...I see. That's... unfortunate."

Unfortunate? That was *it?*

There was a disconnect, for a moment, between his thoughts and feelings. His mind turned in circles as he tried so desperately to convince himself it wasn't true – that it couldn't be. And all the while he felt his chest tightening, like icy fingers closing in on his heart and beginning to squeeze. His breaths came sharp and fast, and the air was too thin to properly catch them.

"There has to be a way," he croaked. "I never even got to say goodbye. Please... let there be a way for me to say goodbye."

He looked up into the blurred face of the Riftmaster. With nothing he could say, and uncertain of what to do, the slightly older man simply stood, listening. Finally he shook his head.

Bailey's face grew hot with embarrassment as the tears began to trickle down his face. Bailey turned his back on the other, and found himself sinking to his knees, waist deep in snow, trembling.

He felt a hand gently rest on his shoulder.

"Believe me, you wouldn't be the only one looking for a way home. But... It's usually better to just forget about it, than die trying to find one."

"You don't understand, there's... there's so much I should have done. Should have –"

"I know. I've heard it all before. I understand, but..."

His voice wasn't cold, but Bailey still felt a sharp stab of anger. Anger at himself, for never saying goodbye... anger at the Riftmaster, for being so painfully and utterly average... Anger at Seven-horn, for giving him false hope. Anger at the Rift, even though he didn't even know what it was. But that hardly mattered now.

"You should have just left me to die in the snow."

"If you really wanted to die, you could have lain down in the snow and let yourself long ago."

The Riftmaster's voice was firm, but not unkind. Still, Bailey looked up at the man in a stunned silence, wondering if he really cared that little. After a momentary pause, though, he continued.

"...You had a drive in the storm – a will to survive that kept you on your feet and walking, when you could have easily died. Surely that isn't all gone."

Bailey was vaguely aware of fat snowflakes that began to flutter from the heavens, refreshing the pristine whiteness and renewing the cold. They set the perfect mood for his misery.

"And... might I add... – though optimism is never the best idea in the Rift – you never know. One day, you might be dropped back on Earth. I know of some who got to say their goodbyes, however late." The Riftmaster shifted, looking thoroughly uncomfortable. "I forget; is it better to live in hope or die hopeless? If you had a life worth mourning, perhaps try to treasure it, instead? Or perhaps it would be easier to just forget? I don't know. Everyone handles it differently."

Bailey's chest heaved in the thin air. The newer tears felt hot against his face, but the ones sliding down his chin felt piercingly cold against his skin. Those that fell had solidified to crystalline jewels by the time they hit the snow. He shivered violently – but the icy chill felt like the least of his worries.

"...You'll figure it out. Eventually."

The man turned his face towards the sky. Bailey got the impression he'd had this conversation many times before.

Bailey found a part of him bitterly wondering just how long had the Riftmaster been away from Earth to care so little. ...Five years? Ten?

Had he been born out here, in the Rift?

"C'mon. Let's get out of the snow. There's another blizzard coming. Look at the mountain-crawlers."

The greatest of the large creatures had begun tipping their faceless heads upwards to wave their feelers towards the sky, catching some of the snowflakes on the tips of their searching tendrils and long, wiry whiskers. With deep and trailing cries like the whalesongs of Earth, others followed – heralding the coming of another storm.

The babies chimed in with shrill wails – the eerie chorus

carrying far over the mountainside.

Bailey had almost forgotten that they were there, but the din they set up was enough both to remind him, and fill him with a surge of primal fear.

He almost didn't want to go, but slowly – with his body feeling as leaden as his heart – he wrenched himself upright and onto his feet. He pulled his mask back on – the herbs made breathing easier, and sobbing less taxing. His face hidden away, Bailey felt just a little bit better about crying away his woes.

Almost automatically, Bailey stumbled after the Riftmaster, and back towards the village.

The rest of the journey was a shambling blur of cold and silence. Vaguely he remembered stopping halfway up the trail, ripping off his mask and vomiting up a stomachful of thick black goop. By the time they reached the opening in the mountainside, the sky was pelting them with shards of hail that left welts in the exposed skin of his face and pockmarks in the snow around him.

It was still nothing compared to the hole in his chest.

From that point, Bailey simply followed the guiding hand that took hold of his arm. Eventually even his shudders gave out.

Rather than heading back out onto the mountainside and towards Seven-horn's home, they pressed deeper into the village and followed a spiralling corridor that descended under the village hall.

He slipped, he stumbled; he felt the familiar feeling of cold water soaking through to his skin. The tips of his fingers and toes were soon numb.

Their destination turned out to be nothing more than a cramped little room.

There Bailey was ushered quickly inside and seated. The aroma of warm herbs and woody, rich burning filled his nose, the light of the bright, lilac flame filling his vision.

Although he was still sniffling, he felt his aching lungs gratefully receive the incensed air. Soon, he was asleep where he sat.

• • •

Bailey slept fitfully and dreamt so vividly that, for a moment, he almost believed he was back on Earth. The dream was short and, in any other situation, it would have been painfully mundane. But he knew even as he dreamt that something was very wrong. He was home – fully home, at his parents' house. But he was alone. It was dark outside other than the starry sky.

In a panic, Bailey pulled his phone from his pocket and called each of his parents in turn; something he hadn't done in months.

But no-one answered; the sound of its fruitless ringing bored into his waking mind.

When Bailey awoke with a jolt, he was on his side, the Riftmaster already waiting for him. With a long stick he stirred some kind of mysterious concoction that smelled spicy. It looked a little different to Seven-horn's, but not by much.

He didn't feel hungry, although he knew that he should. The image of home, still fresh in his mind, had left a hollow feeling in his stomach.

The young man didn't get up for a while, and simply watched, eyeing the mixture suspiciously. After his breakdown yesterday, Bailey's heart felt surprisingly numb, although he wasn't sure if that was better. In any case, he tried not to think about where he was.

Instead, Bailey kept his mind on the other pains.

He ached, his skin stinging where it was dappled with marks from the hail, and there was a bitter taste on his tongue. His eyes prickled and stung, scratchy with the dried remnants of his tears.

His rosy cloak was dappled with flecks of black; he could smell bile. The young man was desperate for some kind of a shower. He could almost feel the filth caked on his skin.

Before he had the luxury of wallowing too deeply in self-pity, the Riftmaster finally noticed that he was being watched with bleary eyes.

He grinned.

"You're awake!" he said excitedly, quickly pouring the liquid he was mixing into a bowl. He offered it to Bailey, even though the young man was still lying on his side. "Here. I'm not as good a cook as Seven-horn, but you should try and eat something."

Slowly, Bailey forced himself upright, though his muscles screamed a sharp protest as he moved. Bailey winced vaguely as he took the bowl. He looked into it, tilting the bowl so that he could see the contents, and as he did so he caught a glimpse of his reflection.

He was a mess.

His usually well-groomed black hair was sticking out in every direction, clumpy with sweat. His tawny skin had paled in the cold, and was blotchy with hail-marks. His face had become just a little more gaunt; tired, chocolate-coloured eyes set back in his skull.

Stubble was beginning to grow in a scattering across his chin and cheeks.

In comparison even the Riftmaster, with his messy hair and explosion of freckles, looked remarkably well-groomed.

Bailey glanced up at his host, who waited expectantly. He looked back at the bowl, and tilted it again slightly so the contents rippled. At least this one looked *slightly* more like a soup. There was more colour to it. It was, however, more watery, and didn't smell quite so strong.

The Riftmaster looked down at his own food.

In the uncomfortable silence that followed, Bailey began to eat. The Riftmaster did the same. It wasn't an unpleasant meal; and certainly, Bailey preferred it to the mysterious black mush.

"Feeling any better?" the Riftmaster asked, once Bailey had drained the bowl. He spoke as though he thought Bailey was suffering from a particularly bad cold, rather than the loss of… well… his entire world.

"Not really," Bailey finally answered.

"…Ah. Alright."

There was another long pause. At least, Bailey thought, in a bemused sort of way, that he much preferred the quiet to the Riftmaster's overly-enthusiastic yapping. This thought, however, was followed by a creeping feeling of guilt. This man, he remembered, had told Seven-horn to look after him. He'd saved his life, and invited him into his home. In turn, all Bailey had done was eat his food and feel sorry for himself. All the Riftmaster had done was try to help; but none of it made sense. Why?

"Why are you helping me?"

There was a pause. "This is a dangerous world for anyone; not just humans. If I hadn't brought you to Seven-horn, you would have died," Riftmaster said carefully. "Call it... a sense of duty, maybe."

Bailey watched him doubtfully, waiting for more.

The Riftmaster took another long sip, and sighed as he saw the look on the young man's face. "I saw the light of the Rift as I was heading back to the village with a herbalist party. It was close by, so I followed it. Originally, I'd hoped to just bring you to safety, and let you go on your way. But that changed when I saw you were human. As I said before, it's been too long since I met another–"

"How long? You keep saying that, but... how long has it been?" Bailey interrupted him before he could finish.

The Riftmaster paused, hesitating for a long, hard moment. "Well, give or take, but... It's been almost a thousand years."

Bailey took in a sharp breath.

"You see... well... humans rarely survive in the Rift." The Riftmaster looked Bailey dead in the eye. "If the first planet doesn't kill them, usually the heartache does. If they survive, though... the Rift's energy stays with them. It extends their life with every leap between worlds."

Bailey's blood ran cold as he thought back to the fear; the agonising pain of realising that there was no way back. It was a feeling that still clutched at his heart, right up to this very moment.

He could hardly imagine feeling like that forever.

But Bailey remembered also the desperate will to survive that had driven him on through the otherworldly blizzard despite the cold.

He didn't know which of the feelings was stronger – but knowing that there were others who had succumbed to heartbreak before made the thought of his death feel just a little more real, and a little less appealing.

"There are many on Earth who would kill for the Rift to take them," the Riftmaster continued. "To spend an eternity worldhopping... to learn the secrets of an endless number of planets... to travel across the infinite cosmos and leave society behind. But the truth is, it's a hard life that no one's ever prepared for."

"What about me?" Bailey asked in a small voice.

"I think with the right guidance, you could make it out here, Rifthopper. I really do."

"How?"

"Well… I could show you the ropes, give you a leg to stand on. And maybe one day, you'll be able to find your way back to Earth." The Riftmaster poured out just a little more of the herbal soup for himself, then offered some to Bailey. But the young man shook his head. As he placed the pot back on the fire, the Riftmaster continued. "I've been thinking… it's been such a long time since I've taken on an apprentice. Maybe I'm ready to give it another shot."

"An apprentice?"

"Yeah. We'd travel between worlds together, and help each other out whilst you learn the ropes."

"I thought the Rift takes people away at random. That's what Seven-horn said. Wouldn't we end up separated?"

The Riftmaster approached, and extended a hand. "That's right; with one exception." He tugged gently at the pendant hanging from Bailey's cloak – the blue jewel on its leather band, tied so roughly in place, dancing in the light of the fire. With a thumb he polished its gleaming surface, almost tenderly.

Bailey found his attention drawn, again, to the many necklaces that the Riftmaster wore – all of them leather bands, and all of them adorned with different stones and trinkets. There were gems of a myriad colours and textures, some of them polished, and others rough. Some held tiny, presumably alien skulls or bone fragments, others teeth.

He couldn't help but notice the distinctive tip of a mountain-dweller's horn among them.

"…If you wear something that has travelled with me between worlds, then we'll be linked together, and you'll rift alongside me to the same places."

"So… this gem…"

"Yes. Call it selfishness, but… if the Rift took me before you awoke, I feared I might never get to meet you. Seven-horn speaks your language, but it's *me* the Chief is loyal to. Without my guidance, they may well have thrown you back out into the snow."

Bailey thought about the Riftmaster's offer as though he had a choice. "What if I say no? Would I be able to just…

stay here on this planet? Take your place?"

He was answered with a shake of his head.

"Once the Rift chooses someone, they'll belong to it until the day they die. Whether you come with me or not, one day it'll take you away from this planet, too. Then the next... and then the next. It might be in months or years, but you'll go."

It was a bleak look towards the future, and for a moment any brief sense of resolve Bailey felt deserted him. Everything he'd ever wanted to be... everything he'd ever worked for, was suddenly meaningless.

Back on Earth, he'd wanted to be a teacher.

He'd been so close to getting a degree in English literature; following that, he'd planned to start training. Then maybe, by the time he was 25... maybe then he'd be getting somewhere with his life.

But now...

Everything he'd learned in his short lifetime on Earth meant nothing. All of his potential, all of his opportunities... gone. No more girlfriends and dates, tough breakups, or missed deadlines... Never would he be able to get married and see his future children grow up, or their children.

He struggled to think about what would happen instead.

His parents... how would they cope without him? Would life ever be the same for them again? Those 19 years spent raising him, wasted.

And his sister... she was 9; she had a whole lifetime ahead of her. Perhaps she would lead the long and happy life that he couldn't. She wasn't old enough to know what she wanted to do yet, so Bailey would always wonder what she grew up to be. She might get married; their family might grow bigger.

His mother and father would grow old without him, always wondering where he'd gone.

And then... when they died, he would never know.

Even when they *were* all gone, he would still be out here, roaming the infinite cosmos.

Perhaps the scariest part of all of this was the thought that he was, all of a sudden, alone.

...Except that he wasn't, not quite.

At the very least, there was an opportunity here. There was *one* other human living out here, in this wide and empty universe, and by some insane coincidence Bailey was sitting right next to him. It was barely a choice worth asking about. He nodded slowly, eyes welling up with tears.

The Riftmaster beamed, clapping his hands together. "Excellent!"

"So is there… anything I need to do?"

"Not at all! I've already made the necessary preparations."

"Prepar–"

Having finished his soup, the Riftmaster began to enthusiastically ready himself to head out into the snow, packing fresh bundles of herbs into their masks. It seemed like that was it, then. Bailey couldn't help but wonder if he'd made the right decision, but the Riftmaster seemed so certain. And, as always, Bailey had nothing left to lose.

Although he offered a word or two of explanation as he worked – something about needing to tend the mountain-crawlers again today – Bailey found his attention drifting, and he looked around the Riftmaster's chamber.

It wasn't much to look at – unlike Seven-horn's, it was backed into the rough stone wall of the caldera, a little way away from the rest of the village. Everything else was virtually the same, from the clear ice walls to the pink hide carpet. Unlike seven-horn's dwelling though, a leather satchel rested by the door and there was a distinct lack of shed horns readied for use in various daily activities.

As Bailey's gaze drifted to the door, which was far taller than most of the others he'd seen, he realised that they were being watched.

A short figure had appeared at the doorway, a goatlike face peering in. Bailey jumped at the realisation, but he quickly recognised Four-horn. Without needing an invitation, she trotted in and gave the Riftmaster's cloak a tug. She spoke to him in a bleating tone, interspersed with rumbles and pauses. The Riftmaster turned, nodding, occasionally adding an odd note of his own. Coming from a human throat, the mountain tongue sounded a lot more like language – but it was still like nothing he'd heard on Earth.

As they conversed, the Riftmaster's expression became one of concern, and Bailey listened curiously as he waited expectantly for an explanation.

Soon, the goatlike creature hurried back out, leaving the Riftmaster barely enough time to call a farewell.

He slung the satchel over his shoulder before turning towards Bailey.

"The Chief has requested our presence. We've got to go. Now."

. . .

As it turned out, the chief had only requested the Riftmaster's presence, leaving Bailey to wait outside with Seven-horn. The mountain-dweller's ears perked up as he saw the young man, who imagined with a distinct feeling of warmth that the little mountain-dweller was pleased to see him in one piece.

Bailey noticed absently that the little creature had brought his spear, and with a prickle of unease, wondered why.

"Yuman," Seven-horn greeted, as the young man came to stand next to him outside the entrance to the Chief's hollow. It was then that Bailey realised he'd never given the mountain-dweller his name.

"It's Bailey," he said, trying his best to smile at the odd little creature.

Seven-horn paused, ears twitching. Bailey could almost see the translation running through his brain.

"Bailey," Seven-horn corrected himself with a small dip of his head.

Then there was a pause, the mountain-dweller standing dutifully by, although he kept glancing sideways towards the entrance of the dwelling, where the burble of mountain voices – and the Riftmaster – could be heard.

It looked, at a glance, like any other tunnel end, with a small, open archway; but the shed horns of the village people that decorated the opening set it apart.

"Do you know what's going on?" Bailey asked after a time.

One of Seven-horn's ears flicked.

"Yes," he rumbled. Then silence.

"Can you... tell me?"

There was a pause. Seven-horn slowly turned his way and watched him as though considering. "Herb gathering party went down the mountain. Only the apprentice returned. The others, trapped down there."

Seven-horn's ears twitched back, almost losing themselves in his lionlike mane. Big eyes blinked. Tail wiggled. Bailey thought he was beginning to understand the body language of these tough little beasts.

But it didn't take a genius of language, however, to know that the situation was dire.

In any society, people would die without doctors. And this one was built in a climate as tough – if not tougher – than any on Earth; here, the lives of everyone depended on the experience of the few who survived. Perhaps the mountain-dwellers were hardy enough to survive without any healers… but even if they did, there would be deaths.

"I'm sorry."

There was a moment of silence between the two – a moment of mutual understanding between two beings that were otherwise alien to one another. In the quiet, Bailey could hear winds howling, trapped in the caldera beyond the ice.

In the silence, Bailey thought about what he'd heard, and what the mountain-dwellers had done for him. Even though Seven-horn acted at the Riftmaster's command, he had given Bailey shelter and food, saving him from near-certain death in the storm. He wondered if there was anything that he could do to help them; and equally, how the Riftmaster had gained their trust.

"…Is there… anything we can do?" he asked finally.

"That's what Chief wants to know."

Bailey opened his mouth to reply but was interrupted as the Riftmaster emerged from the Chief's hollow. His expression was bleak, and just for just an instant, angry. But it settled to an even firmness as soon as Bailey met his eye.

"Got everything on you?" the Riftmaster demanded.

"Uh… yes?"

"Good. We're going down the mountain."

Bailey felt the colour drain from his face. "Now?"

With a small hop of excitement, Seven-horn bounded ahead to lead the way. The Riftmaster stormed after him, and just one look was enough to tell the young man everything he needed to know. Suddenly filled with fear, and feeling intensely underprepared, Bailey hurried after.

What else could he do?

They were going down the mountain.

Now.

Chapter 4
Into the Depths

Seven-horn led the way as the small party descended down the mountain and into what could only be described as a sub-zero rainforest. A freezing mist enveloped them the lower they trekked, leaving a faint covering of white powder clinging to clothes and skin.

Navigation wasn't a problem for Seven-horn, who must have made the journey many times before, and the humans followed closely in his tracks. Just off the trail, shapes could be seen in the fog. Bailey felt his mind playing tricks on him. Every structure – natural or otherwise – was turned into a jagged monster by age-old icicles. In the barren silence every crunch of snow felt piercingly loud, every breath a ragged gasp.

The air was so cold that it lingered in his lungs, and Bailey was glad for the mask that trapped at least some of the warmth.

His legs were aching, his skin crawling with tension by the time they reached the foot of the mountain.

He knew that it had been many hours since they'd set off, but somehow he still felt unprepared.

The valley beneath the mountain slumbered in quiet dignity, still-thriving plant life encased in ice. The crystal-clear icicles brought out a myriad of colours in the leaves and flowers, whilst the stems lay low in cool blue and purple hues. It was like walking into a surrealist painting – there were colours where there shouldn't be, frost dappling every surface that wasn't dripping in ice, and diamond-like dewdrops that had been there for an eternity. This place had a serene beauty like nothing he'd ever seen.

As they pressed deeper, vines – or, tendrils that looked like vines – poured out of holes in trees and twisted their way around stems. Bailey couldn't help but feel like there was something strange about these and a closer inspection revealed that, unlike everything else, they weren't glistening with frost. These vines were blue, like the other plant life here – but their many tendrils wore a purplish hue, which faded to red at the very tips. He thought for a moment he might have seen one move, but as he turned to look at it, it was still.

The frozen forest was less silent than it had been on the mountain slopes – but Bailey almost wished the quiet would return. Icicles tinkled softly against each other in the mist like ethereal windchimes. Frozen leaves softly rattled against each other. A sprinkle of powder occasionally fell with a quiet hiss. There was no wind, so the sounds could only be creatures moving in the fog, just out of sight.

The layer of snow was surprisingly thin here. Perhaps it was because mountains of snow covered the knots of plant life above them, making the thick woods themselves almost cavern-like. The path they followed was criss-crossed by other creatures' trails; there were clearly mountain-dwellers' footprints, but there were others too. Larger ones, smaller ones, and tracks which were no more than thin squiggles in the snow.

As they pressed deeper, Bailey saw more vegetation, flowers and herbs pushing heads and leaves above the covering of snow. Most clung to roots, or trailed from branches or vines dangling above their heads. All were bent low with the weight of the ice forming upon them.

As they passed through curtains of hanging plants, the icicles upon them softly chimed.

They pressed deeper and deeper into the wood.

Finally, Bailey saw Seven-horn and the Riftmaster stop ahead of him. He hurried to catch up as the two conversed in low rumbles.

When he reached them, Bailey saw the Riftmaster turn his way.

With the exception of splashes of colour on those strange,

creeping vines, the forest here was a lot greyer than the pristine world they'd passed before. It was a lot quieter, too. Suddenly the silence didn't seem so appealing anymore; he wanted the windchimes back.

He noticed, with a prickle of dread, that the strange, creeping tendrils he'd seen almost covered the vegetation here.

There was a whole curtain of them, blocking the trail as they dangled from a low-hanging branch. Without thinking, Bailey reached out to see if he could peer past them, and was quickly stopped by a sharp jab of Seven-horn's spear. He let out a small yelp of stunned shock and looked at the mountain-dweller accusingly.

He raised his hand to suck on a small puncture wound that Seven-horn had left on his wrist.

By way of explanation, Seven-horn reached out with his spear and brushed it lightly against the plants... or... what he'd thought were plants. Immediately, they curled up, tendrils grabbing and grasping, writhing as they tried to pull the object from the mountain-dweller's grasp. He pulled it loose with a grunt. He yanked a few tendrils free in the process – which quickly began to crawl down the spear towards Seven-horn's pad-like little hands.

Bailey stepped back, wide-eyed with disgust, as seven-horn threw his spear at the ground. The severed tendrils quickly burrowed their way into the snow and disappeared. The remaining tendrils in the curtain curled back. There would be enough room to go through now – not that Bailey wanted to.

"What are they?" Bailey asked in horror, voice barely above a whisper.

"Parasites," Riftmaster answered, voice equally low.

"They only live in frozen forests like this one. Usually there aren't as many as this."

"...Meaning...?"

"They have a host."

Bailey's blood ran cold. "A host?"

"There's a creature lives in woods like this capable of forming a symbiotic relationship with these parasites, and using them for its own gain... On its own, it's not so bad. But once infected... it becomes the one apex predator of this planet."

The Riftmaster motioned towards the remains of the curtain.

"They make barriers like this to protect their dens. Usually after a disturbance."

"…And we have to go in there?"

Bailey knew the answer as soon as he looked at the ground – the healers' trail went ahead.

The Riftmaster dipped his head.

Bailey took in a breath, feeling his heart hammering in his ears.

"…What's the plan?" he asked finally, if only to buy himself a little bit of time before the storm.

"We go in. We get the healers. You carry one, I'll grab the other two, and Seven-horn will watch our backs. Then we leave… and hopefully we won't run into the host."

"What if we do?"

"Well then, in that case, I hope you have a thing for cannibalism."

"…*What*?"

"Did I stutter? Let's go."

Bailey felt his stomach drop like a lead weight, and he hesitated, but followed.

What choice did he have?

The three ducked under the curled-up tendrils and continued walking. As the trail continued, everywhere Bailey looked he saw yet more colourless plants and those same creeping tendrils.

Finally, they came to a pile of rubble at the base of a steep slope. Perhaps there had once been a rockslide here. But in between two boulders resting against each other with a small hollow in between, he thought he saw a flicker of movement – four little eyes peered at him, and then he heard a frantic, burbling bleat.

The Riftmaster hurried forward. He squeezed in between the boulders and disappeared from view – there must have been a small cave back there.

Bailey glanced at Seven-horn.

"Will stand watch, here," the small creature rumbled. Bailey turned to follow the Riftmaster, when the mountain-dweller spoke again, quietly.

"Bailey."

Bailey looked up in confusion. The Mountain-dweller

wasn't looking at him.

"Seven-horn?"

"Thank. And… sorry."

Bailey was confused.

"…What for?"

Seven-horn looked sideways towards him.

"This… not your world. We… not your people. You… not even been here long. But you might still die for them."

"…I… Don't have anything else to lose. And I don't really have a choice."

Seven-horn paused as the words processed. "Still… Thank. You a good one."

Bailey dipped his head. "You too."

Although Bailey still wasn't the best at reading the mountain-dwellers, he thought that as the otherworldly creature turned back to his lookout, he did so with a smile.

Bailey heard the Riftmaster call his name from behind the boulder, and squeezed his way past.

After the tight entranceway there was a surprising amount of openness hidden behind the rocky outcropping, a small cave safely stowed away where no-one would find it.

This little alcove was tendril-free. Perhaps this was the only area of the predator's territory where it couldn't fit. After a quick look around, Bailey theorised that it was because there were no plants here for the parasitic tendrils to feed on. At least not plants that grew naturally – bundles of discarded herbs had been piled up by the entrance, seemingly forgotten.

The three healers were huddled together at the back, where a white mountain-dweller lay on his side. A nasty-looking wound on his stomach had been patched up with a strange-coloured poultice. He seemed unconscious. A peach-coloured one with white patches had one leg that was twisted the wrong way. And the last one, who was pale rose in colour with just a few freckles, was apparently the only one in a suitable condition still to walk. It slowly hauled itself to its feet and limped over to them.

A gash across one cheek oozed bluish blood into the surrounding fur.

Its pads were dyed with a strange, bluish tint; it must have been the one tending the others' wounds.

"Take New-horn," Riftmaster said to Bailey, motioning to

the unconscious mountain-dweller. Bailey moved over to the back. The others watched him as he stooped, and gathered up the prone form in his arms.

The other two healers supported one another as they exited the tumble of rocks between the entrance boulders.

Bailey waited for the Riftmaster to squeeze his way out, passed New-horn through, and then did the same.

When they were outside, he took New-horn into his arms again and watched as the Riftmaster hoisted one onto his shoulders, and lifted the other up against his chest. With the rose-coloured one clinging to his head, and the other nestled in his arms like a pair of exceptionally large and goat-like children, his companion began to lead the way back to the village, with Seven-horn bringing up the rear.

Very quickly, Bailey's arms were aching from the strain of carrying New-horn and his fingertips felt numb from the cold. The unconscious mountain-dweller didn't wake up even for a moment. Even when its large eyes were tightly shut though, the smaller pair still stuck out shiny and black like beads on its brows.

He wondered, briefly, what they were for.

Seeing in the dark, maybe? Seeing in thick fog? Or just for attentiveness whilst sleeping?

He allowed himself to relax a little bit as colour trickled back into the world around them. They had passed the strange parasite-curtains and they were nearing the edge of the wood.

The tendrils they saw were thinner, and he noticed them less frequently.

He allowed the faintest trickle of hope to creep into his chest.

Except...

They weren't there yet. The world was still dark. They were still in the forest, surrounded by a thick tangle of roots and vines and frozen flora. And somewhere along the line, Bailey began to hear a slithering sound.

At first, he thought it nothing more than the sound of powder falling from a branch or vine. But it grew louder. He tried to put it down to mere imagination, but a quick glance back at Seven-horn told him that the mountain-dweller had heard it too; he held his spear at the ready. Such a small and makeshift weapon suddenly didn't seem like enough.

The Riftmaster picked up the pace.

Bailey could see the two mountain-dwellers he carried bristling, their ears perked upright.

They were being hunted.

Something slithered through the undergrowth with a crawling sound like a thousand insects moving in the dark.

Finally as they passed through an open clearing, the brightness of the mountain slopes visible as beams of light in the distance, it appeared.

It was a quadrupedal creature, around the size of a horse, with a low and heavy-set bulk reminiscent of a Komodo dragon. Its legs were thick and its feet wide, its body round and... Bailey presumed blubbery, but it was so covered in layers upon layers of writhing tendrils that Bailey couldn't make out its true shape. Occasionally, as the parasites reeled back he thought he saw flashes of a grey-blue hide beneath.

It wasn't the beast's motions producing the grotesque sounds; it was the parasites.

It splayed open its mouth to reveal a toothless grin, that split its head almost entirely in half, and mandibles peeling its lower jaw apart. With flickers of tentacle-like tongues it tasted the air.

It stayed there, trying to pick out the scent of its prey from the scent of the ice.

And then, without a roar, without a gasp, without even a warning – it lunged. It picked out the biggest target, and then with a single violent surge it went for the Riftmaster.

But then, with a piercing squeal, it skidded to a halt and thrashed.

For sticking out of its neck with tendrils writhing around it, was a spear.

"Run! Go!"

Bailey didn't need to be told twice. After a moment's wondering if he should simply leave his precious cargo in the snow, he bolted past the Riftmaster and into the last tangle of trees standing between them and the mountain.

He could hear the Riftmaster hot in pursuit, and a sound like breaking glass as the creature burst after them, knocking icicles free only for them to shatter against its hide.

Seven-horn tried desperately to draw its attention with a

throaty war cry that echoed through the trees. Bailey was running out of breath. He didn't know if he could go on for much longer. He stumbled, foot caught beneath a stray root, and saw the Riftmaster skidding past him and keep going. The eyes of his passengers were round with terror.

In that moment, Bailey thought that the man would turn back towards him – that he'd show even the slightest bit of concern. But no. In a few short moments, he was gone; disappearing out of sight and lost between the trees.

Bailey took that moment to glance back, and immediately wished he hadn't. There it was; pulling itself upright and onto its hind feet before lurching forward for the devouring blow. Blue blood scattered against the ground as it moved.

Bailey suddenly found himself frozen, entranced with morbid fascination by the sight of his own impending death.

With every inch shifting and writhing in so many terrible, yet beautiful, colours, jaws peeled back wide enough to engulf him whole, and four snakelike tongues thrashing in perfect symmetry, Bailey found himself hypnotised by the horrible beauty of it all. He clung to New-horn as though the unconscious mountain-dweller could somehow protect him.

He couldn't even close his eyes to prepare for the end.

Then Bailey found his view blocked by a wiggling tail.

Seven-horn was standing between him and the monster. He was clutching the spear still trailing with limp tendrils, his mane moving softly in the predator's terrible breaths. He shoved the spear into the roof of its mouth and it reeled back, screaming. As the mountain-dweller's arms returned to his sides, Bailey realised that there were tendrils clinging to one forearm, thrashing as they burrowed into his fur.

Bailey caught the mountain-dweller's eye.

The two creatures – of such different worlds – shared the same look that lasted mere moments, but felt like forever.

Seven-horn's gaze jerked up again as the monster advanced once more. The mountain-dweller closed the distance in a few trotting paces.

The predator snapped its jaws, and one tongue lapped at the oozing wound. It lunged, and Bailey saw the two creatures clash in a last, life-or-death struggle.

Then a light filed his vision, so utterly, blindingly bright.

He let go of New-horn as the ground dropped away beneath

him with a feeling like being violently thrown.

The last he heard of that world was the strangled scream of a mountain-dweller.

And then suddenly, abruptly, a fiery pain flooded through his veins. Bailey was dimly aware that he was falling through empty space, silence closing in from every side. That piercing sound that had been present the first time was strangely absent. When he opened his eyes again, the mountain-dwellers' world was gone.

Their mission?

Meaningless.

Chapter 5
The Titanic Forest

By the time that Bailey had struggled upright into a sitting position, the Riftmaster was already scrambling to his feet. Bailey made to do the same, but his vision swam, and he soon slumped back down onto his knees, and let the stinging pain fade from his skin. When he looked up again, his companion was standing over him, mask tucked under his arm and a hand outstretched.

Bailey accepted the proffered hand and eased himself to his feet. Slowly he removed the mask from his face and looked around, baffled and frantic. He felt warm moisture on his face, and drew in a long breath. The air smelled damp and had a sharp, citrusy tang, soothing the ache in his lungs as he breathed it.

But that wasn't what was important right now. "Where are the mountain-dwellers?" Bailey asked frantically. "Seven-horn, he–… I saw him before we…"

"They're gone, Bailey. A million miles away."

The Riftmaster's voice was dry with resignation. There was little room for questioning. As though nothing had happened, he was already brushing himself off and straightening his cloak. His expression was solemn.

Bailey looked around one last time as though hoping one of the little creatures would pop out from under the woodwork but, alas, their former companions were nowhere to be seen.

"But that means they… They'll all…"

Bailey trailed off, crushed.

The Riftmaster had turned away and was scanning the surrounding world. He didn't reply for a while. "I carried two of the healers as far up the mountain as I could. If they support each other, they might make it."

"But... Seven-horn –" Bailey began, voice trembling.

The Riftmaster cut him off, finally looking at the young man. He approached, placed a hand on Bailey's shoulder and, in a slightly softer tone, spoke.

"Seven-horn doesn't matter any more. We're here now."

He gave Bailey's shoulder a pat before pushing past him and craning back his head to look up towards the tree canopy.

"We did all we could, Rifthopper."

Bailey gave the man a long, hard look.

Was it really all for nothing? After everything they'd worked for? Everything they'd done? The last Bailey had heard of his friend was his last scream. The Mountain-dweller had put himself between Bailey and the predator, despite knowing him so little.

Or had he? Bailey knew little of Seven-horn's relationship with the other mountain-dwellers. Perhaps he'd simply been trying to save New-horn. And in that last fleeting glimpse Bailey had of him, Seven-horn's fur had been alive with parasites; perhaps death was the better option.

Perhaps it was human selfishness that made Bailey think Seven-horn cared so much.

After all, he and Seven-horn were beings alien to each other. Why should either of them care?

But Bailey did.

Why shouldn't the mountain-dwellers care?

Bailey turned his gaze away, and looked around, struggling to keep the tears out of his eyes.

Were it not for the situation at hand, this place might have been quite beautiful.

They were in a mossy clearing surrounded by plant life. The leaves here were green flecked with pale autumn yellows, and most importantly they looked... well... like leaves. But it was awfully dark here, the tree canopy consuming any frail rays of sunlight that might have made it through. The glade where they stood was instead lit by huge glowing fruits and massive flowers that shone in a rainbow of neon. Trees as thick as skyscrapers soared off into the abyss above them, dwarfing the two figures on the ground.

The clearing they were standing in was nestled in amongst the roots of a single tree, coiling around them like a massive snake.

Small, serpentine creatures pulsed above them, shimmering with momentary brightness. They soared on undulating sails that channelled the air and kept them aloft. They glistened and glimmered in shades of rose-gold, gathering in shoals around the lantern-like fruit or chasing one another around low-hanging branches. They reminded Bailey of fish in the way they weaved and twisted and gathered with their companions.

The largest groups dipped and dived in hypnotic harmony.

They twittered and shrilled to one another as they flew, filling the dark forest with an excited melody.

With the ground shrouded by a low-hanging mist and the dark abyss stretching above, Bailey was distinctly disoriented; he felt like they were standing on the very bottom of the ocean.

Whenever the young man stepped, water welled around his boots.

It was a far cry from the harsh mountain world they'd just come from.

It almost... *almost* looked *habitable.*

Certainly more so than the mountain's slopes.

Bailey looked down as the Riftmaster's voice broke through his reverie. The man tugged a petal from a flower as big as his torso and approached, holding it to his chest.

Each step squelched softly under his weight.

"Come on. Let's find somewhere drier. I'll figure us out something to eat."

He ducked under a thick tree root and left the clearing, glancing back at Bailey only briefly.

Bailey hesitated for a moment, isolation creeping in. Was it even worth it? Forever hopping from world to world, no home or friend ever permanent... was it even worth keeping themselves alive? If the Riftmaster was telling the truth, Bailey had little to look forward to save for an eternity of letting go.

But he had questions.

He had a *lot* of questions. Might as well have them answered before giving up entirely. And with morbid amusement, Bailey considered the possibility that maybe food poisoning would be a quicker and easier death than starvation.

With a sigh, Bailey trudged after the Riftmaster.

• • •

The shelter they found was a little grotto at the foot of a gigantic tree, nestled in amongst its roots. And it was in good time, too; moments earlier, the heavens had opened. Droplets of rain poured from beyond the treetops with a mysterious fluid that tasted bitter, and mysteriously itched as it touched his skin.

Bailey sat by, watching as the Riftmaster assembled some dried-out scraps of leaf for kindling and lit a fire by striking two shards of mountain-dweller horn against one another. He made the fire close to the wide entranceway, where the roof sloped outwards, and directed the smoke away from them. The glow of the flames mingled with those of the flower petals he'd collected on the way. The objects shone in a wild array of shapes and colours, having been laid haphazardly against one wall.

"It's not perfect, but it'll do for now..." the Riftmaster mumbled to Bailey.

Never stopping for a moment, the Riftmaster set to work on something else. He laid down his leather satchel, usually hidden beneath his cloak, beside the fire. Following that, the man used the cloak itself to cover the entranceway, separating the fire from their sleeping area. When Bailey offered his as well, he used the two to form a curtain that meant even the worst of the raindrops occasionally sizzling on the fire wouldn't find its way through to their sleeping area. To pin them up, he untied yet more of the necklaces from his neck, and with relics of tooth and claw, pierced the hide and fixed them to the wood.

What Bailey had considered mere mementos of his time on other planets, seemed to be integral to the Riftmaster for actually surviving them.

Without his cloak, the Riftmaster still didn't look very

special. His body was relatively lean, with wide hips and a broad chest. His clothes looked cobbled together, patched with various different materials and fabrics, although they were mostly a cottony material that was a washed-out purple in colour. He still wore the pink-fringed, knee-high boots made of mountain-crawler hide. The Riftmaster's tunic ended just above his belly, revealing a covering of iridescent scales, royal purple in colour. The same material could be seen covering his forearms like flexible gauntlets hugging tight to his skin, right up to a loop around his thumbs. The gauntlets disappeared under his tunic sleeves, and Bailey assumed it was all part of the same undergarment. Beneath a loincloth of more mountain-crawler hide, he wore a pair of leggings made of similar scales. A couple of leather belts were tightly wrapped around his waist, each laden with a variety of tools and one long, wicked-looking silver knife resting against his outer thigh.

Bailey's gaze lingered for a while on the weapon, uneasily, but his gaze was drawn back to the Riftmaster as he held out the jewelled necklace that had been used to hold Bailey's cloak in place.

Bailey took it, and closed his fingers around it.

But the Riftmaster wasn't finished yet. Humming as he worked, the man took a small piece from each of the flower petals he'd picked in the woods and – after sniffing, squeezing, and examining the pieces closely – mixed them with some powders and herbs from his satchel. In a palm-sized bowl he mixed in droplets of water from a small waterskin, and closely examined the concoction he'd made, before emptying each bowlful out into the rain.

"What are you doing?" Bailey asked, after a few long minutes of watching in quiet fascination.

"I'm checking for various toxins to find which are edible. The powders cause a chemical reaction and change colours if different elements are present."

Presumably satisfied, the Riftmaster finally offered a thick petal, raw, to Bailey.

"…You can only survive for so long on luck."

After a moment's hesitation, Bailey took it. When that was done, the Riftmaster settled back, gathered the remaining plant matter into a haphazard pile, and finally relaxed against the soft moss of the alcove wall.

Bailey wondered how he could seem so contented after leaving the Mountain-dwellers' world behind. After all, the Riftmaster had lived there a lot longer than Bailey had.

"Cook it if you like. It probably won't taste good either way, but it's not poisonous."

Bailey turned over the petal in his hands, reluctance clear in his motions, but after careful consideration he bit into the glowing petal. He was startled by its bitter, acidic taste, and it took all his willpower not to spit it out on the floor. Pulling a face, he chewed and swallowed.

The Riftmaster ate without so much as a flinch to show any kind of discomfort. "Seems to be plenty of moisture in it, too," he mused. "Not bad. I could get used to this world."

Bailey shuddered, geared himself, and then ate some more.

When he'd got used to the sourness, it wasn't too bad. It had an earthy taste which reminded him of all those times he'd fallen and ended up face-down in the grass. He supposed that wasn't all that surprising.

When Bailey's companion – his mentor, he supposed – had finished, he fed the remains to the fire. Unable to stomach much more, Bailey did the same.

They sat in silence for a while, watching the acid rain as it fell.

Bailey tried not to think about what had happened; and he couldn't help but blame the man sitting opposite him. He looked down at the leather-bound pendant he now held in his hand, and tilted it so that the jewel glinted in the firelight. If he'd turned down the Riftmaster's offer, and removed this necklace... he might have stayed in the Mountain-dweller's world for just a little bit longer. He could have got New-horn to safety and helped the other healers make it up the mountain.

Sure, he... might have Rifted again, and he would have likely died soon after, but... then, at least, it wouldn't have been in vain.

Bailey looked up as he felt eyes on him, and realised that the Riftmaster was watching, seemingly afraid to disturb the silence.

Their eyes locked for a few long moments, and although it wasn't a challenging stare, Bailey felt his breath catch.

Nervousness fluttered in his stomach.

It took a moment for Bailey to realise that the other was trying to think of something to say. After a while, Bailey managed to unhook his stare from his mentor's, and broke the awkward silence for him.

"We... never really got to talk much last time," he said, nervously looking down at the pendant he held.

"Yeah. So... what do you want to know?"

"Do you know where we are now?"

"Not without seeing the stars. We could still be in the milky way, or we could be light years away from any familiar galaxy. The only thing I know is that I haven't been here before – to this planet, that is. We'll have to tread carefully." The man leaned forward to poke into the fire for a moment before, presumably satisfied, settling back again.

So, they were completely blind.

Comforting.

Bailey sighed. "How can you be so calm about everything? Seven-horn was your friend, too. You knew him longer than I did. He's... He died, you know."

The Riftmaster looked up, but his face didn't show any surprise. He sighed.

"I've been through it a thousand times before. You just... get used to it after a while. I think of the things that I did do, rather than what I couldn't. Because of me, the healers might stand a chance of getting back to their village."

"That was after I fell... when you kept running," Bailey recalled drily.

"Yeah."

"Why?"

"If I'd turned back, we'd have *both* been eaten. I've lived too long to die for the sake of someone I've known for a day. That mission was a fool's errand anyway. We should never have taken it. I *knew* we shouldn't have."

In the midst of his own dismay, Bailey recalled the expression on the Riftmaster's face as he'd left the chief's hollow, his face a storm.

"Then why did you?" Bailey asked, his tone accusing. It was almost as though the man had *wanted* him to die.

The Riftmaster hesitated. "The chief was going to have us thrown out of the village, if we refused – cast out into the snow so that we'd freeze. And if we'd done it, well... we'd have proven ourselves a lot more than just a drain on resources. Humans have to eat a whole lot more than mountain-dwellers to stay warm, you know. Not that it matters now."

"How long were you living with them?" Bailey asked.

"Five years – give or take."

"That's a long time."

"I suppose it is," the Riftmaster answered, as though he didn't really believe it. And how could he? Bailey remembered something else he'd said; how it had been a thousand years since he'd seen another of their kind, another human. To the Riftmaster, years must pass by like minutes.

"Has it really been a thousand years since you've seen another human?"

The Riftmaster nodded.

"Probably longer, actually."

Bailey paused for a moment, digesting this, before curiosity and disbelief pushed him to dig further. "Is that when you left Earth?"

"Not exactly. I've been traveling the Rift for..." he paused for a moment, as though silently counting the years. "...Five-thousand years. Again, give or take."

Bailey struggled momentarily to think of something to say. It wasn't, strictly speaking, the strangest thing he'd heard in the past few days. But the Riftmaster was... older than he'd anticipated. One thousand years was a lot, but five thousand was another thing entirely.

"...You've aged remarkably well," Bailey finally said.

This, at least, resulted in a quiet chuckle from his mentor.

Bailey continued. "If it wasn't on Earth, then... who was the last human you met?"

The Riftmaster hesitated. "That... would be my last apprentice."

"There have been others? What happened to them?"

"...Only one, but... we had a... disagreement, and went our separate ways. He might still be out there, somewhere."

Bailey followed the Riftmaster's gaze as he looked out into the rain. A long silence passed between them.

"Five thousand years," Bailey murmured. "That's insane. What was Earth even like, back then?"

Surely, Riftmaster could answer everything asked by archaeologists throughout the ages. He could answer questions on long-lost civilisations and unveil secrets that not even modern technology could uncover.

And maybe one day Bailey could do the same, reminiscing about what he knew as the modern world as it became the distant, distant past. Bailey felt his heart sink once again. He wanted to go back to Earth so badly, and thinking about the world moving on without him... well... it was almost too much to bear.

Oblivious to Bailey's emotions, the Riftmaster chuckled.

"Hold your horses, Rifthopper. Time flows a little differently out here, and it always seems to go slower whilst you're away. ...If... you don't mind me asking, what year is it, back on Earth? If you're... ah... fine with talking about it, that is."

The young man looked up as though startled.

The Riftmaster must have caught onto the expression that crossed his face. He stiffened up, and spoke. "If it's too much to think about, that's–"

"It was 2019," Bailey finally answered, surprising even himself with the firmness of his tone. "January 5th."

The Riftmaster looked surprised as well for an instant, and then relaxed and smiled.

"That's... incredible," he murmured softly.

"What?"

"I still remember the exact day the Rift first came for me. July 19th, 1960. It hasn't even been a hundred years on Earth. Crazy, right?"

Bailey stared at the Riftmaster, unbelieving. "How is that possible?" he asked after a time. So, there would be no ancient secrets or stories of civilisations long-lost to time. Bailey was a little disappointed, but he reminded himself that an ancient human probably wouldn't even speak the same language. And if he did, it wouldn't be English as Bailey knew it.

So in a way, it was lucky.

"I don't know. As I said, time flows differently in the Rift. I ah... don't know the exact science, but my theory is that the further you are from a planet, the slower time passes there. Maybe it's just that different places have different concepts of time. But if you ever get confused, just remember this one rule: time will only ever move forward. You'll never go back to the exact moment you left."

Bailey fell into silent bewilderment. Even if the Riftmaster had only been gone 60 years and not thousands, the youthfulness of his face still made him an anomaly.

Catching the look on his face, the Riftmaster chuckled.

"Try not to worry about understanding it for now, Rifthopper. Just worry about surviving it."

Bailey gave a small nod, but he still wasn't satisfied. He thought for a while. He had so many questions buzzing around in his brain, all of them ripe for the picking. But answering one question only opened the doors to a thousand more.

"Can you tell me more about the Rift?" he asked. "Is it alive?"

"Nobody really knows. You can't study it because it might whisk you away as soon as you've put together all the resources you need to tap into it, or long before. Anyone and anything can become a Rifter, but not willingly. You could be the hardiest creature in the universe, or you could be... well, human. The Rift doesn't pick favourites, and it doesn't seem picky, because most Rifters die soon after leaving their home planet. If you survive, it just keeps bothering you."

"Does anyone on Earth know about it?"

"Not really. There will always be whispers, of course. Conspiracies. Sightings of aliens and cryptids that can never be explained, or rumoured gateways to Hell. But most mysterious disappearances can be put down to murders or kidnappings, and strange lights in the sky always seem to have a logical explanation. Because no human's ever made it back to Earth, the tale has never been told. And even if it was, who would believe them?"

Bailey looked away, thinking back to movies and TV shows he'd often watched as a child. From paranormal investigators to alien conspiracies he always used to wonder, and wish, and marvel, at the possibility that there was something more out there. But as he'd grown older, Bailey had largely lost interest in the unknown. Comfort instead came from knowing the certainties in life and finding the hidden meaning in things right in front of him.

He knew that he wouldn't have believed anyone if they'd told him about the Rift before now.

Deep in consideration, Bailey barely noticed the Riftmaster getting to his feet and stretching languidly. When he looked up, the man was preparing to duck into the little shelter they'd made, but was looking back towards him. "I'm gonna hit the hay. Do you wanna keep first watch?"

Bailey felt exhausted himself and was tempted to simply follow him inside. But at the same time, he didn't know how long the Riftmaster had been awake. He didn't think the man had slept at all during his last nap, and knew that at least one of them ought to stay up. He tried not to think about everything that had happened since then, and instead nodded.

"Sure."

The Riftmaster looked relieved. "Thanks. It's nice having someone to watch my back again."

Bailey forced a smile, although he couldn't help but feel a twinge of sourness at that. *Ironic*, he thought, *that you'd expect me to watch your back.*

"No problem," he answered.

And then he was alone again, staring off through the pouring rain and into the wood. Without the voice of his new mentor and the conversation passing between them, it was far harder trying to stave off the darkness creeping in at the edges of his vision.

He stared into the firelight, and watched it reflected in the shimmering droplets of rain outside, hearing its soft crackling along with the sound of droplets falling on leaves.

He listened to the cries of the flying creatures as they played and fed, going about their lives either oblivious or uncaring to the presence of the aliens in their world.

With his belly full, his heart tired and his eyelids growing heavier by the moment, Bailey soon found himself falling into a light, but dreamless sleep.

Chapter 6
Bailey's First Lesson

This time, awakening was less of a nasty surprise. The citrus-scented air was pleasant in Bailey's lungs, it was warm, and the forest was filled with the sound of strange creatures crying out to one another. And this time his eyes weren't so dry and stinging with tears.

The fire had long since burned itself out, but it looked like someone had taken the ashes that remained. There was only a grey stain where it had been burning hours before, and the rain had stopped.

From the area he had been sleeping, still upright, he could see glowing fruits bathing the forest floor in lantern-like light. He couldn't tell if it was day or night above the forest; the lighting was the same as when they arrived.

Perhaps the days were longer here. Or maybe the nights were. Or, perhaps the tree canopy was so thick that it consumed all incoming light. Regardless of which it was, with the glowing fruits, the forest would always be bright.

Groggily, Bailey rose to his feet, pushing back the hide curtain. But, at that moment he realised with a sudden jolt of awakeness that the Riftmaster was gone. The hollow behind the curtain was empty of anything; even the man's satchel had been taken.

Bailey was alone.

He wouldn't just leave me, would he?

Bailey stepped back, away from the curtain, and let it fell

back into place. He turned and looked out into the woods, breaths sharp with panic. *But he has before.*

Bailey couldn't be alone, in a strange world. Without thinking, he set off into the woods. The towering trees loomed like skyscrapers, suddenly ominous, their roots surrounding him in a floral labyrinth like nothing seen on Earth. With each step he took, freshly-fallen rain welled to the surface of his mossy footprints. When he turned back, he could at least see the way he'd come.

But the Riftmaster was too smart to leave any tracks.

Bailey felt suddenly wary. Through the footprints he left behind, anything could follow him, and anything could find their little hideout. Who knew what lurked in these towering woods?

Finally, Bailey ducked under a tree root, rounded a corner and... almost ran into someone coming the opposite way.

Bailey reeled back, but it was only his mentor.

The young man relaxed, letting out a long breath. The Riftmaster dipped his head in greeting. His brows perked in amusement. "Finished keeping watch?" he asked pointedly, with a light tilt of his head.

Bailey felt his face burning.

"...I'm sorry," he mumbled. For a moment, that was all he could think to say. But then he immediately regretted it. *He* was sorry? No, the Riftmaster was the one who left him alone!

"I'll let you off this time. First day, and all," the Riftmaster said with a grin. His calmness prickled at Bailey's already sour mood. "I'm used to sleeping with one eye open, anyway."

"Where did you go?" Bailey demanded a moment later, spurred on by that fleeting surge of anger.

"I got to work. It's a new world. New dangers. We've a lot to do before we're out of the danger zone..." The man glanced around briefly, as though worried something might jump out. "Rather than floundering, I have a little routine I like to stick to. I call it the three S's: scout – meaning, you figure out the dangers, the area, and the basic necessities... sow – grow, or make what you can't find... And then – only then – you can start to survive. The one thing you can't do is panic and run off in a blind hurry. You've got to think, Rifthopper... if you hadn't left in such a rush, you might have seen the signs I left you, rather than rushing into danger and leaving a trail so easy to follow."

Bailey was about to declare that he wasn't a child, that he didn't need nursery rhymes to survive, when – "...Signs?"

"Yeah. You think I'd let anyone find my tracks on a new planet? You've *got* to be more mindful. To survive, you have to think of everything. Walk on rocks and through undergrowth – as much as you can, avoid anything that will leave an obvious print. Maybe lay down some fabric to muffle them. If you *need* to be followed, leave signs – not trails."

Of course.

Anger and indignation flared briefly in his chest. Whatever sign the Riftmaster had left behind had been far too subtle. It wasn't *his* fault it had never caught his eye.

"What sort of sign? Why didn't you wake me, and tell me you were going?"

In his hurry to find his mentor, Bailey hadn't even stopped to consider the possibility that the Riftmaster had left him something to follow, but then his stomach sank. Before the man could answer, Bailey spoke again.

"I...It was a test, wasn't it?"

The Riftmaster was already shaking his head, but there was a sparkle of glee in his eye.

"You're giving me too much credit. You were dead to the world, and it was just a short scouting trip; I was always within earshot. If something happened, I'd know," he dismissed. "I figured I'd be back before you even knew I was gone."

Bailey grunted.

"You sound annoyed..." the Riftmaster mused. "But hey... from now on you won't forget to look for the signs or cover your tracks. Will you? Let me say this: you won't learn anything if all I do is talk at you. But because you failed to do something, you won't forget to do it the next time. Humiliation is the best road to self-improvement!"

The young man stared in pure disbelief. He wished that for just one moment the man would drop the uppity attitude long enough to realise that he was talking to another human.

"I suppose I won't," he grumbled.

"Though I admit, leaving you to see if you'd figure it out

on your own was a good indicator of your problem solving ability, how well you deal with pressure, and such... So I suppose you're right. It *was* a test. Is that better?"

Bailey peered at him, not sure what the man was trying to achieve. "I suppose," he said with an exasperated sigh.

"Good! Now let's cover up that trail so I can show you what I've found."

• • •

Bailey followed as the Riftmaster climbed onto a buttress root and followed it upwards to the foot of the great tree. There were so many of these massive roots that they formed a natural system of walkways, and it was far easier to navigate them than the forest floor. The forest felt a lot less labyrinthine from up here; intertwining and crossing roots made it easy to change their direction.

Bailey knew now how the Riftmaster had managed to get around without leaving any tracks; the lichens growing from the tree roots were bristly and hard, leaving no imprints. When Bailey looked down, though, he could still see traces of the footprint trail he'd left in the moss, all the way to the hollow beneath the tree.

"Try to remember the way," the Riftmaster panted, offering a hand to help Bailey climb from one root onto another.

They climbed up, hopping and clambering from root to root until Bailey quickly felt lost and exhausted.

But the great tree all these roots belonged to stretched above them, keeping his sense of direction grounded and the path easy enough to follow. It was comforting to know that it would always stand here as a central point to their territory, even if it was only one tree of many. For now, this tree was the centre of their world.

At one point they climbed high enough that a couple of sky-creatures swooped by them, glistening beautifully. They looked so small from afar, but up close, they were around the length of his outstretched arm.

But soon the Riftmaster was leading him back down and onto the ground – into an enclosed clearing where the soil was bared, and little moss grew. It was nestled into a nook on the other side of the tree, huddled into a tangle of its roots that reminded him of a bird's nest.

The Riftmaster's satchel hung from a piece of bark that had been cut loose and pried away from the trunk. As Bailey looked around, he began to dig through it, and pulled out a small armful of leather pouches.

"This hollow must have been formed as the roots of this tree closed around a source of nutrients. Maybe a rotting fruit, or a dead animal of some kind. It's long gone, now, but it left behind the perfect spot for a garden."

"A garden?"

That sounded far too normal to be right.

"Yes. To ensure I never run out of herbs, my first task is always to find a spot to plant some more. If we ever run out of tester herbs, or detoxifying ones, then we'd be in trouble. But first we need to plant a neutraliser. Since the other plants are from other worlds, it'll allow them all to grow in this soil." He tossed one of the pouches to Bailey, who lurched forward to catch it.

When he did, the Riftmaster grinned and chuckled, pleased. "Nice one."

Bailey opened up the pouch, and found it full of small, white seeds.

"I'll poke some holes in the soil, you follow after and drop in a seed. Sound good?"

Bailey nodded.

• • •

After such a rocky start to the morning, gardening was a pleasant change. The Riftmaster scattered the ash from the previous night's fire to act as fertiliser, and then they got to work. At first, they worked in peaceful silence, listening to the sounds of the wood. But eventually, when Bailey was able to relax knowing that they were well and truly safe, he allowed his mind to wander.

Soon, his mood began to settle back into its prior state of disgruntled melancholy. This place may have been beautiful, but it still wasn't home. The Riftmaster alone could never replace his family.

Feeling his heart growing heavier, Bailey tried to strike up a conversation. Luckily, his mentor seemed eager to please –

and the opportunity to boast appeared to be exactly what he needed.

"So, Riftmaster… You must have been to all sorts of worlds. Did you have a favourite?"

The man looked up in surprise – and then grinned. "Of course I do! A lot of them, actually. Would you like to hear about a few?"

Bailey nodded eagerly.

"Well, there was a time that I got dropped into a world where the rivers were more alcohol than water. It was the only thing to drink… So you can imagine how that went."

"That sounds great!"

"I mean… sort-of. Of course, life had evolved to cope with it, so I was the only one that was drunk. Have you ever tried staying alive whilst constantly hammered? It's hard enough on Earth! And the fumes – oh God, the fumes!"

Bailey couldn't help but laugh, thinking back to the wildest nights he'd had back at home. Bailey was never a big drinker, so he'd always be the first one needing to be carried home.

"As luck would have it, I was only there for two weeks or I'd have been in serious trouble. But I swear, the hangover lasted two centuries."

He paused with an embarrassed chuckle.

"I wish I could tell you more. I think I might have escaped a predator by throwing up on it? I'm not sure. That world is all a blur. No idea why."

Bailey caught him wink before he turned back to his work.

"There was also a time where I found myself on a planet that rained diamonds. Now I might be the richest person in the universe!"

Bailey laughed at that. "Are they really any use to you out here?"

"You'd be surprised. Diamonds aren't just pretty – they're hard, too. Many sentient species use them as currency, or in technology, et cetera. Diamonds have got me out of a few sticky situations in the past. Let me tell you about this one time…"

Bailey grinned, and listened to his story.

After that there was a moment of silence as they continued to work, but it was a pleasant silence.

"What about you, Rifthopper? Did you… ah… you

know… have any hobbies or anything…? You know… back on Earth?"

Bailey hesitated, feeling the question weighing on his heart. The Riftmaster was easy to question; he'd been to so many planets and seen so many things that it was easy to avoid the difficult subjects.

But when it came to Bailey, Earth was all he knew.

The Riftmaster hastily tried to cover his tracks. "If you don't wan–"

But Bailey stopped him.

"No, it's okay. I collected old books. Sometimes I went to the gym, too."

It was a feeble answer, and not one that meant much all the way out here. In truth, Bailey could have listed any number of other things; playing videogames, reading, studying, listening to music… but truth be told, he'd never been the type to engage much in hobbies. He had never played any sports, and Bailey didn't feel like explaining the specifics of advancing technology. Things like videogames and the internet could mean that the modern-day Earth could feel just as alien to the Riftmaster as any other world he visited.

But old books… well, those were a comfort to him. He loved the dusty smell of their pages and the elegantly-scrawled names he sometimes found on the inside covers. He loved the old-timey charm of the stories they told, and liked to marvel at how much things had changed since they were written.

"Ahh. That's nice."

The silence returned, and this time the atmosphere was thick with discomfort. After a long while, Bailey broke it.

"Are you sure you won't tell me your name?" he asked again. He tried to keep his tone light, but his voice was weary.

"Certain," the Riftmaster answered quietly.

"Okay… that's alright," Bailey said with tangible disappointment.

The Riftmaster snorted with amusement. "Don't worry, you're not missing out on much."

Yet more silence passed between them as they worked. Bailey picked through the facts he already knew about the Riftmaster to try and find something to talk about. And then it struck him.

"1960, huh?" he supposed that even though the Riftmaster didn't have any ancient stories, he could still have some interesting tales to tell. Still, he… didn't know exactly how old the Riftmaster had been back then, so he would have to guess. "So you lived through the second world war?"

"Yeah. But don't get your hopes up for a story; I was 3 when it started, so I don't remember much. My family lived in Keswick, and my dad managed to get exemption from the army as a conscientious objector. As kids go, I was one of the luckiest. Aside from a few bomb scares, we were pretty safe."

The Riftmaster glanced up at him, the expression on his face unreadable.

"I've been to Keswick!" Bailey said in amazement. "My family used to take me there when I was a kid. We'd go on long walks through the hills, and I… well… I hated it."

The Riftmaster gave a small huff of amusement.

"I miss it now, though," Bailey added after a while. "The views from the hilltops always made it worth it, even if I cried all the way up."

"Did you ever climb Latrigg?"

"Latrigg?"

"Latrigg was a hill overlooking the village. You could see the whole valley from up there – all the way across the lake. It was my favourite place. I used to go up there to get away from my family."

Bailey thought back, but with dismay realised he hadn't. "I don't think so," he said sheepishly. But then, so as not to end the conversation prematurely, added "What was your family like?"

"They were alright. They did the job. Devout Catholics, and nothing I did was ever right for them." The Riftmaster spoke slowly, choosing his words carefully. He was silent for a time after he finished. After a while, though, he continued. "…I suppose I didn't appreciate them as much as I should have. …But I still think I'm better off out here."

The Riftmaster cleared his throat. "What about yours?"

"They were… nice. Relaxed. They were just… a normal family, with a mum, a dad, and two kids. My mum's a firefighter, and my dad works in tech support. My little sister is nine. They all live down in London, whilst I moved up north to go to university in Newcastle." Bailey paused, feeling the lump growing in his throat. He stopped planting for a moment and looked away. "I haven't seen them since summer."

Bailey's voice cracked, and he trailed off.

"If I'd just known it would be the last time…"

The Riftmaster didn't respond, but Bailey felt the pouch of seeds gently removed from his grasp. He looked at the Riftmaster questioningly through bleary eyes.

"That's enough for today… we still need to leave room for the rest," the Riftmaster said gently. "And we still have to gather food before it rains again. Do you want to come with me, or…?"

Bailey shook his head miserably.

"Alright. I won't be long."

•　•　•

After the Riftmaster had guided him on his way, Bailey navigated the tangle of tree roots back to the hollow with relative ease. When he could see what remained of his own trail on the forest floor below, he found it easy to make his own way back.

Right before he entered the makeshift shelter, moving unsteadily down the root, the young man tripped over something. He stumbled down the remaining steps of the natural walkway, and finally looked back at his path to see a mountain-dweller's horn embedded in the root.

With a small grunt, Bailey pulled it free and took it inside.

He sat alone for a time, revelling in the crushing quietness and wishing that it would never end. He heard the rain begin to fall against the leaves outside in a melancholy chorus. Finally, around a half-hour later, the Riftmaster finally stumbled in out of the rain, soaked to the bone and carrying more closed flowerbuds.

Although the Riftmaster quickly shed his outer layers of clothing, his pale skin soon became blotchy, speckled with darker patches – he'd spent too long in the rain.

Together they waited, and waited, but the storm was relentless.

That night they ate together in silence, and this time there was no fire to keep the mood light.

Any exchanged words were few and far between, and they never felt like enough. Their meagre supply of food soon ran out.

Both Bailey and the Riftmaster eventually slept, and Bailey could see from the man's expression that he was fretting – though whether it was about their garden or their lack of food, he couldn't be sure.

When they awoke, the storm still raged.

It was 2 days – perhaps more – before the storm had passed, and the duo emerged as if into a whole new world, their faces paler and their cheeks gaunt, squinting in the lantern light.

Chapter 7
Branching Out

With no rising sun or moon to tell the time, it was easy to lose track of the days; and despite the Riftmaster's initial wariness both he and Bailey soon found themselves settling into a steady routine of eating, sleeping, and tending their growing garden.

Bailey was surprised by just how rapidly the first herbs grew, soon covering the ground with a carpet of tiny leaves and small blue flowers. After that, the Riftmaster sprinkled the last of his toxin-detecting herbs over one half of the garden, and buried some sharp, red seeds on the other.

"It's a gamble," the Riftmaster announced as they did so. "But I'm hoping it'll pay off."

And then all they had to do was wait.

The humans' temporary shelter was beginning to feel more like home than Bailey would have liked to admit, but both knew that it wasn't ideal. With each passing day, the Riftmaster seemed to grow more agitated about finding a more permanent abode, or making this one more secure.

Perhaps most pressingly, the bush from which they picked their floral food supply was beginning to dwindle.

Finally, when he was satisfied that the garden was growing strongly without them needing to tend it, the Riftmaster announced that they were expanding their range and taking a trip.

Rather than donning their worn hide cloaks once again, the

Riftmaster wove some of his leather necklaces into a pair of huge leaves. Ever-resourceful, he made the leaves into loosely fitting waterproof shawls to keep them safe from the acid rain.

And then, with the forest creatures chasing one another high above and his stomach fluttering with nervous dread, Bailey followed the Riftmaster across the winding roots and deeper into the titanic wood.

• • •

Most of the creatures in this world appeared to live their lives on the wing, but Bailey saw a few creatures trundling across the ground below them. Mostly he saw long and millipede-like creatures with legs that moved in rippling waves – presumably, a relative of the similar serpentine beasts that sailed and wound through the trees above them.

Though mostly they were small – well, the smallest being the length of his forearm – Bailey saw one twice the length of a man, resting on a tree trunk with feathered feelers whisking peacefully at the air.

At one point, they heard a distant, booming sound like wind howling in a ravine, and both humans tensed. When the sound was at its loudest, the Riftmaster pointed out a train of rippling lights that undulated through the distant trees. They could only speculate at what sort of creature the sound belonged to.

Bailey found himself feeling awfully small. He was an insect among insects here.

No matter the shape or size of the creature though, all of them seemed to gleam with iridescence or pulse with lights.

Bailey looked down often to see the labyrinthine forest floor beneath them, but rarely could he see all the way to the shadowy ground. He often heard the sound of running water, though, and sometimes he could pick out a myriad of lights glistening off tiny streams and rushing rivers of rainwater beneath them.

As they moved further away from the shelter along the winding roots that curved and arched out of the ground, the Riftmaster marked changes in their path by cutting deep gouges into the wood with his silver knife, or leaving behind a fragment of one of his relics. A half-buried tooth here, a glimmering gem there... In theory, it meant that all they needed to do was change roots whenever they saw a mark in the path beneath their feet. But unless someone knew precisely what to look for, it would be impossible to follow them.

Not that Bailey was particularly concerned about that; the young man didn't think that anything on this world was clever enough to even *want* to follow them.

It was as he voiced these thoughts aloud that the Riftmaster offered a gentle scolding.

"Intelligence comes in many forms, Rifthopper. Unless you remember that, you won't be lasting long out here," he said, raising a hand to shade his face as he looked out at the sprawling path before them. "Just because something can't speak the same language as you, doesn't mean it can't understand."

A pair of flying creatures pulsed in and out of view as they chased one another across the sky, squeaking and twittering. Bailey followed them with his gaze.

"The humans living on Earth are stupid to think we're the only ones. Intelligence isn't a one-way scale like most people think; it's a spectrum."

The little creatures dived and swooped around their tree root, before shooting up into the tree canopy and disappearing among the many lights.

"Look at them. They probably think we're dumb, too," the Riftmaster joked as they continued on.

Soon, the two humans found themselves passing into a forest of undergrowth, towering grass stems and glowing flowers sprouting in tufts from the ground below. Bailey could no longer see the ground for the masses of vegetation growing there, or the canopy for the creatures swimming through the air above their heads. Bailey's vision was filled with a rainbow of neon.

They must have been travelling for many hours before they finally found a place to rest, beneath the intersecting roots of yet another great tree. Here they paused, to discuss their plan of action.

Exhausted beyond belief, hungry, and thirsty, Bailey could only nod and listen.

"We need to scout the nearby area and find a new food

source. Only one sort of plant seems to be edible around here, and even then it's only the flowers. I just hope it isn't too rare."

Bailey nodded.

"When we find something, we'll mark the way, and try to find more. The garden won't be ready to harvest for a while yet."

Another nod.

"–And we need to find a reliable water supply as well. I'm thinking that cutting into the trees will..."

"Mmm-hm," Bailey agreed with a half-hearted smile.

"...I'll keep watch for..."

"Sure."

The Riftmaster's voice faded into a low background murmur as Bailey's eyelids grew heavy.

"...Bailey...? Rifthopper?"

• • •

When Bailey awoke, it was already time to go. Hungry, thirsty, and grumpy, he staggered to his feet and once again followed behind his mentor. Luckily, it didn't take too long to find what they were looking for.

It was Bailey who spotted the kind of bush they sought, and he did so with a shout of joy.

"There!"

The Riftmaster was awfully pleased, and praised him until he felt giddy with glee, even if Bailey half-suspected that the Riftmaster had overlooked it on purpose. He felt like he was learning well; this planet was just harsh enough to keep his mind from his despair, and easy enough to feel the occasional relief that came with being safe in a dangerous world.

And yet, something tugged at his nerves; it felt *too* easy.

The creatures here didn't seem to care about their presence, and Bailey had noticed a distinct lack of predatory creatures. There were few dead things as well, at least on the winding world of roots Bailey and the Riftmaster stuck to. Bailey was almost afraid to see just what roamed the maze-like world of the forest floor.

But they had to go down eventually.

With the first food-bearing bush they found, it was easy to

reach the lowest-hanging flowers by reaching from their walkways.

However, Bailey and the Riftmaster had to descend to the ground in order to find the way to the next one, and in doing so were forced to navigate the treacherous, marshy tangle below. Obviously, Bailey had been on the ground before; but he was certain the area around the first great tree had been far less claustrophobic. Perhaps it was in part due to the Riftmaster's insistence in keeping off the ground so that they could know the world around.

The ground, he said, could be useful as an escape route if they ran into real trouble. But in addition to being easily hunted by creatures that knew the terrain better, if they got lost down there, there would be no way out.

Bailey and the Riftmaster were on high alert as they pushed through towering stems and between moss-covered boulders, navigating the choking mist that clung to the earth. Halfway there, Bailey found himself coming face to face with a harsh dose of reality.

For there, lying at the side of their path was a rotting corpse, as yet untouched by nature.

It looked like a massive bear, with broad shoulders and wickedly hooked claws, and jaws that could very easily have crushed metal. Its teeth were like sabres, and it looked to have had five eyes in spiderlike formation, now no more than shrunken hollows in their sockets. Rather than fur, the creature's leathery flesh was shrinking into a rust-red external carapace.

Bailey hung back, but the Riftmaster approached despite Bailey wishing he wouldn't.

"Well, would you look at that," the Riftmaster said in wonder, as he knelt down by the carcase. "You're not supposed to be here, are you? Bailey, come look."

He fingered its wicked-looking fangs, and stroked a section of its carapace.

Bailey shook his head and held up his hands.

"I'm good."

The Riftmaster gave him a strange look. Then he sighed and continued anyway. "Do you know what this is, Bailey?"

"This world's apex predator?" he guessed, eyeing the dead creature's fangs nervously.

The Riftmaster shook his head. "No," his tone was low. "This is one of us. A Rifter."

Bailey stared at the creature in bewilderment. "You mean it's from another world?"

The Riftmaster nodded. "Do you want to know how I know?"

Bailey looked at him expectantly.

The Riftmaster continued. "It's because I've been to their world before. I might have known this big guy. Maybe even rode it."

He paused, to let that sink in, before continuing.

"That, and…"

He turned the great head slightly to the side with gentle hands – a glowing blue substance was oozing from the side of its mouth.

Bailey recoiled.

"Do they usually do that?"

The Riftmastar followed his gaze, and shook his head.

"Poor guy must have gone mad with hunger. He couldn't catch any of the flying creatures, so he started eating the flowers instead. He poisoned himself."

The man allowed its head to drop before giving its cheek one last pat, then stepped back and studied it.

"It's not all bad, though. In fact, this is perfect! We can use his carapace to make you some armour, and his teeth for some tools. Maybe even a knife! You're overdue for a bit of protection. We might even be able to salvage some hide from his belly!"

Bailey stared at the creature, in all of its peaceful stillness, a sick feeling rising in his belly.

"But… but you said you might have known him. At the very least you… knew where he came from. Shouldn't we bury him? Or… do what they might have done?"

"Hardly. He doesn't care anymore. This is a golden opportunity for us!"

"But that's… so disrespectful…"

"Think of it this way; his body might save our lives one day. I hope that when I die, my remains get to keep someone else alive. Think of it like… I don't know. I'd much rather continue travelling long after my death than be put in the ground and forgotten about. Wouldn't you?"

"I suppose…"

"Remember, Bailey. Earth customs mean nothing all the way out here. By sticking to them, you'll only make things harder for yourself."

Bailey fell silent. Their original mission forgotten, he tried not to think about what they were doing.

As he began to tend to the body, the Riftmaster filled the silence with stories of the world this creature had come from.

"…They lived together in enormous tribes created and governed by a single queen. You might say their culture was… primitive. But they looked out for one another and the Tribe. They were honourable beasts."

He told Bailey all about their lives and their tribes; their hostile world of volcanic ash, and how he had been accepted into their world so long as he looked out for their Queen as they did.

To them, he said, the Tribe was the most important thing. Life was lived in the moment, and death was the end. It was just a part of life; not something to be celebrated or mourned. It was only when the Queen passed into oblivion that the tribe would grieve – and, knowing that there was no hope left, each surviving member would tilt their heads skyward and sing a mournful song.

With all their voices combined, the whole planet would soon know that it was the end of an era, and the song would last until the final voice had fallen silent, marking the day that the last surviving member of the Tribe had dropped dead – perhaps to starvation, perhaps predators.

But they would keep singing until their very last breath.

Bailey listened, and when the time finally came to leave the body, he felt as though he was leaving behind an old friend.

"I hope one day you'll get to serve them as I did. Maybe you'll be able to return his bones to his Queen," the Riftmaster said as he finally turned away, arms piled high with fangs, scales and leathery skin.

The body behind them had been disassembled beyond recognition.

And though it still felt wrong just leaving it there to rot, Bailey had convinced himself that wearing the creature's armour for his own would be the kind of funeral that the creature would have wanted.

. . .

Whilst the Riftmaster focused on putting together a set of makeshift armour, it was Bailey's duty to go and gather food and scout the nearby area. Being on his own was, at first, a frightening concept; and he startled at every small noise, whipping around to face anything that moved just outside of his eyeline.

Soon though, he grew used to the newness. Although he kept to well-known tracks and avoided the area around the carcase like the plague, he found himself enjoying the freedom.

When he returned, he would learn from his mentor how to bind the materials together and measure the desired shapes.

Finally, when he came back after a particularly long trip, the Riftmaster had a gift awaiting him.

It was a set of armour, roughly hewn out of dully gleaming chitin and leather taken from the body of the beast. It had pauldrons and breastplate made of rusty carapace, and plates for his knees, elbows and shins, but was mostly a reddish-black leather. When Bailey took it, it was surprisingly light.

It was by no means impressive, but it was far better than the faded t-shirt and tattered jeans he still wore from Earth.

It felt strange to be wearing more than cotton and denim, but most of all it felt good to be wearing something new.

The Riftmaster also offered a knife, sharpened from a single saber-like fang with a grip carved out and wrapped in leather. He tied it to Bailey's belt.

"You should use it to shave," the Riftmaster joked.

Bailey raised a hand and rubbed his bristly cheek, feeling his face grow hot. He laughed, even if his voice was high with embarrassment, as he tried to think of a good comeback.

But his mentor was, as always, clean-shaven.

For the first time, though, Bailey felt like a true apprentice of the interstellar traveller.

. . .

Days later, they returned to harvest their herb garden. In their absence, it had flourished, and the Riftmaster was both relieved and ecstatic to see the results. He hummed softly to himself as he showed Bailey how to harvest the seeds and the flowers separately.

Later, when they returned to their initial shelter, he showed Bailey how to preserve them by the light and warmth of the fire.

"I haven't had a harvest like this in a hundred years or so. This should last us another few planets, easily!" the Riftmaster told his apprentice, excitement plain to see.

Bailey grinned back. He was beginning to get used to what he thought of as the Riftmaster's eccentricities. His mentor's optimism in the face of such impossible odds was beginning to grow infectious; it was as if Bailey had known him forever, even though it had only been around a month since arriving in the mountain world.

This planet was starting to feel a little like home.

Earth, on the other hand, was beginning to feel like a distant dream, the open wound healing into a dully-aching scar. It was becoming rarer by the day that he'd sit down to think about where he'd come from; it was better to simply close that part off from conscious thought and focus on the now.

Even if it still hurt.

"So, what now?" Bailey asked after a while.

They'd brought plenty of food plants back with them from the source they'd found. They wouldn't need to return to it for a while. That left the potential future open, and Bailey's stomach fluttering with nervous excitement.

"I don't know. Scout some more, I guess. There's still a lot we don't know about this planet. I'd quite like to see the sky... And more food sources couldn't hurt, if we can find them. What do you think?"

Bailey perked up as his opinion was asked. "Sounds good! But... Why the sky?"

The Riftmaster smiled. "Good! Set off in few hours?" he shifted as he considered how best to answer Bailey's question. "And... On most planets I like to use the stars to navigate. Even in places like this it's... just nice to look up and see a familiar constellation. So I'd... I'd like to find a place where we can see the sky."

The man had tipped his head back, and a dreamlike look crossed his face.

Bailey nodded, and scooted over so that he was facing out into the forest. "I'll take first watch." He heard his mentor chuckle softly. "Now that's a surprise." The Riftmaster stood, and there was a rustle as he settled down to sleep.

"Goodnight, young Rifthopper."

"Night, Riftmaster."

Despite being used to saying it, Bailey still couldn't help feeling that the name didn't sit right on his tongue. Pondering it, he stared out into the dark and the drizzling rain, and admired the gleaming lights of this world.

He kept his word, and boldly fended off the drowsiness that threatened to sweep him away.

Chapter 8
The Bigger Picture

As soon as both Bailey and the Riftmaster were well-rested and well-fed, they set off once again, carefully picking their way along the path back to their second base. From their shelter there they chose their next course over a brisk snack to keep themselves energised.

It wasn't long before they were pressing on, following the winding tree roots once again and leaving the known world behind. Bailey felt like they were hardly moving, the trees around them towering like skyscrapers, as still and majestic as mountains. Both humans were largely silent as they moved deeper, listening instead to the sounds of creatures moving in the dark.

After a while, the Riftmaster began to climb onto higher-arching roots, trotting along narrow walkways much more quickly. Bailey soon struggled to keep up and was panting sides heaving as he jogged cautiously after, wobbling precariously along the narrowest roots. At first he was uncertain why the Riftmaster had suddenly picked up the pace, but then he realised that the world was growing brighter. Distant trees were lit by a silver glow that shimmered like the surface of a river.

He could make out the shapes of the leaves casting dappled shadows on the mossy earth, and a carpet of ethereal flowers lit the way.

Silvery shapes could be seen weaving through the light,

glistening and glinting and flowing with their wondrous shoals.

The two humans exchanged glances that were joyous and curious, and hurried on, hopping the small gaps between roots and helping each other climb between them. As they got closer, Bailey could see the reason for the gap in the tree canopy – an enormous fallen log lay in the centre of the clearing, a tangled mess of its roots and branches reaching for the sky. To cover the last distance between them and the silvery shafts of starlight, the two humans descended onto the ground, and then climbed the rugged bark of the fallen log. The tree was so big, and so old, that it had half-sunk into the ground, and its sides were ridged and rough. There were plenty of nooks and crannies to grasp, and ledges that the humans could shimmy their way along.

When they reached the top, their feet sank again into soft mosses.

The Riftmaster pulled back his hood, craned his head back and peered up towards the sky.

Framed by leaves and branches and fish-like creatures flying in a whirlwind, he saw a single star casting its milky light down onto them.

But the sky itself was hidden away beyond the trees.

Bailey looked out, back to the way they had come. The log was the perfect vantage point to see for miles through the towering trees and the glowing flowers, lights softly swaying in every direction, and radiant fruits hanging high above them. Bailey could make out the shadows of the titanic trees which had given them shelter, miles and miles away. The serpentine creatures didn't seem fazed by their presence, and danced around them, crying out and singing softly.

One came so close that Bailey could have reached out and touched it before it swooped away.

The Riftmaster walked out onto a long-severed branch to see if he could get a better view of the stars. Bailey followed, and felt his stomach drop as he saw the forest floor falling away beneath them into a gentle ravine, where a glistening river of rainwater was visible far below.

And yet… the view also took his breath away.

Eventually, the Riftmaster sighed in defeat. There was no way they'd ever be able to climb high enough to get a proper view; Bailey could see only one star through a tiny gap in the tree canopy.

"We should go. We don't want to alert anything that might want to eat us. We're very exposed out here."

Bailey looked one last time out of the forest, committing the view to his memory, and then finally nodded.

He turned back to the Riftmaster, only for his gaze to be drawn back out to the woods by a movement. He looked out, gaze trailing over the lights which suddenly seemed so pale against the starlight. He realised with a shudder of fear that some of them were drawing nearer… and although he passed them off at first as another group of sky-creatures, he realised that they were too oddly symmetrical, like the windows on a train.

Something *else* was coming.

Something *bigger.*

As the smaller creatures scattered with trailing alarm calls, the creature emerged into the light. Like an enormous shark, the length of a steam train, it sailed through the air on undulating fins. Its body was a deep cyan blue, and it rippled with lights, white markings down its sides flashing in hypnotic sequence. Its head was long, pointed and streamlined, reminding Bailey distinctly of the muzzle of a fox.

Bailey felt the Riftmaster's hand fall against his chest, grasping his breastplate, and the man pulled him down against the trunk of the fallen tree.

Bailey's heart pounded.

For a second they saw the creature's head turn, and for an instant, he was certain that it looked their way. But it ignored them, and swooped upwards. They saw the scales of its belly, and waves of lights flashing by as it swooped over them, upwards, until it blotted out the starlight.

Its jaws snapped shut on several of the gleaming creatures, as the fleeing survivors pulsed bright with fright. Most had already scattered into the trees, but the ones that were too slow, or too sick, remained.

As it arced through the sky with a majesty like the greatest whales of the ocean, Bailey heard it cry like the wind howling through the ravine.

Finally, when it had eaten its fill, it began to sink in height, its undulations carrying it at a slower pace. It followed the ravine beneath the fallen tree, and then, when it reached the branch where the humans clung, looped with unmistakable curiosity. It swooped in alongside them, and then with a deep thud, collided with the tree trunk. Bird-like talons on the tips of its sails clung to the tree bark, and the rest folded back on bony fingers. It now hung from the fallen tree like a hooked fish, its intent clear as its eye – or what Bailey took to be an eye – flickered back towards them.

"It's looking at us," Bailey hissed in horrified wonder.

Bailey heard the Riftmaster's breaths, sharp.

They remained where they were for a while, almost hugging one another. But the great creature didn't move; hardly breathed, and didn't even try to reach out and snap them up.

It just looked at them.

After quite some time, the Riftmaster stood, and with cautious steps, began to move along the tree branch. The creature turned its muzzle and made a deep grumbling sound, following his motions.

Then, with a long whine as though frightened by the sudden movement, it let go, and continued its flight through the ravine.

It flew up, and up, and up… and then, with a wide loop, changed course.

It was about to swoop beneath their branch.

"It's scared," the Riftmaster murmured. "But curious. It's never seen anything like us before."

With nervous steps, the Riftmaster made his way to the end of the branch.

The creature banked sharply up, then down, for a better look. It glided in another wide loop about the branch, passing over them, and then once again beneath them. It made a figure of eight, twisting in the air and arced over them with a majesty that took both their breaths away.

As it circled, looking, and rumbling, and finally singing that song of the wind, Bailey caught the Riftmaster's eye. His heart sank… with the moment of terror over, and adrenaline still coursing through his veins, the mischievous look in the man's eye was the last thing he wanted to see.

"What?" Bailey asked. "What are you thinking?"

The Riftmaster looked up as the massive creature passed over them again.

"Something really stupid."

"Oh... no."

Bailey caught sight of the creature's back – its leathery-looking carapace and scales almost like the back of an enormous alligator, swooping beneath them. It was so close that Bailey could almost touch it.

The Riftmaster grabbed Bailey's wrist and tugged him to the edge of the branch. "Think of it like a test..."

"A t–"

Before he could even finish the question his mentor jumped from the end of the branch and dropped like a stone. Bailey had no choice but to follow.

He felt himself collide with the flying creature's back and scrambled for a grip. Panic flared as he felt himself slipping, but then he felt a firm hand grab his arm, supporting him just enough to grab onto a few of its ridges.

The flying beast rumbled in startlement at the impact, but otherwise didn't seem to notice them sitting on its back. It circled one last time and, seeing the target of its curiosity gone, soared upwards into the tree canopy.

Bailey and the Riftmaster clung to the leathery scales on its back as it soared. The sails along its sides lent it stability; the ride was almost as smooth as a journey by train, and Bailey could hardly believe they were in the air.

Bailey saw the glowing fruit hanging closer than he'd ever seen before, but they passed them by. The gap in the tree canopy widened until they broke through it, and a vast expanse of stars opened out around them. The forest sprawled out beneath them as far as the eye could see, littered with lights and reflecting the glow of the stars. A massive moon loomed just above the horizon.

When it was above the treeline, the creature stayed low. Its head flickered from side to side; and it appeared to be looking for a way to re-enter the woods. Bailey could see other lights moving above the forest.

For the first time in weeks, Bailey felt a cool wind whipping against his face. The Riftmaster moved in close so that they could hear each other's voices. "What do you think?" he panted.

"How do we get down!?" yelled Bailey above the winds.

"Don't worry, it'll have to eat soon. Then we can hop off! For now just enjoy the ride."

"How do you know?!" Bailey called back.

"It spends its life aloft. That must take a lot of energy. Look, it's already hunting again!"

They hung on tight as the undulating creature circled and dived towards the tiny shape of an unsuspecting forest creature which had found itself above the safety of the trees. It missed, and gave chase.

"Aren't you worried about leaving our shelter?!" Bailey continued, voice high with panic. If the creature went much further, there was no way they'd ever find their way back to their garden. They were plunging into the unknown once again, and goodness knew what would await them on the forest floor.

"Not at all... We have everything we own with us already! This is no different to Rifting, except we know this planet already!"

The great creature soon slowed, as its prey pulled ahead and disappeared back in between the leaves.

Bailey's heart pounded in his ears. Goodness knew where they were going; but he heard his mentor let out a whoop of joy.

"This is what makes it all worth it, Rifthopper!" he called out above the wind.

"Yeah!" Bailey answered breathlessly, feeling his heart soar. For one heart-stopping moment the creature arced upwards, giving them a perfect view of the forest. Bailey felt like he could see to the end of the world. "Can you see where we are now?"

"Yeah! Do you know about constellations?" the Riftmaster called after.

"Not much. Why?"

"We're in Orion's Belt. This is one of the planets orbiting Alnilam – the central star to the belt. The star we saw from the clearing was Mintaka, one of the others."

"...meaning...?"

The Riftmaster leaned in close – so close that they leaned shoulder-to-shoulder, and his red hair tickled the side of Bailey's face. He pointed to a space in the sky speckled with only the tiniest of stars.

"See that? In the very middle. That tiny star, so pale. Doesn't look like much, does it?"

Bailey strained to focus on the star that the Riftmaster pointed out, and then shook his head.

"That, young Rifthopper, is your solar system. That's Earth's sun. Isn't that crazy?"

It made Bailey's stomach drop to see just how far away they were – how far they'd come. The sheer distance was unimaginable; humanity probably wouldn't reach... or even *discover* the life on this planet for hundreds, if not thousands of years. And that was if humanity didn't wipe itself out first.

"...Wow," the young man breathed. That was all he could think to say.

"You're the only man in the universe, Bailey, to see this. How does that feel?"

Bailey opened his mouth to say 'amazing'. Incredible. Wondrous. That he of all people had been pulled from Earth and managed to survive it. But... there was no way he could ever tell anyone back home. No way he could ever share this story or teach people about the things he'd seen.

"Where is the mountain-dwellers' planet?" he asked, tearing his mind away from home. Seeing the sheer distance had opened a new kind of hole in his heart.

"That would be aaaaaall the way over there," the Riftmaster said with a wide gesture to the opposite end of the horizon. "This planet is a lot closer to Earth than that one was. You can't even see the mountain-dwellers' star from here."

Bailey followed his gaze, looking.

Their ride descended nearer the treetops, and Bailey watched the leaves sweeping by, casting an eye over the distant mountaintops. He'd become so familiar with this world that their little garden, and the tree whose roots formed their shelter, had almost felt like home. It would be sad to leave it behind.

"Can we name this planet?!" Bailey called above the wind.

"What?!" the Riftmaster called back.

"Can we name it?!" Bailey yelled, louder this time. "Since we're the first humans who discovered this place."

"Uh, sure?" the Riftmaster answered. He seemed confused by the notion. "Why?"

"I don't know... it'd just... you know... feel nice," Bailey responded, feeling slightly foolish. "Because we discovered it."

His cheeks burned despite the cold. He didn't know why he wanted to name it, truly. It just... felt like the right thing to do. All the other planets back in Earth's solar system had names. Like naming pets, or cars, or boats; Bailey supposed it was a way of laying claim to things. He'd never really thought about it in that way before.

"Oh. Well, yeah! It's been a long time since I thought about naming anything. I usually ask the locals what they call it. You run out of names after a while. Do you..." the Riftmaster paused in a moment of awkwardness. "Do you have any ideas?"

Bailey nodded.

"I... I want to name it after one of Earth's rainforests, because it's so full of life, and... beautiful, too."

"Go on?"

"...And I've really started feeling at home here." He looked down at the leaves flashing by wistfully. "I'm really gonna miss it when we have to go."

The Riftmaster followed his gaze to the glittering woods slumbering beneath the starry sky. It was a sight that Bailey hoped he'd never forget, not even in the thousands of years he might live.

"Same here," the Riftmaster admitted. "It's been a nice change."

The pair sat in silence for one more moment.

"So, what do you want to name this place?"

Bailey opened his mouth to speak but only a sharp gasp emerged as a bright white light filled his vision. A fiery pain flooded over his skin. All too soon, the Rift had come for them yet again. Bailey heard the creature they were riding bellow with fright, and felt its back drop away from under his feet.

He floated in nothingness for a moment, surrounded by the light of the Rift, and struggled for one last glance of the leaves and trees of this planet he'd come to know as home.

His planet.

"Amazonia," Bailey murmured, leaving the sound to fall on the deaf ears of the earth it was associated with.

Chapter 9
The Rift

The planet on which the Rift dropped them next was a far cry from anything that Bailey was expecting, or hoping for. Their time there passed in a blur as they lived their lives on the run, fugitives from nature itself. It was through a mixture of the Riftmaster's resourcefulness and pure, dumb luck that they survived long enough for the Rift to take them away.

The next world they visited was dying, and Bailey thought he might have caught a glimpse into mankind's future there. It was an image that would haunt the rest of his days, and a message that he would never forget.

It was there that the Riftmaster taught Bailey how to grind the herbs they'd grown into brightly coloured powders. He learned how to mix these powders with water and how to test potential food sources for the various toxins that would otherwise poison them. The Riftmaster also taught him that some of these toxins could be repurposed to use as fertiliser for growing their vital herbs.

"You just need to remember," the Riftmaster told him. "Every planet is different. Some won't have any food, some won't have water. You'll need to learn to filter it from the mud, make food where none exists. The universe doesn't necessarily want you to survive. But there is always another way."

Then he looked up into the sky where, somewhere beyond the smog, the stars would be twinkling.

They next found themselves on an ocean planet, where their journey began somewhat inelegantly. Bailey was startled into a panic as the Rift plunged him face-first into waist-deep water. He surfaced a moment later, coughing and choking.

"Bailey! This way!"

The words were muffled through the water in his ears, and Bailey glanced around wildly, blinking the salt from his eyes. He finally found the Riftmaster, wading out onto the shore with his satchel held above the waves. Once he found his footing, Bailey soon followed, hauling the sodden mass of his cloak ashore.

The Riftmaster dumped his satchel onto the chestnut sand and approached his apprentice.

"Are you okay?"

With the brine lapping around his hands and knees, Bailey heaved deep breaths.

Bailey looked out to sea and aside from a far-off smudge of grey shrouded in mist, saw no sign of land. Two silvery moons hung above the horizon, one of them distant and small, where the other lit the sky. Compared to them, the sun shone faint and pale.

"I… I'm fine," he said, then gulped. "We were lucky to land so close to shore."

The Riftmaster shrugged slightly. "I wouldn't worry, you'll rarely land more than a mile from land."

"A mile…!?"

"Of course. So long as you can swim, we'll be fine."

Bailey shivered. When was the last time he'd properly swum? Five years ago? Six? Seven, even? Either way, it had been years, and he suddenly wished that he'd paid more attention during swimming lessons.

Another wave swelled around Bailey's hands and knees, and he finally regained the sense enough to push himself to his feet. Small, squishy creatures with dappled brown hides dragged themselves frantically back into the waves with flailing tentacles as Bailey squelched over to a muddy bank with scrubby foliage clinging to its surface. He eased off his boots and placed them onto the sand. Shortly after, he shrugged off the waterlogged mountain-dweller cloak, and hung it up on a stray root.

Bailey swore as the root snapped, sending the heavy cloak thudding down onto the sand like a ton of bricks.

It took another few minutes before Bailey managed to hang the sand-covered garment up again.

Bailey finally straightened up to tie the blue stone pendant around his neck, before turning towards the Riftmaster. His mentor was rummaging through his belongings, but stopped briefly to toss a knife at a creature that was crawling slightly too close for his liking.

Unfortunately, he missed.

"Are the herbs okay?" Bailey asked, with a flash of fear. What if the sea had ruined them? Surely without the means to tell what was edible, they'd be doomed. Right?

"They're okay. A little soggy, but they'll do for this planet as long as we can find a good place to grow some more." The Riftmaster withdrew a few clumps of droopy, sodden leaves. "In the meantime, would you like to help me find fresh water?"

"Sure!"

The Riftmaster held out the herbs, and Bailey quickly received them.

"See if you can find a spring. I've tasted the seawater already, and we both know that won't do."

"Why not?"

"Too briny. Which can be useful in its own right, but... not right now. Our first priority is not dying."

Bailey nodded.

"If we can't find any more clean water, we can start to filter the seawater over fire tonight. Whilst you're searching for water, I'll gather firewood and put us together a shelter."

Bailey slung his cloak over his shoulder before the pair trudged away from the shore, rising above the sea level and onto a winding path along the labyrinth of what might have been a reef, once. Enormous fungi with broad, umbrella-like caps grew sporadically on sandy plateaus or in tight-packed clusters across the strangely levelled hillside, their roots leaving enormous fissures in earth and stone. Tough, yellowish scrubs grew from every crack and cranny.

As they travelled, the larger moon had begun to dip towards the horizon, and Bailey's eyelids began to droop.

"Think we could take shelter under one of those?" Bailey

asked, nodding towards a thicket of broad caps. The shady hollow beneath them looked dark and warm, and he doubted that the rain would be able to penetrate the thick cover of fungi.

The Riftmaster followed his gaze, then shook his head. "Too inviting. They'll probably drain us of our insides as we sleep, or put spores in our lungs."

Bailey shuddered.

When the Riftmaster had settled on an ideal spot for his shelter, the pair parted ways. Bailey left his mentor on a sandy plateau shaded by a rocky overhang, no more than a hundred metres above sea level.

Soon Bailey joined the path of a tiny silver stream. He followed it up towards the hilltop, and finally found a bubbling pool near the highest point of the island, gently steaming in the humid air. By the side of the pool, Bailey knelt and filled their waterskin, looking out across their new home.

The island could be no more than a mile across and other than that distant shadow on the horizon, now silhouetted beneath the vast shape of the moon, there seemed to be nowhere else to go.

The moon disappeared over the horizon shortly after Bailey returned, water pouch swollen at his belt. He sat down beside his mentor's fire, ducking underneath the curtain of mountain-crawler cloaks that had been hung across the entrance of their shelter.

"Hungry?" the Riftmaster asked triumphantly as he appeared. His mentor held up a slimy-looking mass by one tentacle.

Bailey nodded eagerly. "Thirsty?" he countered, raising the waterskin.

The Riftmaster laughed. "Ready to test it?"

"Me?" Bailey's skin prickled with sudden nervousness.

"Who else? You'll need to learn sooner or later. Remember what I taught you?"

"I think so."

Bailey took the herbs, the Riftmaster's bowls, and his filled waterskin outside. There, by the light of the smaller moon he could see colour more clearly than firelight. The Riftmaster made a show of preparing the slimy… thing to eat, humming softly to himself.

Bailey smiled slightly as he placed down a bowl, added a leaf, and with the pommel of his knife, ground it to a fine powder.

He poured in a few droplets of water, and the substance fizzed for a moment, but quickly settled. Bailey emptied and washed out the bowl, then moved onto the next. This time, a sprinkle of red petals was ground to dust and added to the mix. The water did not react this time, save for a vaguely purplish tint. Bailey's heartbeat quickened. He moved onto the final pinch of herbs, a small tuft of hair-like root. Once the water was added, he gently swilled the bowl, narrowing his eyes, then raised his head.

"It's clean!" he called towards the shelter.

The Riftmaster's head popped out for a look.

"Are you sure?"

Bailey nodded.

The Riftmaster approached, narrowed his eyes as he inspected the bowl of cloudy water. Finally appearing satisfied, he stepped back.

"Well?" Bailey asked.

"Don't ask me. Only one way to find out."

Taking this as encouragement, Bailey raised the waterskin to his lips, and took a swig. A moment later, he spluttered out the mouthful, sending droplets cascading over the mountainside.

"I thought it was clean!"

"Of biological toxins, yes. How did it taste?"

"…Salty," Bailey raised a hand and wiped his mouth on the back of his sleeve. "…Ah."

"You're getting there, Bailey. You just need to remember the obvious things, the simple things. Even on Earth, drinking seawater would be unwise."

Bailey looked downcast until the Riftmaster beckoned him over to the fireside. "Let me show you how to filter this," he said. "Oh, and keep what you can of the water. The soil here is poor, but the powdered herbs will help with that."

That night, the Riftmaster used a clay bowl to heat their water. Steam soon rose from the boiling pit, dripping from the tip of a carefully arranged Amazonian leaf into the freshly-emptied waterskin.

As the sun reached its zenith, both were blessed with a mouthful of clean, albeit warm water.

Later that day, the world plunged into darkness once more, as the sun disappeared behind the immense body of the rising moon. Bailey and the Riftmaster huddled together by their fire, using one another as a shield against the cold and the unknown.

• • •

The sun never truly seemed to set on this world. But, with the moons dominating the sky, it never really seemed to rise, either. The larger moon rose and fell quickly across the sky, rising in the north and setting in the south.

Luckily, the light of these two moons was bright, gold and warm.

The smaller moon circled the horizon once every few days, rising by only a few degrees each time. This moon never crossed paths with the other celestial bodies. But once a day, just past noon, the larger moon passed over the sun, causing a solar eclipse that plunged the world into near-complete darkness.

It was at that time that Bailey and the Riftmaster decided to rest, aligning their routine with the natural cycles of their new world.

During the hour of the eclipse, it was freezing cold. In their haste to secure other priorities, their cloaks had dried out stiff as boards, and instead the two of them huddled together for warmth.

After that first, sleepless night, they washed and dried their cloaks as best they could in Bailey's spring.

Luckily for them, in all other times it was slightly warm and humid.

Complete darkness fell only during the eclipse. Otherwise, the planet seemed frozen in perpetual twilight.

Bailey and his mentor, though, were content to live their lives by the light of the moons. They gathered their resources, planted herbs on the hillside, and each day filtered a little more clean water from the spring.

Each day when they awoke, the Riftmaster's clay bowl was empty of water, but the filtration process left behind some crystals, uniquely pink and, although Bailey wouldn't have admitted it, quite pretty.

"You know what these are?" the Riftmaster asked Bailey one morning.

"Salt, right?"

"Yes, yes!"

The Riftmaster seemed ecstatic as he carefully wrapped the crystals in a small square of hide along with those he'd gathered in previous days, securing them with a length of leather twine. He handed these to Bailey, who accepted the package in an outstretched palm. "Hang onto these. They'll be more than a little useful."

"What for?"

"Well, there's the obvious things. Seasoning food, preserving meat... You still do that with salt on Earth, yes?"

Bailey nodded.

"Other than that, it can be helpful for disinfecting wounds, too. But more importantly, it can be used to trade. There are Rifters out there who'd give years of their life for even just that tiny pinch of salt. Use it wisely, Rifthopper."

● ● ●

The two of them stayed on that small island until Bailey lost track of the days, but he often caught his mentor glancing out towards the horizon, and the landmass beyond the sea. As they explored the island, grew their plants, and learned what they could about the local flora and fauna, the Riftmaster grew more and more antsy.

One morning, as the sun peeked out from behind the largest moon, the pair were patrolling together through their meagre domain. Their route brought them past the bubbling spring.

"Hey, Riftmaster," he said, with a small smirk. "If I take a dip, will you keep an eye out for me?"

The Riftmaster's eyebrows rose. "Of course I would." He paused. "...Why would you want to do that?"

"Why? I haven't had a bath in months!"

The Riftmaster settled down on a nearby rock, removing his silver knife from its sheath. "The water here is salty. You'll feel even dirtier after than when you got in!"

"So you'd prefer to sit stewing in your own filth? What if

you attract predators?'"

"It's a deterrent," the Riftmaster snorted as he began to sharpen his knife.

"No wonder you reek," muttered Bailey, as he peeled off the salt-encrusted, reeking leather armour from his torso. It clung to his bare skin, and Bailey visibly winced as he removed it. "I don't think that'd put off a hungry predator."

"At least I'll die knowing that I taste bloody terrible. You, on the other hand, will be perfectly seasoned in brine."

Bailey chuckled faintly as he set his clothing carefully aside. A moment later, though, the Riftmaster's voice stopped him. "Aren't you forgetting something, Rifthopper?"

"Oh? Oh, right."

Bailey hastily tied the Riftmaster's stone pendant around his neck once more. It felt cold against his bare chest. He shivered lightly.

After a moment's pause, he started to take off his leggings. It was like removing an extra layer of skin.

As he moved back towards the steaming pool, he felt his mentor's gaze boring into his back. He glanced back as the Riftmaster's voice reached him.

"Feeling bold, aren't we?"

Paying him no heed, Bailey stepped into the pool. "What? You expected me to leave it all on?"

The Riftmaster shrugged, pointedly glancing away out to sea. "Of course not. Just... Be cautious. You don't know what lives in there."

"I know, I know," Bailey said, as he stooped in the water up to his chin, sighing as he felt it wash away the many layers of sweat and grime. He washed his face, running his hands through his hair and sending water cascading down his back. Finally he shook his head. "Why don't you join me? The water's lovely and warm."

The Riftmaster grunted quietly in response and continued to sharpen his knife whilst gazing out to sea.

Bailey sighed quietly, and ignored him for a while as he cleaned himself down to every nook and cranny. "For being so dismissive of Earth culture, you're a real prude. You know that?"

"What, are you looking for compliments? I just think it's better to be armoured, that's all." The Riftmaster paused.

"Especially if the Rift comes."

His mentor didn't look until Bailey left the water and began to wash the filth from his armour. Then he glanced over.

"That'll take time to dry, you know."

"I know," Bailey said. He paused, and then, with a soft huff, spoke again. "What if one of us is wounded? Aren't you worried about infections?"

"...I am," the Riftmaster admitted. He sheathed his knife against his thigh. "I'm more worried about polluting our best water supply, though."

"What do you mean? It's a spring. There's plenty of water to spare."

The Riftmaster hesitated. He once again glanced out to sea.

"Riftmaster...?"

"It's this island. It's so small. There's so little food... What if this spring dries up, Bailey? What will we do? Resources are limited, and if the tide comes in..."

Bailey paused, looking down at his armour. Before he could answer, the Riftmaster continued.

"There's an entire ocean between us and the next landmass. There's no telling what's living out there."

"How long do we have left?" Bailey finally said.

The Riftmaster sighed. "I'm uncertain. The resources here might last a week, perhaps. Or maybe two. Maybe even longer than that, but most of the creatures living here are semi-aquatic. They'll soon learn not to come ashore again; just depends how quickly."

"Perhaps we could build a boat," Bailey said.

The Riftmaster looked up. "I was thinking the same thing."

"Have you ever tried it before?"

He nodded.

"Successfully?"

"On lakes, yes. But an ocean like this..."

"What other choice do we have?"

"Stay on this island, and hope the Rift comes before we starve. Not much of a choice, is it?"

"Well, it sounds to me like the decision's already made."

"Perhaps..." the Riftmaster glanced up suddenly, eyes sparkling. "...Yes. Yes, let's do it. We'll build a boat and sail the archipelago. We'll make it across that ocean if it's the last thing we do."

Bailey grinned.

"Now get some clothes on. You can't help me build a boat if you're naked."

• • •

Over the next few days, Bailey and the Riftmaster worked together to gather buoyant materials. They tested their buoyancy out by setting them afloat in the spring, and durability by sending them bobbing off downstream.

Thankfully, the pair found success when it came to the mushrooms that dominated the hillside. As the days passed, they used vines and plaited lengths of foliage to tie the pieces together. Despite a relatively dainty appearance, Bailey was surprised by just how much the small man could carry. In between constantly stressing over the passage of time and just how long it would take them to reach the landmass, the Riftmaster barely gave himself a break. Bailey helped as best he could, gathering their herbs, storing and preserving food and water so that there would be enough for the journey ahead.

In rare moments of stillness, his mentor would gaze out to sea once again. Bailey knew he was looking to see if anything breached the surface, offering some sort of hint as to what lay below.

The thought scared Bailey more than he'd care to admit.

Finally, though, as the days waned and bellies began to growl, the pair were ready. Their boat was built of mushroom trunks, which although rubbery and a little flimsy, seemed waterproof. It was a rough-looking craft, but with a great amount of swearing and the Riftmaster's deft hand, it held. They'd used their remaining Amazonian foliage for their sails, even though they were yellowing and pale, now. The great leaves fluttered gently in the wind.

You've served us well, Bailey thought, as he grasped the Riftmaster's hand and hauled himself onto the boat.

"Ready, Rifthopper?"

Working together, they pushed off from the shore, each balanced on a section of the raft, gripping the flimsy mast. The seafloor fell away beneath them, as they rode onto the open waves. They left the island behind, and Bailey felt the wind in his hair and the seafoam spraying at his face. He laughed, a wild and manic sound, as they left the island behind. Bailey looked back; from here the great orange caps looked like flecks of paint, and that silver spring glistened on the jagged hillside.

As the Riftmaster struggled with the sails, Bailey turned to help him, and he did not look back again.

The waves felt far rougher out here than they'd looked from the shore, and by the time they'd been out for more than an hour, both of their brows were slick with sweat. But there was still a long way to go. His mentor huffed and panted as Bailey offered him the reins, and stopped to take a long drink.

"Bailey," the Riftmaster said, suddenly, his gaze fixed on the waves. "Don't look now, but…"

Bailey looked up. "Huh?"

"…There's something in the water beneath us."

Bailey's blood ran cold. Despite his mentor's words, he peered over the side of the raft, and into the blue depths. There was indeed something there; deep in the water below them. Bailey saw thousands upon thousands of glistening scales, flashing silvery in the moonlight like a reverse constellation. The glistening scales all moved as one; either they belonged to a single creature, or an immense shoal moving as one.

Bailey gripped onto the mast until his knuckles turned pale with fear.

"What should we do?" Bailey asked.

"We keep going," the Riftmaster said. "That's all we can do."

The creature followed them for quite some time, until the smaller moon had made almost half a turn around the sky. At times, it was simply a twinkle in the depths, but once it rose until it was almost close enough to touch. A great, silvery hide rippling just out of reach. Bailey never once saw its beginning, or its end.

Shortly before they reached the shore, the creature disappeared as suddenly as it had appeared. Bailey stumbled onto dry land, legs like jelly, and skipped in a wild and jubilant dance.

For the rest of their time on that world, Bailey and the Riftmaster sailed frequently between the numerous small islands of the chain, each one a far cry from the last. The feeling of freedom was like nothing Bailey had ever felt before, but even so, his fear of the unknown was all-consuming.

The creature in the depths accompanied them frequently on their travels; Bailey grew used to seeing its silvery scales beneath them. Bailey could only imagine why.

All too soon, though, their time on that world came to an end.

With every jump Bailey felt a mixture of relief and dread, for however cruel the last planet had been to them, the next one they visited could well be worse. So many times they stared death in the face, but with each tiny victory Bailey felt his heart swell with pride. With every world they left behind Bailey felt himself learning, and he soon found himself running out of names.

His time on Earth soon felt like a distant daydream, his grief no more than a dully-throbbing scar. But the Riftmaster's presence helped to soothe it. Although he was no replacement for everything Bailey had lost, he helped the Rift feel just a little more like home. From the moment that Bailey awoke until the moment that he slept, they were together.

When Bailey expressed this, though, his mentor simply laughed it off, leaving Bailey feeling foolish, his cheeks hot with embarrassment.

Bailey supposed it was how he'd survived for so long on his own.

No matter how tough the going got, his mentor always seemed to find a way to pull through.

Bailey hung on every word and lesson. He knew that he would have never survived on his own, and every new challenge and danger only reaffirmed it. Bailey knew, deep in his heart, that he still couldn't.

Independence was a long way off, and Bailey shied away from it.

He tried not to think about it for now.

Secretly, he quailed at the idea of one day going alone – the universe would feel far bigger, and far lonelier, without the Riftmaster to guide him through it.

If the Riftmaster shared his fears, he was awfully good at

hiding it. Bailey supposed he'd had five thousand years to grow used to the feeling of solitude.

The man made no mention of one day parting ways, so it seemed like Bailey's secret fear was unfounded. It was obvious to Bailey that he enjoyed the company. He certainly revelled in the chance to tell stories of the places he'd been and the things he'd seen. And yet, as much as Bailey pushed, there were some stories that the Riftmaster would simply never tell.

Bailey knew stories of wild escapes and glorious planets like nothing he could ever imagine. Giants that the Riftmaster had discovered and tamed, and intergalactic languages that he had learned.

But he never knew what had become of the Riftmaster's last apprentice.

It frustrated him whenever the Riftmaster avoided the subject, carefully redirecting the conversation towards a different story or reshuffling their schedule, returning to work in silence with a faraway look in his eye.

"It's not that interesting," he would say. "You're not missing out on much."

And then, always, without fail…

"But do you know what *was* interesting? For example, did I ever tell you about the time I…"

Bailey sighed, but agreed, knowing that he couldn't afford to get on his mentor's bad side.

After a time, he simply stopped asking.

The Riftmaster's stories, at least, were something he enjoyed. After so many millennia, the Riftmaster had enough of them to fill a thousand books, and although Bailey knew they were most likely highly embellished, he didn't know how much by.

The longer they spent together, the less Bailey worried about saying goodbye. It seemed an outcome that was less likely by the day, as Bailey struggled to make himself more useful and shoulder as much of the Riftmaster's burden as he could.

It soon felt like he'd known his mentor forever.

Before he knew it, Bailey had lost track of time.

He often found himself wondering how the Riftmaster kept track, or if it was all simply guesswork. When he asked one time, the Riftmaster gave him a funny look, and after a moment of consideration said "I don't think you want to know."

But Bailey *did* want to know.

At the very least, it seemed like there was a method in the madness.

One night the two companions were sitting, talking in low voices around their campfire as the bitter winds howled outside. It was then that Bailey felt the familiar pain of fire burning just beneath his skin, felt himself yanked from where he was sitting and felt the familiar mixture of excitement and fear overtake him, as he wondered where the Rift would possibly take them next.

Little did he know, the next world would present a new kind of challenge, and it was one that neither Bailey nor the Riftmaster were prepared for.

Chapter 10
Desolate Sands

This time when Bailey hit the ground, he wound up with a face full of fine, red sand. Hacking, coughing and spitting, he staggered to his feet. He rubbed his eyes, making sure they were clear, before opening them and looking around. The Riftmaster, already upright, held a waterskin his way, even though it was almost empty.

Bailey gratefully took it, and washed the taste of iron from the inside of his mouth.

"I'll never get used to that," Bailey said, once he'd swallowed, and stuck out his tongue.

The Riftmaster huffed in acknowledgement, but the man wasn't looking at him. He was taking a long look at the surrounding world.

"What's the plan?" Bailey asked after a moment of silence.

They were standing on a rust-red plain – or what remained of one. Bailey could see clusters of what looked to be gnarled and towering mushrooms, only hard and skeletal-looking. On the ground, stunted scrubs reached upwards, groping at the sky like desperate fingers.

The Riftmaster had moved over to one of these distinctive mushrooms, its trunk gnarled and strange and littered with dried-out pods, and was running his hands over it. Removing his knife from his belt, he made an effort to drive it into a crevice. After a while though, he stepped away, shaking his head.

Whatever they were made of, it must have been hard as rock.

A wind, sharp with dust, whistled eerily as it rattled through the tips of long-forsaken foliage.

Bailey had finished looking, but when he turned expectantly back towards his mentor, the man had begun to stare up at the sky in silence. Faint but present, Bailey could see the distant twinkle of the stars in the maroon-coloured sky.

When he rested a hand on his arm, the Riftmaster whipped around to face him with a suddenness that made Bailey pull back. The Riftmaster's expression was distant. As though he hadn't been expecting to see Bailey there, his shoulders relaxed slightly as their eyes met. He stared expectantly, as if he was waiting for the young man to explain himself.

"Riftmaster?" Bailey asked after a moment of silence.

As though waking up from a dream, the Riftmaster straightened.

"Oh, right!" He breathed out, shaking his head briefly. "Well, first things first, we need to find water. Follow me. I think I know where we can find some."

Bailey followed as he began to walk, pulling up his leafy hood to keep off the blistering sun. Dust played in the wind ahead of them, and red trails streamed from the tips of distant dunes. Soon they began to climb one; Bailey marvelled at the tiny plants which clung stubbornly to its sides and the ugly, half-buried fungal growths that stuck out from it.

In no time at all Bailey felt his throat growing dry and parched.

Finally they reached the crest of the dune. On the other side, the ground fell away from them and into a vast crater, the base of which was dry, barren and cracking.

Bailey stared in mounting horror, but the Riftmaster gave no indication of disappointment and continued, gesturing for Bailey to follow him down into the valley.

They reached the base of the sand dune and walked out onto the hard, cracked earth. When they were sufficiently away from the banks, the Riftmaster stooped, using the tip of his knife to ease up a couple of the hard surface plates. The ground beneath was damp, and Bailey watched as he began to dig, using a couple of tools to carve a hollow into the earth.

Bailey bent down to help, using his hands to pull aside the hardened sediment.

It took several hours, but eventually they struck water, flowing in to fill the base of the hole.

It wasn't much, but the Riftmaster's relief was tangible. Both were able to drink their fill, and then the Riftmaster filled his waterskin. By that time, the planet was beginning to grow cold. Wordlessly, the Riftmaster led the way out of the crater and they took shelter under a rocky outcrop.

There, for the first time since they'd met, the Riftmaster panicked.

"Oh, I can't believe it. I forgot to gather firewood on the plain. The scrubs would have been perfect. Oh goodness, we have to gather some before the sun goes down. I'm sorry, Bailey. I'm so sorry…"

Bailey felt a spark of annoyance, but also worry; he couldn't quite shake the feeling that something was very wrong.

The Riftmaster had never forgotten anything before.

And so the two headed out into the closing darkness. By the time they returned, their breaths turned to mist in the cold, and both humans had abandoned their leaves and hugged their mountain-crawler cloaks tightly around them as they finally settled down to make a fire.

It took the Riftmaster much fumbling before he managed to strike the spark it needed to light.

Under the pitch-dark night sky, they heard the sound of creatures calling, their voices high and ghoulish wails, few and far between. The Riftmaster stared out into the night, unusually silent. Finally, Bailey tried to break it.

"So… you know this planet, huh?"

His mentor looked up at him, his expression dazed in the half-light. He nodded. "Though… It's changed a lot since I was last here."

"How so?" Bailey asked.

The question appeared to stir something in the Riftmaster. When he spoke again, it was with a lot more thoughtfulness. It was a relief to see his mind back on the present. "It was… a lushly forested planet, the last time I was here. It must be dry season now; the sun is a lot bigger in the sky. And you remember that crater we were in earlier? Well, there are lots of them from ancient meteors. They were all full of water when we –…when *I* was last here."

Catching his mentor's stumble, Bailey opened his mouth to ask, but the Riftmaster sharply cut him off.

"…Even if it's drier now, I'll figure it out. But first things first; I want to see if the garden I made here is still alive, and it's a long walk, so… Get some rest, Rifthopper."

The Riftmaster turned his back on Bailey, signifying the end of the conversation.

Bailey sighed. "Goodnight, then," he muttered. His mentor knew his stuff, and made good company the majority of the time, but… god, could he be frustrating.

The young man hugged his cloak around him as he sank down at the far end of their rocky little shelter, watching the Riftmaster as he continued to stare out into the night.

• • •

As soon as Bailey awoke, it was time to go. They started walking once a sliver of the sun broke the horizon, and kept going well past midday. They stopped at several craters on the way, but rarely did the soil yield more than a handful of damp sand.

The Riftmaster was once again quiet, insisting that talking would be a waste of precious energy. From the shadows under his eyes, Bailey suspected that his mentor hadn't slept at all. So the normally bombastic man Bailey had come to know seemed further and further out of reach. He was driven only by a desire to keep walking, even though there was no guarantee of a reward at their journey's end.

Soon, they had exhausted their water supply, and Bailey's throat became more parched with every breath. His exposed skin grew red with the dust that clung to it. He was sweating in the sheer, blistering heat.

The Riftmaster gave no sign that he had noticed and kept marching on.

As they followed a ravine that might once have held a river, Bailey saw an opportunity to rest in the shade beneath the banks. He stopped, feeling the last of his strength desert him with the pure force of his relief.

"Riftmaster! I can't go much further. Can we rest here for a while?"

To his surprise, the Riftmaster whipped around, his eyes restless, and tone irritable. "We can't stop! We're almost there," he insisted. "Won't be much longer, I promise."

"But...–"

"When we get there, we can eat. If the garden still exists, there'll be food, and water, and shelter. We won't need to walk again!"

"...But what if it doesn't?" Bailey asked hopelessly.

"Then we'll find something else. I'll figure something out. I always do," the Riftmaster growled impatiently. Then he moved on.

Lungs gulping at the dry air, Bailey stumbled after him.

• • •

When the Riftmaster finally announced that they'd reached the Rift garden, Bailey didn't know what else he'd been expecting. Dry stalks hung limply and withered leaves had long since crumpled and dropped under the sun's unbearable heat. Ruts could be seen dug into the ground which had once provided water, but they had dried out long ago.

Even the banks which had once protected the grove from the sun had collapsed.

Bailey stared, gulping painfully – his throat so dry that it clung to itself, and raw with dust. As the Riftmaster walked among the long-dead plants, gathering what could be salvaged, Bailey sank against a half-buried stone, watching as the last of the sun disappeared over the edge of the horizon.

Finally, the Riftmaster picked his way back to Bailey.

"We'll have to keep going. We can't stay here."

Bailey didn't look up at him, disbelief and anger giving way to a tense silence. He didn't reply.

"Bailey? Let's move."

"No," Bailey finally said, voice a low growl. "I'm too tired to move."

"Come on. It'll just be a little further," the Riftmaster hissed, like a frustrated father.

"No," Bailey said again. "I need to rest."

"Later. We just need to–"

"Need to what?! Go on another wild goose chase?!" Bailey broke in, leaving the Riftmaster to stare in stunned silence.

"What the hell are you looking for? You've been acting weird since we got here."

"I'm not looking for anything. I told you, I've been here before, I know this planet. I don't have time for this."

"You literally have forever!" Bailey's voice rose as his anger finally spilled over the edge. "You've lived out in space for five thousand years. What don't you have time for?!"

"I don't have time to argue with *you*. I, for one, want to stay alive."

"Do you? Do you *really*? I find that hard to believe. We've been on this planet a *day* and you've already almost killed us twice!"

The Riftmaster let out a low grunt. "So I forgot some twigs. It won't happen again."

"Oh yeah, and what's all this about needing to have a fire lit by nightfall?" Bailey cast a glance towards the darkening horizon. "And you *never* forget things. There's something else going on here."

His mentor followed his gaze. In the half-light, Bailey could see his breaths beginning to cloud. A look of horror slowly crept over his face, as though he'd finally realised the trouble they were in.

"If we'd just rested in the riverbed," Bailey continued hoarsely. "We could have had some time to scout out more water from safety. We could have lit a fire, and then been safe for another day. Hungry, but safe."

The Riftmaster opened his mouth to speak, but then appeared to think better of it. He avoided Bailey's gaze, even as the young man tried his best to catch his.

"You're breaking your own rules, Riftmaster."

The man still didn't look at him. There was a long and torturous silence, as the Riftmaster opened and closed his mouth like a fish. He seemed to shrink back as he spoke, voice small. "I'm… I'm sorry…"

Bailey relaxed, but not because his mentor's apology had appeased him. It was because he had realised how utterly lost he felt. If the Riftmaster couldn't function out here, how could he?

Bailey's shoulders drooped. He heaved out a sigh, studying the man standing before him.

The Riftmaster looked more exhausted, bedraggled, and out of his depth than Bailey had ever seen him before.

And if a 5000-year-old Riftmaster didn't know what to do, what could a 19-year-old college student possibly add?

"...Let's light a fire. We can burn the herbs from the garden... or, what's left of them. First thing in the morning, we'll find water," Bailey said softly. It felt odd to be taking charge, but they had to have some sort of a plan. Saying the words aloud made their task feel just a little bit less daunting. "...We just need to survive the night. But first..."

Bailey's expression hardened.

"You need to tell me what's going on."

The Riftmaster's expression tightened. Their eyes locked; stormy grey fought with rich and chocolatey brown in a battle of wills.

It was a battle that the Riftmaster soon lost; although Bailey had the sneaking suspicion that he'd let him win. The man turned his gaze away.

"Okay, but... I... I need to find something first. It's not far, I promise. I'll... explain everything when we get there." He paused. "And I'll... I'll prepare things better this time. We're not dying tonight. Or anywhere on this world. I promise that, too."

Bailey sighed, and agreed.

Chapter 11
The Truth

That night, Bailey kept watch by the fireside as the Riftmaster slept fitfully close by. He heard the sound of creatures crying out again, ever nearer, and feared that the small campfire wouldn't be enough to keep them safe. But whatever lurked in the dark was afraid of the light, and aside from seeing the occasional rustle of something moving in the shadows, they were safe.

When the sun came up, it had been silent for a long time.

In the early morning chill, they sought out water, following the man-made grooves in the earth that had once fed the Riftmaster's long-dead garden. As they dug into the hollow that had once been a lake and finally hit a swell of water, Bailey didn't think he'd ever tasted anything so sweet.

Aside from offering snippets of advice on the way, the Riftmaster filled his waterskin in quiet resignation.

After that, it was time to go, and the Riftmaster once again took the lead.

The flowing dunes soon gave way to jagged rock formations in hues of dark brownish red, carved into odd shapes by years of wind and dust.

Further still on their way, Bailey began to notice more orderly shapes hewn out of the rocks. Some of them had sides cut completely smooth or had piles of worn rectangular blocks neatly arranged beside them. As time went on, they saw more and more of these, and the Riftmaster walked faster before finally, finally coming to a halt.

Bailey moved to stand next to him, and followed his gaze. They were standing among a small cluster of ruined buildings, only some of them managing to retain their general shape. All of them were missing roofs and doors, and some had massive holes in the walls. Some were no more than piles of rubble and well-worn bricks.

But it was, unmistakably, a village.

Bailey looked to the Riftmaster for an explanation, to see him cupping his hands over his mouth. "Oliver!" he called, voice wavering, and then listened. His only answer was the wind whistling through the stones. Breath catching, the Riftmaster continued further into the fallen village. "Adeline! Murphy? …Toby?"

Whoever the Riftmaster hoped to find here was clearly long gone, but the man kept on calling, gradually growing louder as he added to the list of names, before finally falling silent.

He paused, peering into the first of the crumbled rooms. Looking past him, Bailey saw only sand.

Growing more frantic by the moment, the Riftmaster turned and hurried to the next.

…And the next.

…And the next.

Finally, Bailey heard a strangled noise. The Riftmaster was standing in the entrance of a ruined doorway, and he leaned heavily against the brickwork. His hands were crossed over his mouth.

Bailey approached.

His mentor disappeared inside. When the young man entered the building, the Riftmaster had fallen to his knees before a shape in the dark. Bailey felt his mouth grow dry. His throat tightened, a nauseous feeling rose in his stomach.

For there, half-buried in the sand, was a human skeleton.

• • •

At first Bailey was afraid to ask who the skeleton had been and how it had got here. It was so impossibly far from Earth; there was no other way than the Rift itself. What Bailey did know was that the Riftmaster had known the people here. He must have known them well.

He needed time.

It took almost an hour before Bailey managed to coax the Riftmaster to leave the ruined shelter, and when he did, his expression was unreadable.

Bailey suspected that he was afraid to keep searching the village, and yet driven by mindless desperation, he did anyway.

That skeleton wouldn't be the only one they found. As Bailey and his mentor searched the rest of the village, they uncovered others, huddled in their homes.

Finally, although they searched, there were no more skeletons to be found. As the sun dipped ever closer to the horizon, Bailey and the Riftmaster wordlessly settled in a relatively intact building at the entrance to the village and built a fire.

The Riftmaster gazed into the flickering firelight for a while in silence, with that same expression on his face. He was hunched over, seeming to fold in on himself. Bailey could see the shadows under his eyes.

He seemed to be trying his best to ignore Bailey.

Despite the fluttering nervousness in his belly, the young man cleared his throat. The time had come to talk; there was no use trying to avoid the inevitable.

The Riftmaster's tired eyes met his.

"So… what is this place?" Bailey asked.

"It was a village," the Riftmaster answered. "It was… *my* village. I lived here with… my last apprentice. This was where I last saw him."

"After your… disagreement?" Bailey chanced.

The Riftmaster slowly nodded. "Yeah. It's… a long story."

"Well, it's gonna be a long night."

The Riftmaster let out a very small, and very fake, chuckle.

"I suppose you're right," he said.

• • •

"I met my first apprentice… hmm… let's say, around four thousand years ago. I'd been in the Rift for only a few hundred years back then. At the time, it seemed like I was unstoppable. I'd lived on all sorts of alien planets and I thought I knew all of their tricks. I could survive anything, but... I hadn't seen another human since leaving Earth. And, well... for a time, I just tried not to think about it," the Riftmaster began, looking distant as he thought back to times long gone. "But of course... I secretly fantasised about meeting another of my kind. I thought about the things we'd do, the places we'd go... The friendship we'd form... But it was a dream that seemed more unlikely to come true with every passing year."

He looked up at Bailey.

"So when he came along... Oliver... so young and fiery... it was almost inevitable that we'd figure out a way to travel together. Our discovery of Rift-binding... that's, wearing each-others' clothes so that we Rifted together, was pure chance. He happened to be wearing my satchel at the time of our first Rift together, and things went from there. We stuck together. You might say from that point on we were joined at the hip. Two peas in a pod. Where I went, he went.

"After nine hundred years, we were almost on equal footing, and, well... You know how humans are." The Riftmaster paused, shifting in embarrassment and smiling wryly like a teenager describing their first kiss. "...we began to fall in love."

Bailey found himself trying not to smile at the thought. But he knew that the story couldn't have a happy ending. The evidence was all around them. So he simply nodded solemnly. "Go on," he said.

"...We had all of eternity to look forward to. But even more importantly, we had each other to share it with."

The Riftmaster paused, falling into a reflective silence punctuated by a quiet sigh. When the Riftmaster continued, his voice was quieter, and soft with wonder.

"...But we weren't alone for very long. After another thousand years roaming the infinite cosmos, we had our first child together."

Bailey looked at the Riftmaster to see if he was joking, blinking once with amazement.

"Wait... How?" Bailey asked. And then it hit him like a rock. Suddenly the story didn't seem so important as answering a single burning question. "Riftmaster... are you a *woman*?"

The Riftmaster's brow furrowed, and he... or *she*... seemed annoyed at being interrupted. Suddenly all of the little things that he'd ignored... the wide hips, the way the Riftmaster's face was always clean-shaven even though Bailey had never seen him shave... made sense.

The Riftmaster sighed, looking at him with clear exasperation. "Rifthopper... We're thousands of light-years away from Earth and its culture. I haven't thought about what I used to be in hundreds of years. All that matters out here is that I'm *human*." His brows furrowed. "...Can I continue?"

Bailey was taken aback... he took the answer as a no, but he had no idea what else to say.

"Uhm... yeah, go on," he said, with embarrassment, before adding in a small voice – "...But your *voice*."

"Speaking in alien tongues does terrible things to your throat," the Riftmaster answered gruffly. "Would you rather I sound prim and proper?"

Though the Riftmaster's voice wasn't particularly deep, it wasn't that feminine either. It was gravelly, and low, and could easily pass for whatever someone wanted to hear. In Bailey's case, it seemed he'd been more willing and ready to accept the authority of someone *he* identified as male.

He'd never even stopped to consider the possibility, for a single moment, that he was wrong; it was a clear and obvious property of Earth's continued influence on the way he thought.

Bailey felt his stomach tighten with guilt.

"No."

He supposed that it didn't make a difference. He didn't even know why it was so surprising. Now that he thought about it, the signs were all there at surface level. But why *did* it matter? They were both human. It was just that the Riftmaster had been gone from Earth for so long that she... or *he* just didn't care anymore. So why should Bailey?

The more he thought about it, and found himself wrestling with reasons for why he should care – the more he realised that it just didn't matter out here.

Bailey had already abandoned other such customs; the evidence was even in the armour that hugged tight to his skin made of alien hide. Manners and customs and prejudices, well – if they didn't help you survive, they meant nothing out here.

So why should he cling to this one?

As Bailey stared, debating with himself, his mentor's expression softened slightly.

"My point is, Rifthopper; I don't care anymore. Whether I'm a man or a woman doesn't matter out here. You can call me whatever the hell you want; it won't make a difference."

The Riftmaster stood above human values in a blissful state of disassociation. He was no longer a woman. But he wasn't a man, either.

He was the Riftmaster, traveller of a thousand worlds.

In space he didn't let such menial things define him.

Bailey's attention was drawn back to his mentor as he continued his story.

"...Using Rift-binding, we brought our baby between worlds with us, but she was not a true Rifter like we were. Her name was Adeline, and Ollie and I raised and protected her as we travelled through a hundred hostile worlds."

Adeline. That was one of the names the Riftmaster had called out. One of the very first. Bailey was beginning to get a feeling he knew where it was going, now. He listened with a mixture of fascination and trepidation.

"Born in the Rift, she was a smart one. We taught her everything we knew, and she learned fast. When she was perhaps fifteen Earth-years, her brother and sister were born. With her to help us, they grew fast and strong. And then there came another... and another... It was a difficult, but rewarding life. We were a close-knit family, bound by blood and the Rift. But it was only a matter of time before things started to go wrong."

Bailey let out a breath that he didn't know he'd been holding.

"There were thirteen of us, when our youngest daughter was killed. She was barely old enough to walk, and obviously not old enough to understand the danger she was in. From that point on, things were... different, between me and Ollie."

The Riftmaster sighed once again.

"We fought, often. He started wanting to find a planet that wasn't so harsh, and leave them all behind. By that time, Adeline was coming up to 300. She looked far older than me or Ollie, with grey hair and an old, wise face. I suspect that's because she shared in *our* energy when we Rifted, rather than going alone. The twins, Toby and Polly, were almost as old as she was. Peggy was probably 150. But just… leaving them behind… I was sure that that was far crueller than bringing them with us.

"But the damage was done. The kids started to whisper amongst themselves, and take sides. One day, we landed here. This lush planet, so beautiful, and habitable. We built our gardens, followed our routines and began to tame this world, but the kids, well… some of them wanted to stay. Ollie and I fell out. We yelled at each other until our throats were hoarse and we both wept."

The Riftmaster's voice cracked. He trailed off and fell into silence.

"Then one night, after a particularly bitter argument, the Rift took me away from them. I left them all behind. And even though I never saw them again, I knew what had happened; whilst I was away from the village, Ollie removed the necklaces binding them to me, and just… let me go."

The Rifmaster made a sweeping hand motion to illustrate his point.

"I can't… I still can't believe it, but… they're all still here. Every single one of them… except Oliver."

He blew out a long breath.

"Those are my kids out there, Bailey. I gave birth to them, raised them, loved them and… now all they are is dust."

• • •

The Riftmaster didn't want to bury the skeletons of his children. It would waste time, he said, and in the Rift, time was too precious to waste. They had to find food, and replenish their water supply, before both succumbed to starvation.

But Bailey convinced him to give the village one more day, to stay back and lay them to rest. The Riftmaster and his apprentice worked together to carry a slab of rust-red stone into the relatively-sheltered walls of a ruined building, where it would remain until the walls fell around it, safe from the biting wind.

They dug into the earth with the tools they had available to them; then, one by one they carried the bones of the Riftmaster's children and buried them, side by side in the village they once called home. Although Bailey felt his skin crawling with revulsion, he didn't complain.

It was his idea, after all.

Despite the fact that the effort shattered his tools one by one, the Riftmaster carved a message into the slab of stone. It took until the sun touched the horizon, and when he finally left the building, he hid his face so that Bailey couldn't see the tears.

His hands were bloodied and blistered from the effort.

As they returned to their campfire to rest, Bailey laid a hand on his arm.

"You know... you're human," he said softly. "You're allowed to act like it every once in a while. It can't hurt."

"Oh, but it does," the Riftmaster answered, voice wavering. "It always does."

"Well... now, at least, you can think about what you did do, rather than what you didn't."

The Riftmaster finally looked up at him, the ghost of a smile playing across his lips.

"I suppose you're right," he said.

Before the sun was finally lost below the horizon, plunging the world into shadow, Bailey risked a glance back at the headstone that the Riftmaster had carved.

IN MEMORY OF ADELINE,

TOBY, POLLY, PEGGY,

PIP, MARTIN, KATRINA,

LILY, EVAN, KAREN

AND LUCY

ALL WONDERFUL CHILDREN

OF OLLIE AND ARI.

ALL FOREVER MISSED.

Chapter 12
The Trial

To Ari's immense relief, Bailey said nothing of having seen the tombstone, and reading the names inscribed. They could only assume that he hadn't seen it, or that out of respect for them, was simply keeping quiet about it.

Ari was glad of it; privately, they felt as though their heart had been torn clean open, chest aching and eyes stinging from shed tears.

They didn't think that they could hold it together if Bailey were to question them any further.

But, as Bailey slept peacefully that night, Ari allowed themself precious moments to remove their proud mask and silently weep.

They and Bailey left the ruined village the next morning, as soon as dawn broke. Hungry and thirsty, the duo struggled back the way they'd come, and arrived back at the old garden just after noon. Here, they were able to uncover just enough water to wet their throats and ensure that they would survive another day. They cut loose petrified branches to put together a shelter.

However, both had grown noticeably thin, and there was little food to be had here, even after hours spent searching for it.

For a time, it seemed like this would be the end. Each day, Ari and Bailey chewed the bitter remains of dried leaves and herbs for what little nourishment could be had, and each night they went to sleep hungry.

For what it was worth, the hunger was a welcome distraction from the hole in Ari's chest.

Soon, the Night-stalking creatures with their eerie wails were growing braver... and it was only a matter of time before one of them stepped into their pool of firelight. In doing so the ochre glow revealed a hairless, canine-like beast with impressive fangs and flesh that clung tight to its bones, standing as tall as a man on six spiderlike limbs. It had no eyes, instead sensitive whiskers combed scents from the crisp night air.

The wiry sensors whisked over the makeshift beds they had made, over Ari's satchel, and then it was moving towards them.

Ari froze, hoping beyond all hope that it would pass them by. As they waited with bated breath, they found themself entranced, unable to tear their eyes away.

Its strange appearance was familiar... and yet, different.

The night-stalking creatures Ari remembered from this planet had been graceful beasts once, formidable and powerful. They had had thick, rippling muscles and luscious fur as they crept under the shadow of ancient trees.

And yet this one was a husk of what its ancestors had been, reeking of sorrow and despair.

Ari couldn't keep back the tingling suspicion that their family hadn't been the only one poorly affected by the change in climate. But they reminded themself once again, that they would never know how their children had perished. Not truly.

Perhaps, each one had lived a long and fruitful life, before finally succumbing to the years creeping in.

The skeletons, after all, were still intact, unscavenged.

It was highly possible, probable even, that by the time the drought hit, humans were long gone from this little corner of the universe.

Ari's vision spun back into focus, and they blinked back the tears that had blurred their vision as the creature before them let out a snort. A wiry whisker traced over their arm, sending shivers down their spine.

Suddenly Ari was on their feet, whipping the silver knife from their thigh. They plunged it into the creature's throat as it began to wail. The noise died into a pitiful gurgle, blue blood dripping from the wound and streaming in rivulets down its hairless chest, hot blood steaming as it met the chilly air.

After a struggle that woke Bailey from his slumber, the Riftmaster managed to kill it by plunging their knife into its chest. But the predator left them with a parting gift... Ari suffered a bite wound to one arm that cost strength they couldn't afford to lose.

But at least they had something to eat, now... right?

Ari made up the necessary concoctions with fumbling hands as Bailey waited, eyes wild, by their side, but to both of their dismay, the Riftmaster's tests showed what little meat it had to be highly toxic.

There was little more that could be done; Ari bound their wound with flame-cured strips of its skin, gathered the sharp fangs from its jaws to make new tools, and then scattered its bones as a warning for the others.

They weren't attacked again.

A few days later, they even ran out of dried-up leaves.

It seemed like this was truly the end... and for Ari, the worst part was knowing it was entirely their fault. Bailey shared a few words with his mentor, struggling to lighten the mood as they thrived on borrowed time, saving what little energy they had left.

At least, Ari thought, as they drifted off to sleep one night, *there are no hard feelings.*

As the days went on, the Riftmaster became more reclusive; their wound keeping them bedridden and shivering with nightmares.

They soon succumbed to an illness brought on by the festering wound and, with nothing to keep up their strength, they grew weaker and weaker.

"I hate it when I'm right," they joked to Bailey one day as they replaced the bindings on their wound, even though their voice was hoarse and movements shaky. Ari noticed tears in Bailey's eyes as he knelt down to help them.

The young man took over most of their daily activities as Ari struggled to recover.

They suffered more with exhaustion and starvation by the day, and soon couldn't even get up any more. Bailey seemed more subdued than he had for a long time, but dutifully he followed the rhythms that Ari had taught him.

The Riftmaster themself quietly hoped that they would get to thank the boy later, but was not foolish enough for optimism. They knew better than anyone that they might be joining their children soon.

At night, Ari dozed fitfully, plagued by feverdreams, as Bailey kept watch. Both of them knew that the beasts out there would smell the sickness.

Silence reigned between them, broken only by the distant, hollow cries of the despairing predators.

In the wake of another distant cry, Ari stirred, and in a moment of lucidity, opened their eyes. Dreams came spinning into consciousness. They knew, in that moment, that they were dying.

And yet even now, the cogs in their brain were turning, thinking, with all the energy they had left, what they could do about it. They felt, in a strange, empty way, prepared for it; and yet… they couldn't go now, not yet.

Ari squinted out at the world, desperately searching for the only scrap of legacy they had left.

Ari's vision was blurred at the edges, and the world beyond the campfire was dark.

Where was he…?

"Bailey," Ari rasped urgently, glancing fervently to and fro. "Riftmaster?"

They heard him call out tentatively, and a quiet shuffling as he came inching closer. His blurred shape materialised out of the dark. By the way he flinched as he drew nearer, Ari could tell that the smell of death hung around them like a cloying perfume.

"There you are… Good." The Riftmaster fell silent, catching their breath. "I need you to… do something."

"What do you need me to do?"

Bailey's voice was shaky, but business-like. Eager to please. Good. It should make their last lesson easier to digest.

"You should know by now… Rifthopper… that sentiment doesn't get you anywhere. It's what killed me in the end–"

"Don't say that," Bailey butted in, much to their displeasure.

"No use sugar-coating it."

Bailey grunted, and Ari got the impression that he was biting back a retort as he nodded for Ari to go on.

There was fight in him yet.

The Riftmaster took a deep and shaky breath, preparing themself. "You need to keep going. You need to survive long enough for the Rift to come for you. And if I die... *when* I die... that will be a lot easier."

Bailey swallowed. He knew what that meant.

"No... That's wrong," Bailey whispered.

But Ari went on, heedless of his moral dilemma. They didn't see the problem; when consciousness faded, they would be only dead flesh. If there was an afterlife, they'd be much happier there knowing that their last deed had been to give Bailey another chance to live.

"There's nothing else to do," Ari said. "You have to keep going. Humanity doesn't matter out here, Bailey. When I die, don't bury me, don't carve me a gravestone. Don't waste your strength. When I'm gone, look out for *you*. Take everything I own. Eat my flesh, make my bones into tools and my skull into a bowl for your herbs." Their voice was hoarse, their eyes watery, and their voice sharp with icy seriousness. "...Survive until the Rift comes for you."

Bailey stared in horror, and met the Riftmaster's gaze.

"No," he said, and his voice was little more than a whisper.

Ari felt their throat close up.

"Bailey... I've already lost 11 kids. Please don't let me die knowing that I'll lose you too."

Bailey didn't answer.

So, that was it then.

Both of them would die.

They didn't talk any more after that. The Riftmaster's consciousness passed once more into fitful slumber, and warped nightmares of the worlds they'd seen.

• • •

From the moment Bailey's eyes cracked open in the first rays of sunlight, Bailey knew he was to suffer alone. The Riftmaster... or Ari, he supposed, lay unconscious nearby, trembling and sweating.

Although Bailey's bones ached to their very core, and his

stomach cried out in hunger, he forced himself up into a sitting position and then to his feet. He moved over to his mentor, rested a hand against his forehead. Through the sweat, and the feeble flutters of his eyelids, Ari's skin was blistering. His breaths were quick, and shallow.

He groaned faintly at even the lightest touch.

Bailey sighed. He lifted his hand from the Riftmaster's forehead, pushed himself to his feet, and looked around.

Sometime in the night, their campfire had burned down to ashes; the meagre shade of the banks around them was not enough. Their shared waterskin had long since drained, squeezed till the very last drop.

With Ari's help, Bailey knew where to find water on this world; what to look for in the long-dried-up rivers to find the tiny remaining springs that had once been a source of life. Food was their main problem. Even now, Bailey felt his skin hugging tight to his bones, his frame emaciated and gaunt. With a shudder, Bailey looked at the Riftmaster, reddened by the harsh light of the sun, racked by tremors and on the brink of death.

Ari's last words rose again to the surface of Bailey's mind; the grave certainty of his tone chilled him to the core. The very thought of what Ari had asked him to do made him feel sick to the stomach, forcing back the snarling hunger. Even in starvation, his appetite deserted him.

Bailey shook his head in disgust, squeezing his eyes tightly shut.

You know I could never do that to you, he thought grimly, slowly opening his eyes. *Not even if I were on the brink of death myself.*

He shivered once again.

But what about you? Bailey's hand strayed of its own accord to his knife; made from the fang of another Rifter; and the armour that now hung so loosely from his slim frame. He felt his blood run cold.

What would you do?

Truth be told, Bailey wasn't certain he wanted to know the answer. Luckily for him, there was not a single person in the universe who could have answered them now.

But... perhaps there was still time.

Ari lay there, racked with fever, perhaps dreaming of those

he had lost. But maybe he wasn't beyond help. Not yet.

It was the morning; if Bailey left for a short while to find water, his mentor would be safe here. Making a decision, Bailey tied Ari's waterskin to his belt.

"I'll be back soon," Bailey murmured, despite knowing his voice would be heard by him alone. Moving slowly, Bailey slung Ari's satchel over his shoulder, and wrapped his thick cloak across his shoulders. He made sure that Ari lay with his back to the incoming sunlight and moved him as far into the shade as he could.

Then, and only then, did Bailey finally leave his mentor behind.

• • •

He returned a little over an hour later, when the sun had risen high in the sky. He had already drunk his fill at the water source, and now brought back the waterskin filled entirely for the benefit of Ari, who lay in the sand exactly where Bailey had left him.

At first, Bailey thought it might be already too late; but when he drew near, he noticed the gentle rising and falling of his chest. He was alive.

Letting out a soft sigh of relief, Bailey gently rolled his mentor onto his back, wrapped a hand around his shoulders, and sat him upright. Bailey gently shook the Riftmaster by the shoulder, but he did not stir.

After a moment of thought, Bailey instead raised his hand and held Ari's head steady.

He poured a trickle of water over his mentor's lips, but the droplets slid uselessly down over his chin and dripped down the front of his tunic. "Come on, Riftmaster..." Bailey murmured hopelessly. "It's water. It'll help, I promise."

Holding him steady, Bailey tried again. This time he didn't miss, but he wasn't certain Ari was drinking, either. After another second spent considering, Bailey gave him a little more, and then held his mouth shut, praying that he would swallow it.

Oh, god... please don't choke, or drown, or...

The Riftmaster swallowed, and murmured something unintelligible.

Bailey blew out a small breath, having to suppress a mirthless bark of relieved laughter. It wasn't much to be excited over. Hell, it wasn't even a proper mouthful. But something was better than nothing.

Over the next hour, with Bailey's encouragement, the Riftmaster drank twice more.

By the time the sun reached its highest point in the sky, Bailey was planning their next step. *I need to find food. But what could possibly be edible in a place like this?*

His first thoughts went back to the enormous mushrooms in the region they'd landed, whose trunks were hard as rock. Back then, it had seemed a waste of energy to try and get to their cores for the fleeting chance of something edible. He remembered that Ari had briefly tried, and failed. But now... It might be the only chance they had. That is, if they weren't all long dead.

Bailey stood, his gaze trailing over the distant horizon. *It'll be a long walk, and I don't know the way as well as he did.* Finally, he looked back to their camp, and his prone mentor still lying by his side. *...and I'll have to carry him there.*

Bailey closed his eyes, taking a deep breath.

But I don't have anything to lose... and if we both make it out of this alive, it'll be more than worth it.

Finally, Bailey came to a decision.

As the sun reached its zenith, he packed until their satchel bulged, and returned once more to the water source to refill the waterskin one final time. He found some of the scattered bones of the night-stalker, and brought them too, knowing that the moment they stepped out of the garden, they would be at risk. Hopefully, re-scattering the bones would help to curb the creatures' bloodlust.

As an afterthought, he tied several of its teeth onto his necklace.

Finally he returned to Ari. He placed one arm around his mentor's shoulders and, slipping the other behind his knees, finally lifted him from the ground with a grunt of effort. Bailey blew out through his teeth and brought his mentor to his chest, feeling his legs already beginning to tremble.

Ordinarily, Bailey was certain that Ari's weight would have been almost unnoticeable, but his brush with starvation had caused muscle to wither, and strength to fail.

Bailey realised as he began to walk how incredibly lucky he was that his mentor was so much smaller than him. Had their situations been reversed, Bailey was uncertain the Riftmaster would have been able to lift him at all. But Bailey held him tight to his chest, soon rejoining the dried-up river.

The journey was slow, and far longer than he remembered; Bailey was forced to stop and rest frequently, settling down to drink and catch his breath. By the time the sun had set, he was hardly half of the way back.

In the distance, something began to wail.

Bailey felt that he had no other choice; he had to keep going, on into the night. If he left it any longer, they may as well both give in to starvation.

He trudged along the ancient riverbed, panting heavily, and holding the Riftmaster close.

The cries of the hunters in the night drew nearer, and still Bailey pressed on.

Occasionally, he'd look up towards the riverbank, and see something hunched there, sending shivers down his spine. He pressed on, picking up the speed until his legs ached and he felt as though his knees may give out. He no longer knew where they were, just that he'd been walking for many hours.

Finally, he was forced to halt, laying Ari on the ground beneath an overhang in the riverbank. Like a cornered rat, he shrank into the sandy wall, gulping at the waterskin, eyes wide. As he sealed it up again, he looked out across the dried riverbed. It was too dark to see to the far bank, or anything at all really… Bailey squinted until a spray of pebbles and sand skittered onto the cracked ground just in front of them.

His blood ran cold.

There's something on the bank above us.

Bailey froze.

He heard the soft scrape of its claws on the rock, the rustle of its tendrils whisking across the sand. Trembling, Bailey fumbled with Ari's satchel, rooting through the darkness to find something within. With the other hand, he drew his knife.

He heard a sniff, and a wheezing breath, and a pale tendril began to creep down into their little alcove.

Bailey heard the softest clack, as two bones knocked together in the satchel.

He didn't even have the chance to hope that nothing had

heard as a wail began, echoing out into the night, setting his ears ringing.

A large creature dropped down with a thump onto the riverbed. It crouched before him on six emaciated legs, whisking tendrils around the alcove, uncomfortably close to Bailey's feet.

Hardly thinking, Bailey grabbed a bone from within the satchel, drew it out, and hurled it with all his might. The creature let out a stunned scream, and backpedalled. Bailey leaped forward, heart hammering, and plunged his knife into its skull. He felt its blood, fresh and hot and black in the night, spilling onto his hand and wrist, where it clung like glue, burning hot and steaming in the chilly air. He tried for a moment to take back his knife, but his blood-soaked hand slipped off.

It snapped at him, snarling, but missing his arm by a hair's breadth.

Bailey finally let go of the knife, and stumbled back, cowering against the alcove wall. He looked around, but all he could see was darkness. The clouds crept slowly by above them, obscuring the stars, as the night-stalker died at his feet.

Other voices distantly answered its dying wail, echoing mournfully in the dark all around them.

Finally, he looked up.

In that moment, Bailey made a decision. He grasped the still-warm creature by its hindmost set of legs, and dragged it to the entrance of the alcove. With the tip of his boot he dragged a circle of its blood around the entrance, and then shrank against the wall beside Ari. His hand beginning to burn, Bailey reluctantly drew their waterskin, and washed the clinging fluid from his skin as best he could.

Finally, Bailey whipped his mentor's silver knife from the sheath on his thigh and held it at the ready, eyes wide.

Shivering, he stared out into the dark and the cold, hoping beyond hope that morning was just around the corner.

Bailey wasn't certain when he dropped off into slumber, but he awoke to red-gold sunlight filtering onto the riverbed, and blissful silence punctuated only by the faint whistle of the wind.

The creature lay where he had left it in a pool of blue blood that had been smeared haphazardly across the riverbed. His ivory knife still stuck out of its head at an odd angle. Bailey looked down, and picked up Ari's knife from where it had fallen beside him. After a moment's hesitation he returned it to his mentor's sheath.

As he did so, he caught sight of Ari's face. He was pale now, ghostly white, although a quick check revealed faint, warm breaths falling on his hand. Bailey gently shook his shoulder, and Ari's eyes cracked open. His heart swelled with hope.

"I've got water," he said gently. "Here. Drink."

The Riftmaster grunted, but did not refuse as Bailey lifted the waterskin to his lips. After he had finished, Bailey laid him back down, and the Riftmaster promptly returned to sleep.

Bailey drank himself, before slinking over to the night-stalker's body to reclaim his weapon.

It was stained black with dried blood, and he had to pull hard before it would come loose with a squelch and a splatter. He wiped it as best he could on the underside of his cloak then returned it to his sheath, knowing that he wouldn't be able to clean it for quite some time.

He salvaged as much of its hide as he could to make fresh bindings for Ari's wound, and skinned its back to make them each a hooded shawl that he hoped would help repel further attacks.

After that, Bailey moved further into the open. He looked back and forth along the riverbed but, from here, was unable to tell how far they had to go. He clambered up onto the bank, and looked out across the plain.

In that moment, he almost cried in relief; for, in the distance, he could see the shadow of a forest of twisted trunks and gnarled caps. It might not have been the first forest they arrived in at the beginning, but it was something. And they were almost there.

Finally, Bailey returned to the alcove. He re-emerged a short while later carrying Ari in his arms, wound freshly bound and body wrapped in a new hide shawl.

Bailey struggled up the bank of the river, which crumbled under their combined weight, and staggered onto flat ground. Then he began the final trek towards the edge of the forest.

. . .

They finally reached it late into the afternoon, and from that point Bailey's first task was to find a safe spot to make camp. He found a small hollow at the edge of the trees, deep enough to vaguely hide them, and close enough to be an easy trek to and from the mushroom forest. Before he left, he built a fire with twigs and a ring of pebbles, just in case he returned after sundown. He lit a few wiry hairs from his mountain-crawler cloak as kindling, and to his surprise, the fire took hold.

He exchanged his blade with Ari's silver knife; if he did find food, he wouldn't want to taint it with the night-stalkers' toxic blood.

Then, Bailey ventured into the trees, searching until he found a mushroom with a slightly slimmer trunk. He tried to drive his knife into it, but found that it wouldn't budge. After working, scrabbling, and scratching for a few moments, it left only the faintest mark.

Bailey moved around until he was standing next to one of the bulbous, green-tinged pods growing on its trunk. He drove his knife into it; it was softer, but not by much. Bailey turned his blade from hand to hand as he reconsidered.

I can't waste time, he decided in the end. *I just have to do it.*

Bailey tightened his grasp on the hilt of his weapon, sucked in his breath, and drove it into the gnarled trunk. He scratched off the top layer of stonelike skin, revealing a layer of yellow-green flesh beneath. This was harder than the outside layer but, in desperation, Bailey gouged, cut, and chipped at its surface until his fingers bled.

Just a little deeper...

He bit his lip to try and distract from the pain, working away at the mushroom's thick outer layer until the sun had long set.

When I get to its centre, perhaps...

The cries of the night creatures began again, far away, but Bailey was too deep in desperation to stop now.

One more cut, and I'll be there.

Bailey kept on going until sweat poured down his brow and his lungs felt raw with gasping breaths.

Just one more...

He gritted his teeth and pushed Ari's blade forward one last time. To his surprise, it slid easily into the centre of the mushroom. Green sap welled to the surface from within, dribbling down its trunk.

Bailey's breath quickened. He fell to his knees, his heart pounding as he rifled through Ari's satchel to find the tester herbs. With shaking hands he gathered the sap into a tiny bowl, and began to mix.

The wait was excruciating, and the encroaching darkness made it hard to see.

And when he did see, he wasn't sure whether to believe.

Before he'd properly registered what the herbs showed, tears began to gush down Bailey's cheeks for the first time in months. Taking another bowl, he filled it with sticky sap, brought it to his lips, and drank.

It was as sweet as honey, with the faintest cinnamon spice that left his lips tingling.

With tears still streaming down his face, he returned what was left of Ari's tester herbs to the satchel, filled the bowl again and added some to the waterskin as well. Then, he slung the satchel over his shoulder, and began the trek back to his mentor.

· · ·

"Riftmaster? Riftmaster, wake up!"

For a single, awful moment, Bailey thought he was too late. He burst into the hollow and knelt by Ari's side, placing the sap-filled bowl beside him. With gentle hands and a faint wince, Bailey rolled the Riftmaster onto his back and pressed the back of his hand against Ari's forehead, sweeping damp locks of red hair back as he felt for a pulse.

Then a soft huff stirred the Riftmaster's sides. A faint cough racked him. Bailey sat him upright.

Ari's eyelids flickered. He mumbled something.

"It's going to be okay. We're going to be alright, Riftmaster. Look…" He raised the bowl to Ari's lips. Ari did not stir.

"Come on… I've found food!" Bailey paused. He looked at the thick, syrupy liquid oozing around the bowl. "…well… nourishment, at least. You can't die now."

Ari's eyes cracked open, and for the first time in days, he

looked up. Bailey tried to meet his gaze, but the Riftmaster stared vacantly off into nothingness. This time, as Bailey tilted the bowl, he drank. Finally, as the bowl was empty, Bailey placed it back on the ground beside him.

"...Bailey..." Ari whispered. "Is that you?"

"Riftmaster...?" Bailey asked, his eyes welling up. "Yes, it is."

The Riftmaster's lips cracked into a faint smile. He let out a small huff, opening his mouth, and then closing it again.

"What is it?" Bailey asked breathlessly.

"Why...?" the Riftmaster asked.

"Why... what?"

"Why are you like this...?"

Bailey couldn't help a tiny chuckle. "Like... What?"

The Riftmaster's eyes flickered. They began to close again.

"Just... this..." he mumbled. Bailey saw his lips move, but his voice had already trailed off, his eyelids finally sliding closed.

"What do you mean?" Bailey whispered back. But the Riftmaster had already drifted back into slumber. "Riftmaster...?" Bailey gently shook him. "...Ari?"

He held his wrist beneath his mentor's nose, and felt the Riftmaster's breaths, long, warm, and peaceful. Bailey's shoulders relaxed slightly. In that moment, he felt as though everything might just be okay.

Finally, Bailey laid his mentor down to rest again, before slumping down by the fireside himself. After binding his raw hands with strips of hide, he passed out almost immediately.

• • •

The next morning, Bailey awoke to faint sunlight flooding the sky. He opened his eyes, blinking, and sat up. He reached for the waterskin, took a drink, and was greeted by the welcoming flavour of slightly sweet, spiced water.

Immediately, his spirits rose.

Bailey was soon on his feet. A moment later he was checking to ensure that Ari was still alive and, to his immense satisfaction, he was. After offering the half-conscious Riftmaster a swift drink of water and briefly checking their surroundings, Bailey set off back to the source of sweet sap he'd tapped into the previous night.

When he reached it, he found signs of a struggle in the surrounding area. Deep gashes had appeared in the dirt around the foot of the giant mushroom, smears of blue blood could be found in the soil and gashes bore deep into nearby trunks.

The previously small gash he'd cut into the trunk had been widened, its trunk crisscrossed by claw marks and assailed by desperate jaws. The mushroom's sweet sap oozed onto the surrounding earth in a river.

Looks like we aren't the only ones getting desperate, Bailey thought, a pang of sympathy sneaking into his heart. *Still... What a waste.*

Kneeling down, Bailey made sure that no bloodied smears had managed to work their way into their food source, before finally bringing the waterskin up from his belt, and filling it to the brim.

It feels wrong to taint our waterskin like this... but this seems like the best way to store it. Hopefully the sap will provide enough moisture on its own to last us for a while. That being said...

Bailey wiped the lid of their waterskin as best he could. It was getting sticky, and cleaning it was going to be difficult. And that was saying nothing of the infections or mould that might take root in the rapidly thickening fluid...

The Riftmaster would have my head if he could see me now.

Bailey let out a small, amused huff.

He probably will, still.

Bailey soon returned to his mentor's side, and spent the rest of the day tending his needs to the best of his ability. The Riftmaster did not awake again that day, but his fever was gradually receding, his violent feverdreams and restless slumber becoming gradually more peaceful.

The next few days passed by uneventfully, with Bailey making numerous trips out into the woods. He used what remained of their firewood, and spent their daytime hours gathering more. As dry as his throat felt at all times, Bailey came to realise that there was no need to expand the search for water. The sap was so thick that it didn't quite quench the thirst, but it was enough to keep them going.

He scattered bones from the night stalkers nearby their

camp, and hung up their hides on nearby trunks to keep them at bay once and for all… but Bailey still heard them fighting during the nighttime, and knew that when he returned to the well of sap the next morning, its wound would have widened once more.

Slowly, but surely, desperation became routine.

Each night, Bailey curled up by the fireside, and though he didn't feel safe, his belly was filled and his throat a little less dry than it could have been. His blistered hands and bloodied fingers hardened into scabs, and he no longer needed to bind them, instead saving everything he could for Ari's wound. Overall, though, he felt more content than he had in many weeks.

One morning around a week later, Bailey awoke to a familiarly fiery sensation flooding through his skin, and the unmistakable feeling of being thrown. He hit the ground face-first, but hardly felt the pain. By the time he opened his eyes to the slightest slits, they were already in another world.

• • •

Ari had no way of knowing how long the world was dark.

The fever came over them in waves, tremors racking them, senses deserting them, and dreams drowning them like a crashing tide.

Occasionally they'd surface into consciousness, gasping for air and drenched in sweat, only to be dragged back under by the surging waters of slumber.

Sensation continued, faint and hazy, as though seen or felt through someone else's senses. The flare of agony that the Rift brought in its wake was enough to stir them into little more than a few moments of wakefulness.

Sometimes, they tasted sweetness on their lips. Then, there would be warmth, a pressure around their shoulders or waist supporting them before once again fading away. They sometimes felt the earth beneath them, catching them off guard and removing any semblance of understanding from their grasp. Once, it was cold and harsh. The next time they felt thick mud beneath their fingertips. Once, the world felt rocky and jagged against their back, sending pins and needles through their fingertips.

Even then, Ari's body remained still, rooted in leaden torpor.

Opening their eyes showed no more than a blurred haze, though sometimes a shadow crouched over them.

When their eyes were closed, figures swelled in the darkness. Creatures and humans surrounded them, muttering in tongues Ari had yet to understand. And among the crowd, they caught sight of a familiar shape.

Ari struggled to their feet. Hands grabbed at their wrists, holding them back, down against the earth. They thrashed, struggling free to run after her.

In their mind's eye they saw curly red hair framing a pale, freckled face. She turned towards them. Eyes widened, mouth formed a silent gasp of stunned shock that mirrored their own.

Adeline?! Adeline!

No matter how hard Ari tried to cry out, no sound seemed to emerge. Still, they reached out an arm, trying desperately to catch her, to hold her, to pull her close. Their daughter did the same. *Adeline...?*

The feeling of hands gripping their wrists tightened.

They traced the curves of her face and memorised the pattern of freckles across her button nose. The way her eyes sank into her pale face as she aged before them in seconds, the way the skin hugged the outline of the skull beneath... the very same skull they'd held in their hands...

Ari came to a halt as they realised the figure before them was no more than their own reflection. And then they were alone. So terribly, and awfully, alone.

Just as she had been.

In the stillness, Ari felt those disembodied hands let go of their wrists. And suddenly, any and all connection to the world outside their troubled psyche was gone. Ari sank down in the dark, bringing knees to their chest and staring out into the nothingness.

Faces flitted before their very eyes, passing from memory into obscurity. Creatures and monsters danced around them like a grotesque Riftworld parade.

And yet, they couldn't lift a finger. Ari's body felt heavy as lead.

They sank once more into a blanket of unseeing,

unknowing nothingness.

They continued fighting through nightmares as the fever ran its course. They replayed the fight with the night-stalker in their brain a thousand times, warped and twisted beyond any recognition.

Often the night-stalker shifted, body changing into a thick, leathery biped. Its mandibles cracked violently as it tried to fling them off its serpentine neck, knife-like forearms raking at nothing, clipping leaves and gouging the forest floor. Ari fought violently, gripping its neck, striking with silver knife.

They saw Adeline looking up from the forest floor with horrified eyes, blood oozing from a wound in her forearm.

The twins, Peggy and Toby, cowered in a tree above the battle, faces twisted into picturesque terror, whilst Oliver kept shrieking the name of someone who no longer existed.

"Aria!"

As the creature finally fell into a growing pool of its own blood, the world faded away to a faint, hazy blur. Something cold was pressed up against their lips. They tasted something earthy and sweet, and heard the lingering echoes of a soothing voice.

"Come on, Riftmaster… Please drink….."

Ari ached to return to the cold darkness of slumber, knowing all too well that consciousness hurt. But, as the nightmares began to fade and lucidity returned, the Riftmaster was denied their wish.

The next time their eyes cracked open, the sunlight gleamed beautifully through blurred patterns of luscious leaves, and they felt a carpet of mosses and flowers beneath their fingertips.

They didn't know how it had happened.

All they knew was that, somehow, they kept on living.

Chapter 13
Out of the Frying Pan

Bailey lay for a few seconds on the ground, winded, before jolting upright. It took a few more seconds for him to assess the situation and come to terms with the overpowering surge of emotion that quickly followed. For a moment he simply combed the soft moss with his fingers, and picking up a fragrant flower to stare at it as though worried it would vanish before his very eyes.

Soon he was staggering to his feet, punching at the air with a closed fist and letting out wild peals of laughter.

"We're alive! Riftmaster, we survived!"

His mentor's name suddenly felt strange to say out loud. It had been a long time since the pair had spoken properly, and privately, over the course of long hours spent taking care of his mentor's every need, Bailey had begun to think of him as Ari. Even now, though, Bailey was certain he would be scolded should the Riftmaster find out.

In the meantime, though, he was still hungry, his throat dusty and dry and his skin caked in dried mud, but he was alive. *They* were alive.

Panting, he scrambled over to the Riftmaster's prone form, still lying in the grass. He was unconscious, but breathing.

A moment later, Bailey was rifling through the Riftmaster's satchel to retrieve the sticky, sap-covered waterskin, and pouches of tester herbs. With some difficulty he tied them all onto his belt, and set off. Now that they were in yet another new world, water was the most important thing; and luckily he didn't have to search for long before he came upon a bubbling hot spring in the centre of a mossy grove.

He tested the water as the Riftmaster had showed him, and although he had done the same on numerous occasions, he panicked as he second-guessed his judgement. *It hasn't been that long since I did this, but it feels like forever.*

A quick swig revealed the water tasted strongly of minerals, and slightly sour. But other than that, it didn't seem dangerous.

Once he was certain it was safe, Bailey couldn't stop himself from drinking more. Even though it was hot on his tongue and tasted strange, he couldn't remember the last time clean water had been so readily available.

Finally he filled the waterskin, rinsing it as best he could of the sticky sap.

From the surrounding trees he gathered bundles of strange, purplish leaves, distinctly alien flowers, and odd, bulbous-looking seed-pods.

As he headed back towards the Riftmaster, Bailey began to feel a prickle along the back of his neck, and felt a distinctive paranoia that sent chills down his spine.

It felt like he was being watched.

When he arrived back in the clearing, he mixed his foraged vegetation and the tester herbs with frantic quickness. The seconds the mixture took to settle felt like an age, but he watched unblinkingly.

To Bailey's chagrin, none of them were edible... or, at least, he didn't *think* they were. Although he briefly considered trying to nudge the Riftmaster awake to make sure, the idea quickly died as he glanced over and caught sight of that deathly-pale face, deeply lined with exhaustion. Bailey laid what he'd already tried against a tree root. Growing ever more frantic, he once again left the clearing. He plucked a few wrinkled fruits and used the knife on his belt to sever sections of plant stems and roots.

A movement caught the edge of his vision.

Bailey turned to find that there was nothing there. Fear was beginning to crawl up and down his spine. And perhaps even more pressingly, as he once again returned to his mentor Bailey realised that his prints were leaving an ever-deeper trail in the mud; that in his panic, he had forgotten the very first lesson the Riftmaster had taught him. There was no way that he could cover them now.

He hurried on his way, back into the clearing where he'd left the Riftmaster.

Ari had moved. Stubborn as ever and seemingly filled with a renewed sense of vigour, he'd forced himself upright and into a sitting position. He watched Bailey with barely-open eyes and a vacant expression.

This time as he tested the plant matter, Bailey let out a small sound of glee; one of them, a tough section of root, proved edible. As he carried on working, so too did a few leaves, and a handful of small blue berries.

Although he was half-tempted to eat the berries himself since they looked the most appetising, Bailey forced himself to ignore his growling stomach. Instead he crushed them up with a few drops of water. This Bailey fed to the Riftmaster, getting his attention with a gentle shake of his shoulder.

Always as he worked, Bailey was dimly aware of that creeping presence.

Only after the Riftmaster had swallowed his meal and fallen back into a noticeably more peaceful sleep did Bailey return to the rest of what he'd gathered. He crammed a few leaves into his mouth, chewed, and then spat them out again with a gag. Even if they weren't toxic, they tasted foul.

He gave the section of root a tentative nibble.

It was just wood. Not toxic, just wood.

Finally, with a sigh, Bailey went to gather more berries. He heard a rustle in the undergrowth as he set off. He thought he saw movement – the twitch of a branch, the tremble of a leaf – but there was never anything there when he turned to look.

Finally, heart pounding, Bailey arrived at the berry tree.

He reached out for the lowest-hanging berries, only to find that they hung just out of reach. As he struggled and stretched trying to reach them, the young man heard a rustling sound somewhere behind him. He froze, and then slowly turned, to see that a stand of flowers had slightly parted. A leaf fluttered from a piece of brown wood.

Bailey moved slowly, trying to inch in closer to see what was hiding there. There was another rustle. What Bailey had taken to be a protruding branch shuffled back. The flowers bounced and returned to their former positions.

Silence.

Bailey moved closer.

More silence.

He was almost there – finally, he knelt.

Trembling slightly, he reached out and brushed away the flowers. And there, standing staring at him frozen in equal fear, was a tiny rat-like creature, with a slender body and woody brown scales, with long and pointed ears folded back against its long neck. Strangely, it was wearing a leather band around its neck, adorned with a few colourful feathers. It met Bailey's gaze with slitted, snake-like eyes and backed away again. Bailey held up his hands to try and show that he wasn't going to hurt it.

It followed his movements with a small twittering warning, and waved the end of its tail so that he could see it. It was segmented with large, glistening scales and tipped with a wicked barb like a scorpion's.

Even if the creature was only around two feet in length, Bailey was certain that that barb would contain some kind of venom, and he didn't want to risk anything.

Bailey stepped back.

With no more need for stealth, the little creature's scales moved – colours shifting in the light with hypnotic quickness. What had once been woody brown rippled with waves of iridescent green and purple, flushing over its long body. Stiff, quill-like scales trembled softly against its back, perking up to make it appear bigger, and then rattling a soft warning like a rattlesnake.

Seeing that Bailey was retreating, it pricked its ears and swayed curiously, colours settling into a more muted purple that blended better into the mossy ground. It took a cautious, curious step forward and then sat up on its haunches. For a moment it appeared to be considering, then it crossed its small forelimbs over its chest, and bowed, extending one paw out towards Bailey.

With a jolt of shock Bailey realised he'd seen the gesture before, when he'd first met the Riftmaster.

With hasty awkwardness, Bailey copied it.

A flush of bright cyan moved over the little creature's body, its quills perked up before flattening smooth against its spine, and the tip of its tail twitched. Seemingly no longer afraid, it moved towards him, scaly nose twitching. It made sounds as it did so, shrill squeaks and twittering almost like birdsong. Bailey guessed it was trying to speak to him. It rippled around him in cautious examination.

In complete shock, Bailey remained where he was, following the creature's scrutiny with a nervous gaze.

"I... I can't understand you," he said helplessly.

It looked up at him, narrowing its eyes slightly. Then Bailey let out a cry of shock as it shot up his leg, little paws sticking to his clothes like the feet of a gecko. He balled his hands into fists and stood stiffly with fear, but knew better than to try and throw it off. Instead he just let it complete its inspection until it was seemingly satisfied, then felt it climb up to sit on his shoulder. It looked at him and he turned to look at it.

They stared at each other for a few long moments. Bailey watched its nose wrinkling until it finally got bored and turned tail.

It began to patter away, but paused.

With a toss of its head, it beckoned towards the way he'd come. Did it want him to take it to the Riftmaster? Did it *know* the Riftmaster?

"Wait," Bailey said.

Although it obviously didn't understand, it watched him.

Bailey pointed up to the berry tree hopelessly. His stomach let out a pitiful growl.

The little creature's quills quivered. It seemed to take a moment to consider. Then it twittered at him, like a bird. Bailey nodded, although he didn't know what it was asking. But it seemed like he got it right, anyway. With feline grace, it scaled the vertical trunk of the tree, running directly up the trunk with its gecko-like pads clinging to the bark.

Bailey soon lost it among the upper branches of the tree. Shortly after, a berry-covered twig dropped from its heights. Bailey stooped to pick it up with relief.

The little creature soon returned as well, carrying a single berry in its mouth. It gratefully clambered onto Bailey's arm as he offered it, and lounged on one shoulder with its tail wound around his upper arm.

As Bailey set off towards the Riftmaster's clearing, it held the berry in its forepaws and gnawed.

Bailey ate too, as he walked, smacking his lips with distaste. The berries were sour and earthy, although the inside juices were slightly sweet.

Still, they were bearable.

And right now, Bailey didn't think he'd ever tasted anything better.

• • •

Ari awoke soon after Bailey and the scaly little creature returned to his resting place. There was much snuffling, and Bailey watched warily as the little thing climbed over his mentor's unconscious form. As the Riftmaster stirred, it shot away from him and instead perched atop Bailey's head.

The Riftmaster's unfocused gaze trembled, then fixed on him. He didn't seem to notice Bailey's new friend at first.

"Water," he grunted.

Fizzing with excitement, Bailey handed him the waterskin, and what remained of the berry branch. It was the first time he'd spoken properly in many days. Even now, his brow was slick with sweat, but his eyes were clearer than they had been in a long time.

After the Riftmaster had finished drinking his fill, he was about to pop a berry in his mouth, then hesitated. "Is it edible?" he asked cautiously.

Bailey nodded, beaming.

He heard the creature on his head chirp sharply in protest.

"Don't worry, I checked," he said proudly.

The Riftmaster gave a small huff of surprise. "Well done," he praised.

Bailey watched as he ate, and though he felt his stomach crying out, he knew that the Riftmaster needed it more. Besides, even the small meal of berries he'd eaten earlier was enough to make him feel slightly nauseous, and he didn't know if that was because of the berries or the fact that he hadn't eaten so much in so long.

Already, his mentor was looking better. He even cracked a smile, and after he'd finished eating, quirked a brow and nodded towards the little creature on Bailey's head.

"So, who's your little friend?" he asked finally, tossing the remaining twig aside.

Bailey shrugged. "I thought it knew you," Bailey said, with a trifle of nervousness entering his voice. "Do you have any idea what it is?"

The Riftmaster shook his head, shuffling a little closer to examine it. "No idea. I've never seen one of these before. What makes you think it knows me?"

Bailey heard the creature's quills tremble softly.

"Are you sure?" Bailey asked, perturbed. "It greeted me in the same way you did."

"You mean like this?"

The Riftmaster placed his hands over his chest, and again made that strange gesture. By the way that the creature's forepaws raised from his hair, he guessed that it was doing the same.

"Amazing," breathed the Riftmaster, his eyes lighting up with excitement.

Bailey blinked in confusion. "What does that mean?" he asked.

"That's a greeting used by some experienced Rifters to signal that they're sentient, and ask if you are as well. With so many intergalactic languages, it's the easiest... and sometimes only way to communicate with fellow Rifters."

"So Rifters run into each other quite often, then?" Bailey asked in surprise. In all the worlds they'd passed through, they'd only ever seen the dead one.

Ari sighed. Bailey saw tiredness in his eyes, but also a faint spark of his old self resurfacing there too. Bailey heard a hint of the old excitement enter his croaky voice.

"Not usually. But sometimes... there are planets where the Rift seems to collect, called Riftworlds, in which hundreds, sometimes thousands of Rifters and Rifthoppers, collide. You'll come across them quite often. It's as though they attract the Rift, somehow, but no-one knows why. When you've lived as long as I have, you'll have found yourself passing through many Riftworlds. You'll stay in some longer than others, but they're all amazing. You never know what you'll find there."

"That's strange. Has anyone ever tried to find out why?" Bailey knew he shouldn't push his mentor too hard when he was so fresh out of the sickness, but he felt that this was important.

"As I've said before… the Rift is virtually impossible to study because you can't predict it. But Riftworlds are the closest we've got."

The little creature that had perched itself on Bailey's head began to move – he let out a small grunt of pain as it wrenched its sticky paws free of his hair and dropped onto the ground. It bounded away from him, putting a few metres of distance between them before turning back, flicking its head pointedly.

The Riftmaster huffed. "Looks like your little friend wants to show us something."

The little creature spun in an excited circle as it waited for them to get the point.

Ari began to try and drag himself to his feet, but Bailey pushed him back down. The man bent over in a coughing fit, and when he looked up at Bailey, there was a haunted look in his eye, and a smear of blood at the corner of his mouth. He hastily looked away and wiped it off.

"Come on. You've got a long way to go before you're better," Bailey said with a sigh, thinking for a moment. After a while of hesitation, he stood up and told the Riftmaster "Lie back."

As Ari did as he was told, Bailey bent to scoop him up. He ignored the sheer embarrassment on his mentor's face that was probably mirrored by his own. He'd carried the Riftmaster before, but this was the first time he'd been *awake*.

"Aw, come on! I'm not that old!" the Riftmaster growled, red-faced. "I can walk by myself!"

Bailey sighed, shaking his head slightly. *Ah, Riftmaster,* he thought, bemusedly. *If only you knew…*

"Stop moving! You're too sick to walk by yourself."

"No I'm not…! We could just stay here! There's food here! Besides, it's a waste of your energy."

On failing to struggle free, the Riftmaster folded his arms like a bad-tempered child. "*You're* the apprentice. You should do as I say."

"No… Not this time. Sorry, Riftmaster."

The Riftmaster finally stopped struggling and allowed himself to be carried. Bailey followed the glimmering little creature as it bounced like a living jewel deeper into the woods. An awkward silence followed.

Finally, Bailey spoke.

"I'm just going to take you somewhere safe. Then you can relax."

"Yeah, yeah. I just hope your little friend is trustworthy."

Bailey sighed. "Well, I don't have a better idea. We need to get you somewhere warm, just in case night falls."

"I know," the Riftmaster responded softly, voice low. He hated feeling so helpless. Usually he was the one in control.

Bailey kept walking for a while. The trees were beginning to thin, and he could see light shining ahead of them at the edge of the treeline.

The Riftmaster silently watched the world go by. His eyelids began to droop, but Bailey could tell he was fighting to stay awake. Bailey wished he would just let himself drift off into slumber.

"You know," the Riftmaster said finally, eyes squinting against the growing brightness.

"Hm?" Bailey glanced down.

"Sometimes I feel like you stick to the rules better than I do."

Although the Riftmaster didn't look at Bailey, the young man thought he detected a hint of pride, and for now, that was enough.

Chapter 14
Flora's Abode

Bailey decided, secretly, to name their vibrant little guide Flora, for now. She (or, Bailey liked to think of it as a she) seemed to take on every colour of the rainbow, more vibrant than any flower in the woods. Her most dramatic changes seemed heavily influenced by her moods, although she appeared to linger mostly within the spectrum of iridescent green.

With the Riftmaster held safely in his arms, Bailey followed Flora to the very edge of the wood, where she waited for them just beyond the trees. Before them was a wide and flat plain, in which grasses of deep purple and cyan swayed softly in a warm breeze. Dark clouds swirled overhead, dappling the land with shadows cast by a distant sun of rich aquamarine.

The mauve sky was flecked by a faint smattering of stars.

The distant horizon was slightly curved; it was an odd, and almost disorienting sight, but Bailey knew he was looking at the shape of the planet itself.

The meadowland before them was scattered with small structures; mounds of earth and shelters built mostly from wood, little huts in all sorts of shapes and sizes. It looked like the outskirts of a tiny village, though most of the homes were built far enough apart that the owners would be able to live a solitary lifestyle. Many of them had gardens – dramatic clusters of plants, herbs and flowers that stood out from the cool tones of the world with colours of reds, yellows, greens, and some that even glowed.

Beyond all the huts and crude homes, Bailey could see somewhat natural-looking structures of various metals and stone clustered closer together, glistening in the sun. Bailey could see a few pillars of smoke rising from these buildings, and beyond these, a dome built of sleek black crystal, towering, and imposing. When the light hit the surface of the dome, its many-faceted surface shone with rainbow colours.

Bailey couldn't quite make out the buildings further into the town, but here each structure seemed mismatched to the rest, in wildly varying styles and qualities of build, from little log cabins to simple mounds of earth. Bailey assumed that these homes had been made of materials that could be easily found on this planet's surface.

He heard a thunderclap, the sky filled for an instant by an arcing brightness, and then he saw a pillar of lightning strike somewhere beyond the dome.

"Riftmaster, look," he said softly.

Although Bailey wasn't sure when he had fallen asleep, Ari jolted awake. He blinked several times before Bailey saw his face split into a broad grin. "Welcome to your first Riftworld, Bailey."

Bailey began to walk forwards, making to move towards the town, but was drawn back by a sharp squeal. He turned towards their escort, to see that Flora was staring at him and, with a flick of her head, redirected him. Bailey stared wistfully out towards the dome, shimmering in the pale sunlight. Then he turned to follow the small creature.

She led them around the edge of the meadow, along the treeline. Bailey saw a few Rift-creatures look up as they passed. An almost-humanoid creature with enormous eyes, a large mane of spines and huge, pointed ears watched as they went by, pausing before continuing to tend its garden with a flick of a long, spined tail their way. A chunky reptilian creature flared dazzling fins at them as they passed the rock where it was basking. Noticing Bailey looking, it raised one huge paw to its chest, and bowed its finned head in a familiar motion.

They passed a sandy-toned quadrupedal creature digging in its garden with masterful efficiency. The desert-looking creature was short and stocky, with thick front limbs and small hind limbs. It reminded him almost of a small bear, but for the low hanging cheek pouches that ran along the sides of its body almost to its haunches. Its ears were small, its eyes tiny, beady, and black. With a dextrous tongue it harvested the roots it was looking for, stored them in its pouches, and then spat a few seeds into the hole.

This one gave the rat-like creature they were following a low growl that wobbled the pouches at its sides, narrowing four eyes as they passed.

Their guide twittered back, gesturing wildly in a way that Bailey wasn't sure was respectful.

With a snort, the cheek-pouched alien started to fill in the hole with big paws.

Finally, they came to an oddly-shaped little cabin, built of wood so old that it was beginning to rot, and covered with cyan moss. The garden outside was overgrown, its leaves wilting. Their guide disappeared inside, through a hole in the side of the cabin. The main doorway was small – he would have to duck to enter – but surprisingly wide. It must have been made for a smaller creature than they were. Bailey let the Riftmaster go for a second, sitting him down on a nearby rock.

"Careful, Rifthopper," his mentor warned as he began to feel over the door for a way to open it.

Opening the door revealed a home that was smaller than he was expecting, perhaps owing to the thick walls. It was tall enough for him to comfortably move around, albeit with a slight hunch, with about as much room as an average-sized camping van. But it was cosy and warm, with a musty smell. Surprisingly well-lit, too – a fist-sized crystal, glowing cyan-white, had been wedged into the ceiling between two support beams. Animal hides had been laid out at the back for a bed, and the walls were lined with trinkets – mostly marbles and statues, and pieces of what looked like broken scientific equipment. Especially strange were the surplus of broken geode pieces. Flora waited for them on a shelf, where a small mound of fabric scraps had been piled up, but every twitch of her tail disturbed the dust and Bailey soon found himself sneezing.

It must have been empty for some time.

Bailey looked up at the rat-like creature curiously, and she stared right back.

Clearly, the pile of fabric on the shelf had been put there for her benefit – and Bailey realised then that the hole in the wall she had entered through had been intentionally made, and covered with a little flap of wood on a hinge. Whoever had lived here before them had been looking after her... and they must have been taken by the Rift.

Unless...

Bailey's attention was again drawn to the band around the creature's neck, shimmering in the crystalline light. He'd taken it, at first, to mean that she had been someone's pet; something that he'd thought more likely by her sheer confidence around them both.

But... there was a problem. She was *sentient*.

What if she, too, had had a Riftmaster to guide her? But now she was on her own. Her master might have been separated from her, and now she was alone until the Rift came for her. But then... why was she still wearing her binding?

Bailey found himself thinking of the worst-case scenario; that Flora's old master, or perhaps mentor, had died.

It was a possibility, at least. Bailey couldn't be sure; all he could really do was wish Flora's former partner luck, wherever he might have found himself among the stars.

But was her mentor's death *really* the worst-case scenario? After all, he'd left this home behind. If he hadn't, they might still be out there in the woods, slowly freezing as night fell.

Bailey tore his gaze away from the little creature as he realised with a sharp jolt that the Riftmaster was still waiting for them outside. The young man stood, nodded a thanks to Flora, and then went to get him, feeling her eyes following him all the way.

• • •

Bailey worried at first that the cabin's last owner might come storming in one day, and demand his home back. But to his relief, that outcome seemed less likely by the day. Bailey spent most of his days out foraging, and to his relief the Riftmaster's health kept on improving.

The infected wound on his arm gradually began to heal, and the ensuing sickness faded in one last bout of violent fevers.

Bailey began to learn the surrounding neighbourhood, and practiced his greetings. Without bothering to ask for the Riftmaster's advice, he began to scout the surrounding area, find more potential food sources, and even plant neutralising herbs in their garden outside. He found more water sources; and to his relief, there were plenty of hot springs – all of them evenly spaced, evenly sized and perfectly round. It was admittedly quite strange, but a blessing nonetheless.

Bailey soon began to think about ways to communicate with Flora, who, in the Riftmaster's absence, became a near-constant companion. He began to point to objects and sound out their words. "Bailey," he would say, gesturing to himself. "Human."

One day he'd point at a tree.

"Tree."

And a flower.

"Flower."

But the little creature had the attention span of a butterfly, and as soon as she'd finished one botched attempt at speech she'd show her displeasure by showing waves of red and spitting and hissing in frustration. Within minutes she'd be off doing something else.

She often twittered at Bailey conversationally on their foraging sessions, producing sounds in ways that Bailey was certain meant something. But he, himself, was at a loss for what she was trying to say to him. It soon became clear to Bailey that learning alien languages was no mean feat.

After a while, his attempts became fewer and farther between.

But the companionship was a nice change. Flora showed Bailey all the berry trees she knew of, and all the fruits that she fed on – some of which were even edible to the humans, too. In all of his scouting expeditions Bailey didn't go near the town centre, and he caught the little rat-like creature sometimes looking at it, her nose wrinkling and ears laid back.

Bailey reasoned that it was better to stay away for now; having never been to a Riftworld before, it would be better to explore with someone who knew what to expect, and most likely knew a few more languages than Bailey did.

Still, curiosity tugged at the pit of his stomach.

They often saw the same light flashing across the sky, and lightning striking at the earth sometimes frighteningly close. This, Bailey came to understand, was the Rift. Sometimes its comings and goings would be foreshadowed by earthly tremors; earthquakes were common here, and though not all of them were severe, it was the wooden homes and the scattered huts of the town's outskirts that suffered the most.

But the inhabitants of these houses came to one another's aid when they needed it; he saw the cheek-pouched alien carrying materials from the woods, and several beings gathered where the reptilian being's home had fallen around it.

Working together in wordless harmony, they managed to free the beast.

In this part of town, no-one could speak to one another, but everyone seemed to understand as they thanked each other with silent bows.

Bailey came to understand why the walls of their shelter were so thick. The foundations buried deep into the ground, they were safe from even the worst of the earthquakes. The longer that Bailey spent here, the more he felt at home. There was strength in numbers to be found, and although he couldn't communicate with his neighbours, he began to enjoy their presence.

When he spoke about the earthquakes to Ari, he was dismissed.

"All Riftworlds have them, some worse than others," he said. "It's nothing to worry about. I've lived on Riftworlds for centuries without any trouble, although... they do seem to be particularly frequent here. It's something to do with the Rift, I think."

Bailey still wasn't fully convinced.

One day soon after that Bailey returned from foraging to see that part of Cheek-pouches' home had fallen in. The alien stared for a while, and then wearily started to put it back together, taking a thick log in its jaws. Bailey moved over, and it looked up in surprise. With dextrous fingers that could put things in place infinitely better than its jaws, Bailey helped the otherworldly beast fix up its home.

Then after, both of them nodded their heads and went their separate ways.

Bailey returned home with a spring in his step and Flora uttering shrill protests in his ears despite the smile on his face.

Time passed by almost unnoticed.

Bailey's herb garden was soon fully grown, the shelter almost carpeted in plant life. The young man picked his way through to the door and, upon opening it, found that the Riftmaster was awake, upright, and waiting for him.

As he began to unload what he'd gathered from the Riftmaster's satchel and let Flora take her place on her shelf, Bailey excitedly began to tell the Riftmaster about everything he'd done, and everything that his mentor had missed whilst bedridden.

Ari listened, sometimes with a smile, other times with surprise, but always with a faraway look in his eye.

Chapter 15
The Riftworld

When the Riftmaster was fully healed, his wound now no more than a series of scars across one arm, he finally left their little dwelling to explore the surrounding area for himself... and help tend the garden that Bailey had started to grow. With plants growing wildly even in a single night, Bailey opened the door one morning and found that it was almost impossible to leave.

"Didn't you think about trimming them!? This is the messiest 'garden' I've ever seen. It's a wonder everything is still alive, and... are those thorns!? Did you cut down the last garden before starting to plant things? ...Oh my God."

It seemed Bailey still had a lot to learn, but despite his face growing hot with embarrassment, he was eager to improve, and helped his mentor harvest the flowers and seeds. He'd missed the sound of Ari humming as he worked. He'd missed seeing his face – however gaunt – and his smile was a welcome sight.

Bailey found himself releasing a breath that he didn't know he'd been holding as the pair set out into the sun.

He hadn't expected to feel quite so relieved.

Ari was, of course, curious about the residents of the surrounding area, but seemed even more curious about the city beyond. With a healthy dose of caution, of course. The Riftmaster waltzed through the scattered homes of the surrounding neighbourhood to admire and greet their residents, as Bailey trailed after and recounted as much information as he could about them.

Which was to say, not much.

Cheek-pouches greeted them on the path with a grunt as he plodded the opposite way, pouches stuffed to almost twice the size of the creature. He nodded to Bailey, and growled softly at Flora as he disappeared among the trees.

The lizard-like creature watched them with a flick of his tongue as they padded by. Bailey bowed, outstretching a hand, and the chunky green beast waved its fins and did the same. And then there were others: the newest arrival was a small, fat, feathery creature that waddled around and stole food from everyone else's gardens. A large, hippo-like creature lumbered around on two feet heaving snorting breaths like it had just run a marathon. A serpentine lizard on two extremely impractical legs wobbled and whisked its way away from them.

Wandering in a group, Bailey, Ari, and Flora drew more than their fair share of eyes in this part of the neighbourhood.

"So," Bailey asked as they returned to their dwelling. "What do you think?"

"Such variety," Ari said wonderingly. "But I want to check out the town. I've never seen a Riftworld so densely crowded before."

"Towards the dome?" Bailey felt a familiar thrill of nervousness despite himself, but also felt his heart beat a little faster with excitement. He'd been curious about the town since the day they'd arrived here. "Do you think you'll be able to understand anyone there?"

"Probably. I know more than my fair share of languages. There has to be someone there that speaks one of them."

"I don't think that Flora will like that, though. She always shrieks if I walk that way."

"Flora? You mean your little friend? I wonder why."

The Riftmaster seemed suddenly hesitant about heading into town, and insisted that they should probably research more, perhaps try to learn the language of the small creature accompanying them so that she could tell them what to be wary of. But Bailey didn't want to waste their time on this world; they'd spent too long dawdling already whilst the Riftmaster healed.

No doubt the Rift would be coming to pick them up soon.

"Besides," Bailey coerced. "We might never get another trading opportunity like this one. You have plenty on you, right? Crystals... salt... herbs... you even have those diamonds you were telling me about."

Bailey caught Ari's eyes light up, and knew he had him hooked.

"I suppose that's true..." he said at length.

To Bailey's relief, he needed little more convincing.

When they returned to their shelter, their focus was immediately on preparing what few possessions they had to take with them. The Riftmaster gave Bailey a few words of advice as he hid his satchel under the mountain-crawler cloak.

"Keep your knife within a moment's reach. Stay alert, and anything you own, keep it hidden. You can, and will, be pickpocketed if you don't. Whether the culprit's as small as a mouse or massive, you'll be just as screwed. All set?"

Bailey listened, and nodded.

The Riftmaster looked him over, and then moved the knife Bailey carried from his waist to his chest, so that it was hidden.

They gave each other a nod, and then set out. As they left the hut, Bailey stopped to speak to a curious Flora as she hopped between his head and left shoulder. Bailey gestured to the dome. Flora shook her head – one of the only human expressions she'd learned.

Her spines quivered, letting out a sound like a rattlesnake. Bailey nodded gravely back at her, and she curled back, the end of her tail twitching. Her scales stormed with clouds of pale green sweeping from nose to tail.

She twittered at him in a commanding manner, shaking her head repeatedly.

Bailey kept on nodding.

Then they stared at one another for a moment. Bailey began to walk again.

Flora let out one last shriek of protest... but she knew she'd been outvoted. A moment later she crawled down his collarbone and onto his chest, grumbling low to herself. From there, he expected her to drop to the ground, perhaps scamper off somewhere – but a moment later she had vanished under his cloak. Bailey let out a small yelp of surprise as he felt her cold scales against his skin, and realised that she'd found her way into his clothes and hidden there.

At least she was coming with them.

He heard her tweeting occasionally in a disgruntled manner, but other than that was quiet. Bailey ignored her, and kept on walking.

• • •

The inner part of the town was like a maze of metal, the shapes smoother and overall style of building far more unified. Some looked, for all the world, like natural formations of stone or metal. Others were like the crystalline dome in the centre and emerged from the ground like hollow stone igloos. And others still were metal structures intricately welded together into a hollow shell. But some were big, some were small; some even had carvings or wooden signs that seemingly signified businesses, although there was far from a uniform style or language for these and Bailey found it impossible to figure out what any of them meant. They were arranged purposefully to make a winding maze of streets and back alleys.

In all the dwellings' varying sizes, it took Bailey a while to realise exactly what he was looking at; but then it struck him. The majority of buildings here were meteorites which had fallen to the surface of the planet, which had been reclaimed and then repurposed, hollowed, and lived in.

The ground was packed hard by thousands upon thousands of feet, and was devoid of any soft grasses or mosses, the earth beneath a faded lilac.

The more Bailey looked around in wonder, the more he wanted to see, but remembering the Riftmaster's warning, he walked on and tried to keep focus, hugging his cloak tightly around him.

The streets, although not too narrow, were bustling.

There were so many different faces and creatures to take in that Bailey quickly found himself growing overwhelmed. The crowd parted around them like they were never there – and although some creatures made Bailey feel dwarfed, he also had to keep an eye out for the ones that scampered by at his feet.

He accidentally kicked into a scaly feline creature that glared accusingly at him, and then hissed before marching on. He narrowly avoided stepping on a small, cyan-skinned humanoid that darted beneath his foot carrying a lump of metal in spidery arms.

Shortly after, Bailey threw himself out from under a massive grey creature lumbering through the crowds with a long and striding gait, feeling its way along with slimy tendrils.

And all the creatures with glowing markings meant that his vision was filled with lights.

Before he knew it, Bailey had lost the Riftmaster entirely. He stopped in the middle of the street, looking around frantically.

To his right creatures skittered by on six legs or scrambled on three, and to his left a massive millipede-like being marched by on thousands with a unified tramping like the sound of earthbound soldiers passing by. The smaller creatures hitching a ride on its back stared at him.

He was lost, and trapped, surrounded and yet completely alone.

Bailey felt himself begin to panic, his heart pounding, hair standing on end, as he stared fearfully at the creatures washing their way around him, not knowing where to turn or what to do, which way was forward or back…

Suddenly, Bailey let out a sharp yelp as something grabbed him by the shoulders and pulled him out of the throng. Breathing heavily, and in a near-panic, he turned to see that it was only the Riftmaster standing just apart from the crowd.

From here Bailey turned back and watched in wonder everything weaving around and through each other. The big and the small, the short and the long. The creatures that scurried and hopped and ran.

A few of them huddled by their homes in mismatched groups of two or three, talking amongst themselves.

"Isn't this amazing?" Ari called over the hubbub. "Look at them all! This is insane!"

Bailey followed his gaze. Now that his panic was subsiding and he had the chance to truly think, this place really was a wonder. He finally had the chance to observe, to look around, mouth agape as he caught his breath, and truly take it all in.

He could see the dome, even more massive up close, just beyond the next row of buildings.

Whilst a lot of the town seemed natural, as though the meteorites had been hollowed and used exactly as they'd fallen, Bailey could clearly see that the dome, with its glistening black crystal, had been built. Supports of black meteorite metal held each facet in its place. At its base, smaller structures of the same crystal rose up out of the ground.

The town seemed layered by class; on the outskirts were the Rifthoppers, who cobbled together houses out of what they had available to them and lived in relative solitude. More experienced Rifters, who'd learned enough language to pull together tiny cliques seemed to live in the outer circle, in homes carved of stone or meteorite.

So... what was the inner circle for?

Presumably, it would be the aristocrats of the Riftworld. Experienced Rifters who'd seen worlds the likes of which Bailey could never imagine. They could speak enough languages not just to form allegiances but to rule, to govern in an otherwise lawless place.

The Riftmasters.

"Are all Riftworlds like this?"

"No, not at all! I've never seen one so densely populated," the Riftmaster repeated, his curiosity clear.

"Do you recognise any of them? Understand any of them?" Bailey asked.

The Riftmaster took another long look around. "I know a few of these species, but there are lots even I don't know. As for language, well... we'll just see. Let's keep our heads down for now."

"Okay. What next, then?"

"Let's just explore, for now. Learn our way around. I want to find some traders."

• • •

Once they'd started looking, traders weren't awfully hard to find. In addition to a couple of smithies, alchemists, and crafting workshops, Bailey and the Riftmaster soon found a large courtyard that seemed central to the town's market scene.

All around, alien creatures peddled their wares. In one corner a large, almost dragon-like beast coiled around itself was making jewellery from its own rainbow-coloured feathers and iridescent scales. A short, squat creature with large antlers decorated with rings and jewels was selling what looked to be rough leather satchels made to fit a variety of sizes and body types. There were plenty of stalls selling tools, and a small number were selling (or trying to sell) shrieking aliens in cages.

As Bailey stared in horror at the sight and hoped (but also doubted) that none of them were sentient, the Riftmaster gave him a nudge and said "You should get yourself one of those satchels. Do you still have that salt?"

Bailey withdrew a small leather parcel from under his armour, resulting in a grin from his mentor. It felt like a lifetime now since they left the island chain; and yet the salt it yielded would still serve them.

Bailey followed his mentor over to the stall and watched as the Riftmaster removed a small pouch from beneath his cloak. He emptied a couple of small jewels onto his palm, and offered them to Bailey. "Here," the Riftmaster said with a wink. "Just in case you see anything else."

Upon receiving them, Bailey admired the glistening objects for a few moments.

"Diamonds?" he asked.

"Yeah," the Riftmaster answered with a grin. "Now cover them up. You don't want to be robbed."

His mentor gestured with a small nod of his head over to a nearby stall.

"I'll be over there if you need me," he said. "I know their language, and I'd like to ask about that dome."

Bailey nodded, and smiled. "Good call."

As the Riftmaster moved away, Bailey took his time picking from the bags which were available. He didn't want it to be too cumbersome, and a great many seemed more like saddlebags for quadrupeds than satchels that would work for him. Others were meant to attach to a belt, and others still were weird and wacky shapes. Bailey was intrigued to know just what kind of a creature *those* were made to fit.

Bailey offered the antlered merchant the little parcel of salt. It took the parcel in spindly fingers, slowly unwinding the twine and examining the salt crystals with an enormous, orange eye. The merchant folded the parcel back up, tying it carefully back up, before tucking the salt under its robe.

Then the creature pointed with a long and spindly finger at a small satchel in front of him. Bailey blinked.

"Er, no," he said, pointing to the one he wanted.

The creature pointed once again at the smaller satchel.

Bailey pointed to the larger one.

The creature outstretched a hand, flexing long and bony fingertips. Bailey shook his head, gesturing wildly to the creature's robe.

I already gave you the salt!

It gestured again with its fingertips.

After a lot of gesticulating and a moment in which Bailey looked around wildly for the Riftmaster's aid, Bailey finally relented.

He offered a single diamond to the strange creature, who, after holding it up to her eye and squinting hard, gave a huff of acceptance and bowed her thanks. Bailey quickly picked up his chosen satchel and threw it over his shoulder. His good mood soured, he trudged off to find the Riftmaster.

He wandered cautiously as he searched, admiring the sheer variety in wares. There was a lot of jewellery, and raw materials like teeth, bones and small meteorites. Most of the clothing on sale was made from leather, fur or scales. He supposed that, in many cases, these were easiest to take between worlds. Tools and weapons were being sold interchangeably.

After a short wander around, he found the Riftmaster speaking with the rainbow dragon-like creature as she deftly wove her scales into leather twine using her claws as needles, the end of her feathered tail twitching as she listened.

The Riftmaster himself was speaking in tones that were throaty and raucous. It sounded more like he was coughing than speaking. After a long explanation, the creature responded with a few deep, rasping woofs that seemed to reverberate through her entire length.

The Riftmaster ended the conversation with a bow and an outstretched palm, and then waved Bailey over as the draconian creature looked his way.

"Got everything you need?" Bailey asked as he approached.

And then, as an afterthought, added: "I got the satchel."

"Oh good!" he said, sounding relieved. "I think I've had enough for one day. Let's head home... We can carry on tomorrow. We have a lot to talk about in the meantime."

As passers-by looking at the market bumped and nudged him aside, Bailey was inclined to agree.

"If we're still here tomorrow," Bailey added.

The Riftmaster glanced at him strangely.

"Don't worry, Rifthopper. I have a feeling we will be."

After a long glance his mentor's way, Bailey allowed the Riftmaster to usher him out of the marketplace, and this time the crowds didn't seem quite so frightening.

Chapter 16
Intrigue

By the time they had arrived back at the shelter, foraged enough to make a meal, and put together a campfire to cook it on, it was already dusk. Bailey and the Riftmaster had decided long in advance to cook their food tonight, not only to give themselves time to discuss their venture, but also to provide warmth and a little bit of light.

When they were all settled, had a pot bubbling over the fire, and had managed to coax Flora out of his underarmour, Bailey felt that the time had come to speak up.

As the rat-like creature curled up on his lap, Bailey cleared his throat, drawing Ari's attention to him. "So," he said. "The dome?"

"The dome," the Riftmaster responded thoughtfully, as he used a twig to stir the sweet-smelling concoction on the fire. "Turns out, it's a research facility. They're trying to study the Rift."

"How? I thought it was too unstable to study," Bailey reminded him.

"It is. But there's something strange about this world. It's drawing in Rifters from all across the universe, and apparently, none of them are leaving."

"I wonder why."

The Riftmaster grunted, poking at the flames with another twig before feeding it to the fire. "Same here. It seems to be a recent thing, too. The Rift was acting normally up until a few decades ago. Then the Rift just… stopped taking people away. It was a slow thing. Nobody really noticed until more and more Rifters started showing up, and fewer of them left. The town is growing bigger, and bigger."

"That must be how they're managing to research it," Bailey guessed.

"Undoubtedly."

"Do you think they've found much?"

"Apparently they've had a few breakthroughs."

"Think you'll be able to find out what they are?"

The corner of the Riftmaster's lips quirked into a small smile. Bailey got the sense that he was plotting something. "Of course."

"How?"

The Riftmaster paused for a moment, seemingly lost in thought. "I'll need to explain a few things first…" he said thoughtfully.

Bailey nodded, and waited patiently, getting the feeling that he was in for a long lesson. When the Riftmaster finally spoke, he picked his words carefully.

"…You see, the class system of this town is based on languages. It makes sense, of course… the more languages you know, the more allies you can make and the easier trade will be. Employment, even. It's the case with a lot of Riftworlds.

"At the very bottom are the poor saps out here, who can't even talk to each other. In the working class are those that can make a few friends. They might not know many languages, but they know enough to get by and raise their status a little. And then at the very top are those that can understand almost everyone, somehow. Those that know enough languages to make work chains. The ones who can tell the smithy what to do, then take their work to the tailor, and then the shopkeeper. The ones who can make, and keep the order are the ones at the top… they seem to form a bit of a governmental body, here."

"Right. And they're the ones doing the research? They sound like the clever ones," Bailey noted.

"You've got it. No point in doing research if you can't share it with anyone. The folks in the dome have a system. Those who know three or four languages can make a clique, but know more than that and you can make a team."

"What about you?" Bailey asked, with a twinge of excitement, and a little bit of jealousy.

"Fifty-four. Maybe a couple dozen more, if we're counting the ones that I'm not so fluent in."

"Wow."

"Eh. It's not that impressive. I've known Riftmasters who've learned hundreds. I was a slow bloomer when it came to languages. Ollie did a lot of the heavy lifting, back in the day." The Riftmaster wouldn't meet his eye, as he said that. "Besides, one day, you'll know just as many."

"Probably not for a few thousand years."

"Maybe. But we can get you off to a bit of a head start whilst we're here. You collect... books, right?" The Riftmaster looked up at him finally, a note of excitement creeping into his voice.

Bailey looked up with interest. "Old books, yes," he said. "Why?"

"I got you something." The Riftmaster began to rifle through his satchel, pushing all of his little pouches and tools aside before withdrawing something and holding it out for Bailey.

"You did?"

Bailey held out his hands to receive the object, which was wrapped in some sort of thin hide. Bailey unfurled it with mild trepidation at a nod from his mentor. Inside, of course, was a book, bound in what looked to be grey snakeskin of some kind. It was very small, with a plain outer cover, and it looked fairly worn.

"What is it?"

"It's a journal. A Rifter's journal."

As he opened it up, the pages smelled of dust, and they were yellowed with age.

The words inside looked to be hand written, and some were covered with ink splotches and stains in various colours.

The writing was in a strange language; each letter was a circle or series of circles linked by intricate curves. And yet it was full of diagrams – of plants and creatures, and maps of the stars in galaxies that Bailey could only dream of. He stared for a while in amazement, before finally looking up at the Riftmaster.

Flora, seemingly curious, scrambled onto his lap to look at the book herself.

She pulled herself onto one of his forearms and using the tip of her tail barb, began to carefully rifle through the pages herself. She seemed especially taken by the illustrations, and although the position was uncomfortable, Bailey took the time to let her look.

"What does it say?"

"I don't know," the Riftmaster said with a wink. "I'm not much of a reader, *but...* I was thinking you might be able to help me translate it. It's written in one of the most common languages spoken in the Rift – Renohaiin, it's called. The species that use it have colonised a few galaxies and from what I've seen, they're fairly common on Riftworlds, so... it should come in handy. Good practice, too."

"How can I translate it?"

"I'll teach you the Renohaiin alphabet, and the basics of the language. We can get some paper and a pen in the market, and then... well. You can get to work."

Finally, Flora finished looking and left it open on a diagram of what looked like a planet's inner layers, with a few drawings of crystals and meteorites. She hopped down from Bailey's lap and appeared to lose interest.

Thinking nothing of it, Bailey carried on flicking through the pages with fascination. He paused on one page for a while, feeling a lump forming in his throat all of a sudden. For there, staring back at him on the page, was Seven-horn Speaker.

Looking over his shoulder, the Riftmaster looked surprised, and then beamed. His eyes flickered over the page for a second.

"Well, would you look at that. Looks like we weren't the first planet-hopping friends they made."

Bailey sniffed.

"Thank you."

"Aw, don't mention it," the Riftmaster said, with a dismissive wave. "Looks like the food's done; we should eat."

Bailey watched as the Riftmaster poured out two bowls of the fruity soup. Rather than taking one for himself immediately, though, Bailey put his aside and asked, "Can I have your tester bowl?"

The Riftmaster drew the smaller bowl out of his satchel and held it out to Bailey.

"Sure. Why?"

Bailey poured some of the steaming mix into the little bowl and put down on the ground. Flora, who'd spent the conversation watching the pot and sniffling at the air, sat upright, and crawled off him.

With a small, pink tongue, she began to lap up her share.

"She was hungry too."

The Riftmaster grunted with amusement.

Only then did Bailey raise his own bowl to his mouth, his thoughts reeling with the events of the day. He almost couldn't wait to get started.

• • •

As planned, the next day Bailey and Ari returned to the town market, and managed to get hold of a few pens and a stack of parchment. Whilst Bailey took up the foraging duty for the day, the Riftmaster settled down and wrote the basics of the Renohaiin language.

He wrote down the alphabet, the sounds they were associated with, and common words to look for in the journal like 'rift', 'stars' and 'flower' as well as an introduction to basic grammar. As Bailey sat down for the first time on a log with the book on his knee, notes on one side, and blank parchment on the other, he quickly found himself becoming overwhelmed.

Maybe I'm not approaching this right, he thought. *I need a better workstation.*

After relating his idea to the Riftmaster, Bailey went inside, instead lying on his belly on the scraps of hide that served as his bed. Flora watched curiously as he set up, but this, at least, was more comfortable.

But it still wasn't right.

After a while, she joined him, using her sticky paws to turn the pages. She came to the same page as before with its diagrams of a planet's inner layers, then nudged it towards him with the end of her nose. She placed a paw in the centre of the planet, so that he couldn't turn the page, and looked up at him expectantly. Bailey watched her with a trifle of irritation, but as he looked at the page, despite the diagrams, Bailey was unable to translate a single word.

"I'm gonna have to start from the beginning. Sorry, Flora."

She stared back, blankly.

Really what I need is a desk, Bailey thought irritably. After that he set off into the woods, looking for the perfect shaped log, rock or tree stump to work at.

The moment he put everything down in his chosen spot, an earthquake sent all of his papers scattering in every direction over the forest floor.

It was as though the universe itself didn't want him to find the perfect place to study.

After a while, he came sulking back into the shelter. Unsuccessful at his search, he slumped back down on the bed and flicked through the pictures in the journal. *No, what I really need is…*

He stopped himself. *…to stop procrastinating. That's what I need to do.*

Once Bailey had called himself out, he forced himself to stop looking for problems, and began.

He started out by finding all the instances of the words that the Riftmaster had listed, and made notes on the pronunciation. Finding that of no use, he changed strategy and instead translated it to the English alphabet, letter by letter.

After only four pages, Bailey was left with nothing but lines upon lines of gibberish with just a few understandable words; most notably 'rift' 'stars' and 'flower'.

After a few excruciating hours, Bailey felt completely out of his depth, and decided to take a long walk.

· · ·

On returning, Bailey was no closer to an answer. Finally, he called over the Riftmaster, and although at first the man was reluctant, Bailey finally managed to get him to offer up a few hints.

"See this one? Yeah. Looks a little bit like Rift, doesn't it? Well, that means 'Rift walker', and that's their word for Rifter. And that 'star', there? That word means 'starscape'.

And that title? *Maps of the Stars*. Use what you know to tease out hints to what you don't."

An extra word or two here, a bit of advice here.

Bailey scribbled everything down. Soon he was spotting words left, right and centre. By the time the Riftmaster wanted to sleep, Bailey felt like he was beginning to crack the puzzle.

Over the next few days, Bailey's knowledge of the Renohaiin tongue grew – the gaps became smaller, and more and more words and sentences came together.

But if the Riftmaster had asked, Bailey still wouldn't have been able to put a sentence together. He found himself becoming impatient and irritable as time went on, carrying out his task in painful monotony.

The more he knew about the language, the more alien it seemed to become. Bailey had no idea how so many Rifters learned so many languages without help. He found himself equally as grateful for the practice as he was irritated that the Riftmaster just had to spring this on him.

Even Flora, who lounged across his shoulders diligently and watched him work, occasionally succumbed to boredom, and began to bat at the end of his pen with stubby forelimbs.

One morning, after a long studying session, something clicked. He had his first complete sentence. And then, another. And another. Everything was coming together; making sense more and more.

After a while, Bailey called out to the Riftmaster again.

Expecting it to be a call for help, the man turned towards him expectantly, and slightly wearily.

But with a thrill of pride, Bailey didn't ask for help. "It says here that the Rift always takes you to planets with living creatures of their own," he said.

The Riftmaster nodded in surprise. "Yeah, that's… right," he said, sounding impressed. He considered for a moment. "Except for Riftworlds."

"Yeah, that's what it says here." Bailey paused, tapping at his notes with the end of a finger as he and his mentor studied one another for a moment. "Why?" Bailey asked shortly after.

The Riftmaster shrugged. "I… don't know."

"I wonder if it has anything to do with the research they're doing in the dome," Bailey said.

"Maybe," the Riftmaster said. He approached, and looked over Bailey's shoulder at the notes he'd made. He nodded approvingly as his eyes scanned the papers.

"We should go," Bailey said.

Ari quirked a brow at him. "We should," he agreed. "...And then maybe when we get back, you could start on page 2."

Bailey laughed, albeit a little sheepishly. "...Yeah."

. . .

When Bailey and the Riftmaster reached the base of the dome, it was even bigger than they'd been expecting. Towering a hundred or so feet tall, and entirely composed of sleek black crystal, it was quite a sight to behold.

The dome, too, was just the roof; it was held up by sleek pillars of meteorite metal, carved – or perhaps naturally formed – into intricate shapes that were more art decor than functional.

There were many entrances, not just the one; all of them decorated with meteorite arches. And rather than the crowds that moved endlessly through the streets of the outer circle, the beings here seemed to simply mill around in small groups.

Before they had left, Bailey had filled his satchel with fabric and allowed Flora to hide in it; but here, as she peered out and looked up at the dome... it seemed to dawn on her, fully, where they were going. With an offended shriek, she leaped out of Bailey's satchel and fled.

"Flora!" Bailey called.

"Don't worry, Bailey. She's smart. She'll find her way back home," the Riftmaster said, although there was an edge to his voice as well.

The Riftmaster told Bailey to wait a little way back as he went to talk to an alien that seemed to guard the door... or perhaps it was simply on its break. It stood, tall and proud, covered with blonde fur that had been groomed into elegant curls. Four thick, muscular arms ended in meaty hands like those of a bear, each finger tipped with a wicked talon.

A pair of wide and heavy-set hooves meant it would be difficult to knock over if they tried to barge on through... not that they'd want to; it was more than twice Bailey's height.

It glanced Bailey's way only once, scrutinising him with a single eye that sent shudders down his spine, a fan of four pointed ears pricking forward and fanning out from either side of its head. Bailey flinched, wondering if the display was supposed to be a threat, yet the Riftmaster seemed unperturbed. He approached with unflinching confidence and a speedy half-bow. After letting out a few croaking rumbles and high-pitched barks – presumably testing for languages it knew – the two finally began talking in high and whistling voices that made Bailey shiver with discomfort.

Even so, he watched the display with fascination.

A few minutes later, Ari returned, covering the few metres between them at a brisk jog. "They're letting us in," he said, sounding amazed. "The head researcher already knows we're here, apparently."

Bailey watched the curly-haired biped step aside with a few heavy clopping sounds from its hooves. It gave a gracious bow as they passed by, folding both sets of arms across its chest.

When they were through, and after ensuring the door had closed behind them, Bailey said in a low voice "That sounds awfully suspicious."

Ari didn't reply. They were standing in a long hallway, tiled with plates of sleek black crystal and pillars of meteorite. It was lit by glowing crystals like those in their shelter, encased here in orbs of glass that lent the laboratory an eerie, sterile dimness. It was extremely clean, and strangely quiet; even the few aliens that talked amongst themselves did so in hushed voices. "Straight ahead," the Riftmaster translated the guard's instructions. "Then when the path starts to curve tightly, take the stairs."

The corridor's curve meant it was difficult to see what lay ahead of them. It was disorienting, and it took a while to realise that each corridor was built into a wide spiralling shape, intersected by archways leading to labs and further, alley-like corridors. Each pathway was gradually sloping upwards and curving, but the subtlety of it all made Bailey feel ever so slightly dizzy. At the very centre of the building, each corridor came together in a series of intertwining spiral staircases.

As they reached the top of the stairs, Bailey and Ari

stepped out into a wide observatory, with gadgets and gizmos and all sorts of trinkets scattered around different sections of the room.

From some, the sound of electricity fizzed. In others, crystals in glass orbs sparked and began to glow. Researchers of all shapes and sizes worked with their respective equipment and jotted down information, with others scampering to and fro carrying odd items. Whilst not all of them wore clothes, Bailey noted that most wore odd, glowing crystals about their necks, the same as the one that lit up Flora's shelter, and the corridors below.

Bailey was too invested in looking around for a while to realise that there was someone waiting for them.

He looked ahead only as he felt the Riftmaster nudge him. His attention was drawn then to the edge of the observatory where, approaching them slowly as though they were venomous snakes, was a man. A tall man, with a broad chest and thickly muscled arms. He towered over the diminutive Riftmaster, who seemed to be trying his best not to meet his gaze. Long, blond locks fell around his shoulders and traces of a beard clung to his chin.

He looked to be in his mid-thirties, but Bailey knew better.

Uncertain of what to do, Bailey glanced towards his mentor.

The Riftmaster remained where he was, staring in barely-disguised horror.

"Aria," the stranger said, snapping Bailey's gaze towards him instead.

He... *knew* Ari. By *name*. But that could only mean...

"Oliver," the Riftmaster greeted stiffly.

Chapter 17
A Familiar Face

The two former lovers faced one another for the first time in over a thousand years.

Bailey, the researchers, all the world around faded into the back of Ari's mind. Their only thoughts were of the man before them. Horror, bewilderment, maybe a brief flash of relief; the cocktail of emotion was enough to make them feel nauseous.

Even Oliver seemed lost for words, scratching the back of his head with a baffled expression.

Ari tried to avoid looking into his eyes, glancing everywhere but. Oliver was almost a foot taller than them, so it was easy enough to do.

From the few grey strands of hair in his beard to the golden ring on his left hand, Oliver hadn't changed a bit since they'd last met.

The Riftmaster's face began to redden more quickly than they were prepared for, but with well-practiced ease they wiped any lingering expression. With difficulty, they cleared their throat, straightened their cloak and puffed out their chest.

"It's been a while," they said with a small sniff.

"It… has," Oliver said. His voice was deep, with a faint American twang.

Just as Ari remembered.

Oliver cleared his throat before speaking more confidently, as though gathering himself ready to return to business. "I thought you might end up here eventually."

He paused, looked up, and forced a smile.

"I almost hoped you wouldn't."

They didn't know if he was joking or not but Ari laughed anyway, a sharp sound that was devoid of mirth, to cover up the brief look of dismay. A few heads turned their way throughout the observatory, and their manner became more sheepishly subdued.

Ari fell silent, glancing briefly at Bailey before hastily looking away.

Finally, Oliver appeared to notice Bailey's presence, looking directly at him, and then taking a few steps nearer.

"...And who's this?"

Ari grunted. "You can ask him yourself, you know."

Bailey met Ari's gaze for an instant, before offering a hasty greeting in the form of a bow and an outstretched hand towards Oliver.

"I'm Bailey. I'm his apprentice."

"His? You mean Aria's?" He took a long glance over the Riftmaster, who stared back at Oliver warily. "...I suppose I can see why – but you do know tha–"

"He knows, Oliver. He knows," Ari broke in drily. "He knows everything." Their expression hardened.

They and Oliver's eyes met, a moment passing between them.

His gaze softened slightly. "Ah. I see."

"And please..." Ari added, their voice a low growl. "Stop calling me that."

Oliver looked momentarily baffled by the prospect. "But... it's your name. What else am I supposed to call you?" he asked, with a small, dry laugh.

"You know full well what to call me, Oliver."

As the Riftmaster scowled, their eyes like shards of ice, Oliver moved swiftly on. He first cleared his throat, then clapped his hands together.

"So you're *Aria's* new apprentice. Wow... I didn't think I'd ever see the day. And quite a handsome young fella too, aren't you?" He ruffled Bailey's hair whilst the young man stood statue-still in stunned silence. "Have you been in the Rift long?"

Bailey shook his head.

"Only a few months... I think. I sort-of lost track."

"Is that right? Well, you're lucky. Of all the teachers you could have had, you probably ended up with the best. Aria taught me almost everything I know, you know."

Ari looked away as Oliver tried in vain to catch their eye.

"I think we should go," the Riftmaster said suddenly. He turned his back on Oliver, and glanced at Bailey almost pleadingly.

Bailey looked back at Ari in dismay.

"But..."

Ari understood; this was an opportunity, one of the most valuable things to find out here. Here was the chance to learn about the Rift – something that had evaded them for centuries, and yet they were about to simply turn and walk away from it?

But Ari didn't need to learn. What they needed, right now, was to get away from their ex. They needed to think. They had to get out of here. This didn't feel right; the memories were choking them, throttling their already weary heart. Their eyes prickled with fresh waves of tears.

They needed to take a step back.

"I... We – we can come back tomorrow. Promise," Ari stammered, through quick and heavy breaths. "I just... have to get out of here. Clear my head. Please, Bailey."

Their eyes locked.

Bailey met their gaze and finally gave a hesitant nod, expression heavy with disappointment. As they began to walk, Bailey followed.

Oliver's gaze burned into their back as they left, and he sputtered after them. As they came to the top of the staircase, a wave of relief washed over Ari, until they heard what their former apprentice had to say.

"Wait a minute... At least let me give you a tour. We've learned so much about the Rift...! We're even starting to *control* it, Aria."

Ari heard Bailey stop dead in his tracks. And suddenly, Ari felt their mouth drying up, the hairs along the back of their neck standing on end. When they turned back to look for him, they saw that Bailey's full attention was on Oliver.

With one foot raised ready to descend the stairs, Ari hovered, and then took a step back. Their hands slowly closed into fists.

"I'm not going," Bailey said, as they turned around fully.

Ari felt their cheeks burning, their shoulders tensed. Part of them didn't care whether or not Bailey followed, but the rest of them couldn't leave him alone with Oliver, of all people.

It was growing difficult to contain it all. They could hear their heart pounding in their ears and it was growing difficult to see for the tears that they wouldn't let fall.

"We might never get this kind of chance again. I want to learn about the Rift. Don't you see? This could be what I've been looking for! This might be a chance for me to go home to Earth."

"No. You're coming with me," Ari said, sternly. "Don't you see? You'll never be able to get back to Earth. None of us will. We're all stuck out here. The Rift is beyond our control. Messing with it is only asking for disaster." They turned on Oliver now. "And I *said* stop calling me that! My name is Riftmaster! *The* Riftmaster. I'm a different person to the one you knew. Bailey? Let's go."

They turned away again, and took a single step down the stairs, wordlessly threatening to leave as though Bailey was a disobedient child. Then they turned back, cheeks red and eyes stormy with hurt pride, but expression still even.

Bailey still didn't move, remaining where he was with his feet firmly planted.

Ari remembered that just this morning, they had wanted to look at the research just as much as he had.

They had gotten Bailey's hopes up too far.

Ari watched Oliver walk forward until he was beside Bailey, and lay a hand against his back. Even though Bailey stepped away, the Riftmaster flinched as though they'd just been bitten.

Oliver sighed.

"You know I always hated that name... Don't be like this... please. I have it all under control here," he soothed, as though he'd dealt with this a thousand times before.

But Ari wasn't going to fall for it this time.

"If you'd just let me show you the things I've managed to do – what we've created... *Then* you'd believe me."

Oliver turned towards Bailey before continuing... Although Ari couldn't help noticing him give a last, pointed glance in their direction before he did so.

"...Don't worry, she gets like this, sometimes. Give her time, and she'll come to her senses... In the meantime, let me show *you* around–"

Snide son of a–

Ari broke in with a sudden flare of rage.

"No. Stop that! Nobody's showing him around. Nobody's researching the Rift. No-one's doing anything! Especially not with *you*." They sucked in a breath, clenching their fists until their knuckles turned white. They struggled to stay calm, breathing in long, deep breaths.

"I can make my own decisions, you know!" Bailey spluttered.

"I know you can make your own decisions! It's whether they're the *right* decisions that I'm worried about. Come with me, now!" Ari's voice was becoming taut as they struggled to keep it level. They began to waver, expression full of betrayal.

"No!" Bailey said stubbornly, his voice even, but firm.

"Rifthopper!–"

Oliver broke in. "Why don't we just start to cool it down and–"

Ari silenced him with a glare that could have stopped bullets. Then they turned back to Bailey.

"I'm not letting you go with *him*! I know his tricks." Ari's eyes narrowed. "He'll act like he's got things all under control, he'll tell you what you want to hear until you're wound around his little finger. He'll only care until he has what he wants and you're right where he needs, and then he'll rip it all away and leave you at the mercy of the Rift," they hissed, as they felt their heart begin to break anew.

They felt tears beginning to flow, pouring in rivers down their cheeks, and although Ari tried to hide them, rub them away, and remain angry, they couldn't hold back the stifled sobs that shook their sides. "The Rift can't be *controlled*. He'll manipulate you, then take everything from you, Bailey."

They'd lost everything because of this man. He'd taken away their family, their security, and thousands of years from their life.

They couldn't let him take Bailey away as well.

The anger on Bailey's face melted away in that instant, leaving only guilt in its place as Ari's mask crumbled away.

Ari struggled to wipe away the tears, pawing at their

cheeks burning red with embarrassment and shame.

"*Aria!*" Oliver's voice was full of stunned anger, as though he'd had no idea. "That's not... I can't believe you'd..."

Ari saw their ex slump down a little bit, his mouth open. Oliver trailed off, and moved just a little closer. Suddenly, all the aloof calmness faded, and it was his turn to look betrayed, wearing an expression of pure disbelief.

"Do you mean it?" Oliver asked quietly. "Do you *really* mean it?"

Bailey quietly moved away from them both, but Oliver didn't seem to notice.

"Every word," Ari said gravely.

"But... after everything we..." Oliver trailed off.

The Riftmaster stared at him with glassy eyes for a moment before turning their back. They could imagine that their hunched form was the picture of pure humiliation. "We should take this somewhere else. *Some* folks around here are trying to work," they muttered.

A moment later Ari was descending the staircase, their steps quick, leaving the laboratory behind them. The only thought in their brain at that moment was that they had to get away. They had to get out of here. The air felt thick as it filled their lungs, and they struggled to breathe it, and their blood pounded loudly in their ears. Their chest ached like it had never ached before. They could hear their footsteps echoing along the seemingly endless corridors and the gasping sounds of their own breath.

For the first time in years, they felt utterly powerless, and afraid.

They picked up speed as they heard footsteps running behind them, fleeing like a wounded animal.

Oliver quickly closed the distance, but Ari heard him panting by the time he caught up. Finally, they felt a strong, firm hand grab their wrist, yanking them to a complete stop.

The Riftmaster whipped around to face their former lover, teeth bared and hair bristling, cheeks burning.

"Let go of me!" they spat, and to their relief he did.

Ari heard more footsteps as Bailey halted, panting, wavering in his tracks some distance away.

But then, finally, Ari raised their gaze and looked up at Oliver, to see that his face, like their own, was etched and lined by years of woe. His expression was solemn, eyes dark and shimmering.

Ari finally spoke in a voice as cold and brittle as ice.

"Stop acting like nothing happened. I had a family. A *new* family, one that I hoped would last for eternity, that I'd never have to lose. Then I woke up one morning and it was gone. It was you, wasn't it? You took their bindings. You... let me go."

Almost 3000 years Ari had known Oliver, and loved him. But, Ari knew better than anyone that when the Rift kept human lives going for so long, it was inevitable that everything within them had to end.

"I... didn't expect the Rift to come for you so soon. But the world we were in... it would last them for all eternity. They needed a place to settle down, Aria. They were growing old, whilst we were still young. They couldn't keep Rifting with us."

A hundred human generations could have passed in the time that Ari and Oliver had spent together. And yet they had seen only one.

"But worlds change, Oliver. The world they lived in... the world they *died* in... It's a desert now. I went back there, and... I don't know if they died naturally or if the dry season came and took them, but... we couldn't know if the planet would remain stable we were gone. If we'd just brought them with us–"

"You went back there?" Oliver's voice was suddenly laced with horror. He opened his mouth to say something more, and then stopped, letting out a heavy sigh.

Ari nodded, choking back a sob.

Oliver opened his arms to invite his former lover into a silent embrace, but Ari simply turned their face away. So instead, Oliver took it upon himself to close the distance and take the Riftmaster into his arms. Ari grunted, struggling momentarily, their skin crawling with discomfort. But then... they gave in. Ari buried their face in Oliver's chest, and they felt Oliver rest his chin atop their head. They were quiet for a few moments.

"You know, they were my kids too," Oliver said quietly, sadly. "I just wanted to do what was best for them. That's all I ever wanted."

"I know, but *I* was the one who buried them. Every last one of them," came Ari's muffled response a while later. "...I'd hoped to find you there too. At least then it'd be *over*."

"...I always knew you were bad at letting go, but... I didn't think you'd hold on for this long."

Ari let out a muffled scoff. "You act like I didn't *want* to let go. I wasted thousands of years on you... Don't you feel even slightly guilty?"

"Sure. But I wanted to do what was best for *them*. I don't regret it."

"Even though in the end, it didn't matter anyway? They're dead, Oliver. Maybe *because* of you."

A small alien researcher hurried past, shooting the embracing humans a bewildered look. Ari felt a sudden wave of awkwardness wash over them. They pulled away from Oliver a moment later.

"You know, this is a research facility," Ari said a moment later, wiping their nose on the back of their wrist. "This seems more than a little inappropriate."

"I know. Maybe we should find somewhere more private? We have a lot of catching up to do."

Ari didn't want to spend any more alone time with Oliver. They didn't know what sort of 'catching up' he wanted to do, but they didn't think they'd like a single moment of it. "I'd rather not," Ari huffed with a roll of their eyes, stalking back towards Bailey with a small nod.

Taking his cue, their apprentice walked towards Oliver, putting himself between the two of them, for now. "How about taking us on that tour instead?" he asked cautiously, shooting a glance in Ari's direction.

Ari was too tired to protest, and simply returned the look to Bailey.

"Oh? Oh yeah," Oliver cleared his throat. And although he feigned eagerness, Ari could sense his reluctance, and knew that he really just wanted to spend time with them. But they weren't falling for it. Not today. "...Yes. A tour! Of... of course. Follow me – I have a lot to show you."

Oliver turned to lead the way, with Bailey following closely, and Ari trailing behind. The young man tried multiple times to catch their eye, but Ari avoided his gaze.

Chapter 18
Reconnection

Oliver led them along one of the strange, spiral corridors and through several side passages. Aside from the main spiral structure of the lower labs, there were numerous doors and arches to branching pathways, and little rooms where smaller research experiments took place, and newer Rifters were recruited and taught.

Away from the larger corridors, the laboratory felt almost mazelike. Bailey quickly lost track of where he was going.

The structure of the building was disorienting; but as he went, Oliver explained the reason for its odd curves.

"The observatory is built from a thin layer of the crystal that makes up the planet's outer crust. The architecture here is non-euclidean; in your terms, that means the planet is so small that we have to keep the geometry to a curve. This sort of spiral structure happens to be the most efficient way to do it. In addition, most species, human or otherwise, find this layout disorienting, so it's an added defence mechanism to protect our more sensitive research from less... experienced Rifters."

"How did you build this place?" Bailey asked in wonder.

Oliver chuckled. "This place was built over thousands of years using techniques far more advanced than anything seen on Earth. It's been here for as long as anyone can remember. A lot of the research that has happened here over the years was lost with each new generation of Rifters, but its purpose remains. I didn't build it, though."

"Of course you didn't," muttered Ari.

Oliver ignored him and led the way into a small room, where several researchers worked diligently. A small, slimy frog-like alien hopped between a few different devices, taking readings, pressing buttons, and moving small crystals between devices.

"Let me start by admitting something; we have no idea what causes the Rift. What we do know is that it's a rare kind of residual energy which seeks out and exclusively targets living beings, like lightning. We don't know where it comes from, but after someone's been struck once, they become a vector for it. You can't control it, or encourage it. But using the rift-binding technique me and Aria developed, true Rifters can share it with another and bring them into the Rift," Oliver explained, glancing sideways at Ari.

"I think 'developed', is overselling it. And it's not really a 'technique'…" the Riftmaster muttered.

Bailey decided to ignore him. "True Rifters?"

"Yes. Those who are taken from their home world at random, rather than being taken along. Those Rifting exclusively through binding get a taste of what the Rift can do – but it's a diluted form. Their life is extended, but not unlimited, and the Rift will never come for them if their binding is taken away. Right, Aria?"

The Riftmaster sent Oliver a scathing glare.

"…okay. Moving on."

Oliver shoved the little, frog-like alien aside with a startled squelch and hastily moved over to a piece of equipment that was almost like an art piece, a pristine structure of black metal towers, glass orbs filled with flickering plasma, and exposed wires.

"We have a theory that these planets – Riftworlds – have something to do with the Rift. Apart from the Rifters here, these planets have no inhabitants of their own. But… drill just a few metres down into their crusts, past the planet's outer layers, and you can find these."

Central to it all, Bailey saw a fist-sized black crystal, wrapped in a coil of wire and encased within an orb of glass.

Oliver's fingers began to move, nimbly pushing buttons in well-practised sequence.

He paused before finally pulling a lever, causing the exposed wires to light up as they flooded with white-hot heat. The machine hummed softly as it worked. "Now, these crystals... are different. They're temperamental, brittle, and need to be charged with electromagnetic energy or they're basically useless..."

As Bailey watched with fascination, the stone reacted to the coils of wire, its inky surface paling to lilac, and then to cyan blue-white. It began to gleam and glow, the air surrounding it shimmering with heat, at which point Oliver raised the lever and let the wires cool. "But..."

Bailey glanced sideways at Ari, to see that even he was watching intently.

Oliver raised the glass orb from the crystal and carefully plucked it from its nest of wires. He hissed softly in pain – it was still hot to the touch – but the smile on his face was triumphant. "After all that, they can be used to neutralise the Rift. If you wear one of these against your skin, the Rift won't come for you so long as it's charged. It's what we've been using to study the Rift – it's because of these we've managed to make so many breakthroughs."

Oliver's eyes lit up as he continued.

"If we succeed here, we could open up all sorts of possibilities. We could travel immediately across the planet, visit worlds that we've left behind... and maybe even allow new Rifthoppers the chance to return home."

He looked directly at Bailey, until the young man felt his cheeks burn. But even then, he couldn't help imagining the possibilities, and felt his eyes well up. This could be just what they'd been waiting for. But now was no time to fantasise.

"So... you think it's this research you've been doing that means no-one is leaving?" Bailey asked.

Oliver hesitated. "Well... yes and no. Supposedly, the Rift started slowing down long before *my* research had showed anything concrete. It's been going on for decades, unnoticed until fairly recently. But so has our research, in its various stages and forms. Rifters have been coming and going from this planet for thousands of years. Who's to say we're not the cause?"

Bailey gave him a hard look. "That doesn't answer anything."

Oliver looked briefly uncomfortable. "What I mean is that it's possible. Likely, even."

Ari broke through his thoughts as he finally spoke up. "I've seen the other researchers wearing those crystals. If you're so invested in your research," he pointed out. "Why aren't *you* wearing one?"

A fleeting look of wariness crossed Oliver's face, so quickly that Bailey almost didn't notice. But the Riftmaster did, and Bailey saw his eyes narrow slightly, knowing that he had the higher ground.

Oliver answered quickly – and reasonably.

"As I said before, they're brittle. That makes it hard to harvest good-sized crystals without breaking them, so I leave all I can for the more important staff," he said.

"I don't know, you seem pretty important to me," Bailey muttered.

"Besides," Oliver continued, paying him no heed. "The Rift's slowdown means that, statistically, it's unlikely that I'll be leaving anytime soon, so I try to trust in that. I'm living proof of my theory that there's been less need for them lately."

"Do you really not have a clue why that is?" Ari asked.

"Between you and me, that's what we're trying to find out."

The Riftmaster scoffed. "Sure you are. If it's between you and me, why are you telling us all of this? You know I'd rather die than keep your dirty little secrets."

"Call it a sense of duty," Oliver said. "And an overdue apology."

That shut him up; Ari's face reddened.

"Besides, I don't know of another Rifter in the universe I'd rather have on my team than you, Aria."

The Riftmaster's expression soured. "I *knew* you wanted something. You always want something," he growled.

Bailey looked at him in dismay. This could be their chance! This could be what they'd been waiting for! "If he doesn't, I will!" he broke in, almost without thinking.

At this, Oliver laughed condescendingly, as though Bailey was a mere child. "I'm sure you'll be a big help," he said with a chuckle.

Bailey's face grew hot with embarrassment.

The Riftmaster's expression darkened, his eyes flickering. He seemed to consider for a moment, and Bailey felt his chest grow hopeful. He exchanged a glance with Bailey, and finally spoke up. "I'll consider it," he said finally. "We need to talk first. Bailey?"

Bailey nodded, considering what he could say. He turned towards the Riftmaster, awaiting instructions.

"Let's go," Ari said.

Bailey hesitated, but finally nodded.

They made to leave the room, but just as they reached the door, the Riftmaster turned back.

"And one last thing," he said to Oliver. "Call me Aria one more time and you'll be sorry. I'm the Riftmaster – to you and everyone else."

Bailey smiled, a little smugly, before adding "He means it," with a wink in Ari's direction.

Ari smirked back at him, but Oliver laughed obnoxiously.

"Again with that trash? You know I always hated that name."

They left, Ari's face a storm. They were going to have a lot to talk about.

As they left the laboratory, the ground began to quake, and the two humans carried on until the shudders became too much. Then, they huddled together on the open pathway as panic ensued around them. Signs fell, merchants' wares went flying, and chaos reigned.

Bailey was fearful of what they'd find when they returned to the Rifthoppers' district of town; he didn't think there'd ever been one so intense before.

• • •

By the time they finally made it back to their home neighbourhood, Bailey was exhausted; both from the walk itself, and Ari's constant complaining. "I just feel like he's up to something," he kept on saying in an exasperated growl. "Sure, I could be a huge help, but I'd rather cut my arm off than help *him*."

There was a pause as they both trudged onwards, through droves of aliens frantically trying to rebuild makeshift shelters and free their silent friends.

"It sounds to me," panted Bailey, "like you'd rather hold things back from him than learn them yourself."

"Who wouldn't?" snapped the Riftmaster impatiently. He reminded Bailey, amusingly, of a stubborn child. "I'm just getting a bad feeling about this."

"I think you're just hung up on the fact that you'd have to work with your ex. Don't get me wrong, I completely understand that. I've been there."

The Riftmaster looked sidelong at Bailey sheepishly, and the young man knew immediately that he'd hit the nail on the head. "No..." he said sheepishly, before a moment later asking in a much smaller voice, "Was it really that obvious?"

"Pretty much... I'm sorry. I mean... It's not like you handled his appearance very well."

"Right. Well..." Ari sighed, seeming to give up on his frustration. Instead, he looked simply defeated. "I've spent the last thousand years trying to forget about him. When you've known someone that long... When you knew them inside and out, and when they could say the same for you... it's a little hard, shall we say."

"You don't need to forget him to move on from him," Bailey said.

"I don't need this lecture. I don't need to take his offer. I can stay away. We can live together and keep learning by ourselves. We don't need any of his fancy equipment or the laboratory. It might take longer, but we can do it. The Rift isn't going to come for us any time soon."

Bailey sighed with exasperation. "You don't know that. The Rift's coming more rarely, but it might still come. We should make the most of this opportunity. You could just... you know. Avoid him."

"I know," the Riftmaster grumbled. Then, a little more quietly, "I know."

"Well then...?"

"I just... don't think I'll be able to stop myself falling into the same trap. He knows exactly how to wrap me around his finger. And when he said he was sorry, I... I think he meant it. I'm already falling for it, Bailey. After all these years he still has me."

Ari sighed, and Bailey fell silent too. As he walked, he thought about how best to change the subject. Pressing the issue seemed, at this stage, unwise. But... on the bright side, the encounter had left him with a few burning questions that could be a good change of tone.

"What's the deal with your name, anyway?" Bailey asked finally, trying to keep the tone light.

Ari shrugged. "Aria was my Earth name. I've left it far behind me."

"Why do you hate it so much?" Bailey risked. "I mean... I saw you wrote Ari on the gravestone. Is that any better?"

Ari didn't seem surprised. "I prefer Ari. That's what the kids called me. It's less... well... you know. Formal. 'Mother' just didn't feel right at the time."

"Mm-hm."

"Oliver always acted like my name was such an important feature. It was like he thought that, without it, a part of me was inhuman. He always did want me to be more ladylike, but... that's not me. I don't want who I used to be on Earth to define who I am out here."

Ari chuckled before continuing.

"That's why I like just Riftmaster. It's all-encompassing. I don't *need* to subscribe to human values, and Riftmaster could mean anything and anyone. It's not exclusive. It was the 'master' part that always bothered Oliver."

"...Things have sure changed a lot since you guys left Earth."

"Have they? I wouldn't know."

Bailey found himself lost for words as they finally opened the shelter door. They were greeted by the sight of a bed piled high with blue berries, and a sheepish looking Flora hunched in the corner, rippling with waves of white and green.

Bailey stared at her. In all the excitement, he realised that he'd almost completely forgotten about her! He was relieved that the clever little beast had managed to find her way back home.

What made him most curious, though, were the offerings she'd left them – enough berries that they were covered on foraging for the day, at least in terms of food. Although whether it was an apology for running off or a bribe to ensure *they* didn't run off again was beyond him.

As they settled down for the night, they talked a little more about Oliver.

"I know he's not right for me," the Riftmaster admitted with a sigh. "We want different things from each other. We always have. He always hated how I'd jump into things, even after weighing out the risk. He was always the one to play it safe. He was the thinker, the one who figured things out. I was the jumper, who took risks and reaped the rewards."

"Sounds like you made a good team."

"When we stopped arguing, aye. But it should never have been anything more."

Bailey let out a soft *hmmph* of acknowledgement. "He doesn't seem like a bad guy, though. ...Not *wholly*, at least," Bailey added quickly. He recalled, with a prickle of annoyance, that the man hadn't seemed to respect him very much at all. But he also recalled the very real emotion that Oliver had shown Ari when they'd talked about their children, and during their embrace. "...Maybe you should give him another chance. Not as a lover, just as... well... a friend. There aren't many humans out here, and it'd be sad if two of them hated each other."

"Hmph. Maybe."

"Or... Maybe you could just use the opportunity to spite him."

The Riftmaster chuckled at that.

"*That* sounds like a better idea."

Bailey grinned back, snorting softly at the thought. Although he hated to admit it, he would have liked to see that too.

The Riftmaster's laughter gradually trailed off into thoughtfulness. Bailey's eyes began to drift closed as he succumbed to drowsiness. He was brought back to attentiveness as the Riftmaster spoke once again.

"You know what?"

"Mm?" Bailey asked sleepily.

"...I'll give it a shot. I'll head down in the morning. It's about time I started figuring things out about the Rift."

"Sounds like a plan," Bailey answered with a yawn.

"Meanwhile, you can carry on translating that book of yours."

"Yeah. Be careful around your ex, though... okay?"

The Riftmaster smirked lightly, a welcome change from his more recent attitude. "I've dealt with worse things. I'll be fine. Wanna hear about them?"

"Mm-hm."

"Once upon a time I wound up on a planet with oceans of acid! You've seen nothing like the beasts on there. Horrors, every one of them! Let me tell you, Rifthopper..."

Bailey allowed the Riftmaster's obviously-embellished tale to lull him into a deep sleep, the last thing he saw being the glowing gem embedded in their ceiling.

Chapter 19
Rediscovery

To Ari's surprise, and distaste, Oliver was already waiting for them when they reached the research facility the next morning.

Despite themself, they felt their stomach tighten as they met his eye, a sour expression lingering on their face and in their pursed lips.

"You actually came," Oliver said, and Ari was uncertain whether it was shock or disappointment in his tone.

"Yeah, I keep my word. Unlike some."

Oliver's expression tightened. "It's good to see you," he said drily.

The Riftmaster snorted.

"Can't say the same for you."

Oliver grunted. He closed his eyes for a moment and breathed deeply as though to steel himself for the obviously difficult task ahead. When he opened his eyes again, he wore a resigned expression, and held out a hand, which Ari scowled at, before glaring up towards the man in question, in particular eyeing the golden ring on his finger.

"You think I'm going to take your hand, just like that?" they hissed. "…Because I'm not."

"I'm trying to take you to your station," Oliver said.

His tone was cool and brittle like ice. Ari already felt their blood growing hot, but they weren't going to let it reach boiling point. Not yet.

"Well, I have eyes," they answered smoothly. "I can follow."

"It might be busy, and you don't know the way."

"I don't care. I can ask for directions."

"If you insist," Oliver finally relented, to Ari's relief. Their shoulders relaxed slightly, and as he began to lead the way they followed suit, entering the building and following its disorientingly twisting corridors.

As Oliver had said, it was a lot busier today; they almost lost the head researcher several times as he pushed and shoved through the crowds ahead of them, leaving Ari to dip and dodge and wind their way through the crowds. Whenever an unsuspecting Rifter shot them an accusing look, they'd cycle through an apology in as many of the interstellar languages they remembered from the top of their head.

"I'm sorry, I'm sorry, excuse us..."

It was never wise to make a scene in strange worlds, much less Riftworlds.

But they supposed Oliver must have a reputation around here. The creatures in question quickly moved on, presumably to continue with whatever errand they were running in the first place.

By the time Ari caught up with Oliver, they were breathing heavily, and the smug expression on his face told them that he'd been waiting for quite some time.

"Just show me what to do," Ari said, exasperated.

Oliver shrugged as he led the way through a wide archway and into a round room full of strange machines. The mirror-like floor was crisscrossed with wires, orbs of glass containing crystals sat in nests of tubes. There were a few platforms roughly hewn from rocks or constructed from wood, which clashed mightily with the sleek crystal design of everything else. These makeshift workplaces were arranged with different crystals, some glowing, some not, some pointy, some round, some tiny, and some larger than a clenched fist.

As Ari passed one of these tables, they slipped a small, black crystal point into the palm of their hand and then into their satchel.

By the time they caught up with Oliver, they almost couldn't keep the smirk from their face.

Oliver showed them to a cluster of machines like those

they'd seen the previous day. Other creatures, some of which Ari recognised, pattered around the room, rearranging wires, replacing broken crystals in the machines, and pulling levers. Some previously dark crystals began to glow or flicker with a neon shine. In the corner of the room a crystal shattered with a near-blinding flash of light.

Ari blinked, dazed, squinting as their eyes re-adjusted.

They saw that the creature responsible was a small being, about as tall as Ari's waist, with large ears and enormous, glassy eyes. Mottled fur of red, baby blue, and yellow gave it a round appearance. It didn't appear to have any forelegs at a glance, but as Ari watched it hastily yanked the lever back and reversed the buttons with a long and dextrous tail.

Its ears laid back and it bared small fangs as it hopped over to them dejectedly.

"I was looking for someone to show our newest researcher the ropes," Oliver told the colourful furball, in a strange yet familiar tongue.

The little creature perked up, looking at Ari with its large, jewel-like eyes. They sent shivers down Ari's spine.

"Really?" it responded, in a voice almost painfully shrill. It bounced eagerly up and down on the tips of its toes.

"Yes," Oliver said. *"I don't think you're cut out for the job, though, so she'll be replacing you, instead."*

The little creature's ears flicked. It froze.

Ari looked up at Oliver coldly. *"Are you serious?"* they asked, so that the little creature would understand.

Oliver looked up sharply, as though shocked that Ari had been listening in. *"We can't afford mistakes. The crystals are too hard to come by to spend our time breaking them all."*

The little thing looked from Oliver, then to Ari, then Oliver again.

"Well?" Oliver went on. *"Get out."*

"You can't just…! Where will it go?" Ari asked, in English this time, as the little thing began to hop away to shut down the machine it had been working on, and gather up the shards with the tip of its tail.

"Wherever it wants – I don't particularly care. There are plenty of other things for it to do," Oliver said, ignoring the creature as he swept over to the machine.

As it returned, passing close by Ari's heels, they bent down, causing it to pause as they met its eye.

Its ears pricked as Ari whispered into its ear.

"I'm sorry," they murmured, again.

The little creature let out a small, and whistling sound that Ari took for a sigh.

"It's okay. That one's always like this," it said, twitching the tip of its tail towards Oliver.

Ari nodded.

"Don't I know it."

The creature let out a twittering sound that might have been a laugh before hopping away.

Ari rose to their feet and reluctantly followed Oliver over to the now-cooling machine. They allowed him to show them how it worked, what each of the levers and buttons did, and what the wires were for. He told Ari what changes to look for in the crystals and the different kinds of stresses they were working to put them under.

It was a delicate operation, but if their experiments with this machine were, by some miracle, successful, Ari was to take the glowing shards elsewhere to see what else could be done with them. Milking them for stored energy, for example. Linking them up to other machines to try using them as power sources.

The possibilities were virtually endless, and Ari's mind was spinning by the time they actually got to work.

The Riftmaster moved to and fro, gathering crystals in their arms and putting them in the glass orbs before amping up the power, which began as a low hum and then escalated into a throaty roar.

They were aware, all the time, of Oliver's eyes boring into their back.

Finally, after some time, their first crystal made a dull creaking sound, and then shattered, bursting the glass orb with it and showering the floor with glistening shards. It flashed with a bright bubble of light, but this time Ari turned away before they could be blinded again.

"Well," Ari said, stretching their arms above their head, and offering a knowing smirk. "I guess you'll just have to fire me. It's been simply a *joy* working with you, really."

"Okay, let me be straight with you. I know you did that on purpose, so I'm doing nothing of the sort!" Oliver shot back.

Ari shrugged, an impish glitter in their eye. "Whatever you say… it's your funeral. Now, how do I fix this thing?"

Oliver hurried over, removing a tube from their hands and placing it back into the machine, presumably where it was supposed to go. He looked them dead in the eye, and Ari felt their heart stop even as they glared back defiantly.

"Ar… *Riftmaster* Aria. Listen to me."

Ari gritted their teeth, and listened.

"You're acting like a child," Oliver said, causing their insides to momentarily quiver with rage.

"And you, sir, are acting like a pompous–"

"Don't say it," Oliver broke in. "Listen."

Ari let out a breath, but remained quietly seething.

Upon realising that they weren't about to protest, Oliver's shoulders relaxed, and he spoke. "Do you know why I chose you for this?"

"I just assumed you wanted me to give you another chance," Ari said. "…Which I'm not. So don't get your hopes up."

"No. Riftmaster. It's because I trust you. I know full well what you're capable of. You're smart. You're resourceful. But most importantly, you're human. You're not gonna eat me as soon as my back is turned."

Ari felt the sharp edge of their rage dull.

They looked Oliver up and down, from the wrinkles around his old, tired eyes, to his greying beard, and still mostly-blond hair. And then the worn, tattered clothes he was wearing. For an instant they saw the same person they'd taken under their wing all those years ago.

They knew better than anyone else here that Oliver wasn't a scientist. He was a thinker but he always had been too afraid to take risks. And more than anything else, he was just as lost as everyone else out here.

Finally, Ari let out a breath. "Is that why you're so cruel to the other Rifters?"

Oliver blinked slowly. He uncomfortably stroked the side of his beard. "You talk about them as though we're all the same. But we're not. Other planets have different ways of thinking, different morals. And how are we to know which… which… *aliens* are safe to talk to?"

"We don't. But we can let them know *we* are. It's a lot

easier than trying to assert yourself all the time."

Oliver let out a huff.

Ari sensed that they weren't going to get any further on the matter. From what Ari had seen, this Riftworld had a clear hierarchical structure and Oliver obviously had found his place in it for a reason, as backwards as his methods were.

After a moment of studying Oliver's expression, Ari turned back towards the machine.

"So, are you going to help me fix this, or what?"

• • •

Bailey awoke later that morning to find the Riftmaster already gone, and Flora still fast asleep on her shelf. For a moment, he looked around, floundering in the aloneness for a long moment. After a while, he hauled himself to his feet and stretched languidly, popping his head out of the doorway, and blinking in the morning brightness.

Still, his mentor was nowhere to be found.

Although mostly indifferent, Bailey was a little disappointed, and slightly annoyed that the Riftmaster hadn't even given Bailey the chance to see him off.

Bailey heard Flora grunt as the light broke through the folds of sleep, and her snakelike eyes opened to slits. She glared his way, stretched, and let out a long yawn that bared small white fangs.

"Morning," Bailey said to her.

The small creature let out a small chirp in response, curling her segmented tail over her paws and resting her chin on it.

"Looks like it's just gonna be me and you, today."

Flora's eyes flickered as she seemed to consider, then glanced down at the Riftmaster's empty bed, and seemed to understand. But as though to disprove his words, she immediately let out another snort, rolled over on her back, and fell asleep again. Her hide shifted and changed until she'd copied the exact pattern of the hides beneath her.

Bailey chuckled softly at the sight.

Looks like it's just gonna be me, then.

With another yawn, Bailey ate some leftover fruit for breakfast, and then began to prepare all of his notes, and the journal. Another quake shook the earth, and Bailey needed only to hold the papers down to stop them from scattering.

Then he returned to his work, to find that the journal had been opened. Bailey sat back down and took a closer look at the page in question, which seemed to be Flora's favourite. With surprise, Bailey realised now why that was. The diagrams of crystals and the inner layers of the planet's crust – were things that he'd seen or heard about in the laboratory.

This page must be on Riftworlds! he realised with a mixture of shock and eagerness. Bailey took the book into his hand and looked from the page, to the notes he'd compiled so far. He didn't have *much*, it was true, but it might just be enough to make a start.

"Alright, then. You win! I'll start with this page today."

As he spoke, Flora materialised out of the darkness beside him, and excitedly wormed her way under his cloak. He felt the sharp edges of her quills prickling at his neck.

"Careful! What do you want?" he asked.

She twittered excitedly in response.

"Alright then. If you've got nothing to add, I'll make a start."

A grunt.

From that point on, the little creature allowed him to work.

• • •

It was hard getting back into the rhythm of studying, but with the help of his previous notes, Bailey found it at least *slightly* less tedious than last time.

Occasionally his mind wandered to whatever the Riftmaster might be getting up to at the lab; was he doing okay? Had he managed to find Oliver alright? Had he learned anything useful? Bailey could only hope that the Riftmaster would soon return and enlighten him on whatever he'd found out.

In the meantime, there was plenty to work on, and Flora seemed mostly content to simply let him do his thing. At some point, she crawled back up onto her shelf, curled up, and went to sleep.

The only disturbance was another earthquake that juddered the walls and rattled everything that lined the shelves. Bailey was beginning to get the sense that they were becoming more frequent, but he didn't dwell on it. Perhaps it was simply something to do with the seasons here.

After that one, Flora awoke, and pushed her little flap aside to exit the cabin, leaving Bailey to study alone. Although he waited for her, she didn't return.

Translating was a slow, and daunting process. After several hours, Bailey stopped for a snack, and as he tried to take a drink realised that his waterskin was empty. He left the cabin, and looked for one of the many tiny, evenly-spaced ponds that flecked the plains to refill it.

As he drank by the side of the pond, he looked into its depths, and thought. The pond had no visible bottom; it was just a black hole in the earth filled with life-giving water. There were no fish, or frogs, or little insects flitting over its surface. What Oliver had said rang in his ears; that the Rift only took Rifters between planets that had their own forms of life. Perhaps, Bailey thought, this planet's could all be found in subterranean caves or rivers.

After drinking sufficiently and refilling his waterskin, Bailey returned to work.

• • •

Once the machine was repaired, Ari got back to work, and they, as Oliver had predicted, quickly got into the swing of things. Although the technology here was quite foreign to them, it was crude, and simplistic enough for them to get the gist fairly quickly.

They experimented with different levels of energy, putting the crystals into the machine in different ways, and even cramming multiple crystals into the same glass orb.

It didn't seem like there was much to experiment with, but they felt as though they'd figured out a system.

Although, they couldn't resist a few more breakages whenever Oliver gave them the opportunity, mostly just to see what would happen. It seemed the more power was put into the crystals, the quicker and more dramatic the explosion, with the largest creating a substantial flash of light. It wasn't until a large crystal cracked, shattering another glass globe and sending shards scattering over the laboratory's floor that they realised, exactly, what the flash was.

Glistening fragments scattered across their workspace and the control panel of their machine. Ari plucked one carefully out from where it had come to a rest under the lever. As they did so, Ari felt pins and needles shooting up their fingertips and through their tendons, stinging and burning even though the crystal's surface was as cool as ever.

Familiarity sent Ari jolting back, dropping the crystal to the ground with a soft tinkling sound. They waited, looking around, but the laboratory remained as it was.

Immediately after, Ari's face split into a beaming grin despite their still-pounding heart.

When Oliver returned shortly after, his horrified expression made them want to do it all over again.

"Riftmaster?! Come on, I thought we were past this!"

"It was an accident, sorry," they lied. "But look at this!"

They stooped to pick up the brightly-glowing shard, and this time as they picked it up, the tingling feeling was more bearable. They offered him the crystal before dropping it into his outstretched palm.

"Well?"

"Oh, yeah," Oliver said, as though uncertain what sort of reaction Ari was looking for. "That happens when you break them."

"It's full of Rift energy, Oliver! And when the crystal breaks, it releases it all in a... well, an explosion!"

"Yeah. That's right."

"Do you know what that means? We could make use of these crystals, Oliver. Repurpose them..." Ari returned the lever to its neutral midpoint, and let the whirring sound of the machine working gradually fade. "So, do you want me to write this down, or what?"

"Hmmm. Yeah, that would be helpful." Oliver paused for a moment, as though to consider. "I take it – from your conversation with that thing earlier – that you know the Renohaiin language?" he asked after a moment. "It's the most widely used language around here, so we use it to scribe."

"Are you joking? It's the most widely used language in the known universe! Of course I know it."

With the Renohaiin conquest rapidly expanding across the universe, Rifters would be hard-pressed not to end up on one of the empire's planets eventually.

Now *that* was a story he'd never told Bailey before.

"I'm teaching it to my apprentice," they added.

"Oh, good," Oliver said absently. "Well, scribe it in that. Make sure no-one else makes the same mistakes."

"Mistakes?"

"Yeah, mistakes," Oliver clarified, sourly, as he stooped to pick up the glowing crystal shards. "We can't use these again. They're too volatile. I'll need to dispose of these, then I'll put you onto a different task."

"What? Why?" Ari was baffled.

"You think I haven't noticed you pushing your luck?"

"Aren't we supposed to be experimenting? Coming up with results that are new and interesting?"

"Within reason, Aria. This is an outlier, and it doesn't count."

That name, again. Ari bristled slightly. "'Within reason'? What even is the aim of these 'experiments', Oliver? Because it certainly isn't to understand the Rift. The results you want have no variation – they're all the same."

"The... crystals you produce correctly can be used in other, further experiments, Aria. You're not looking at the bigger picture."

"Then why record the 'results' if none of them matter? We could *use* this, Oliver. Isn't that what you want?"

Oliver didn't answer.

Arms full of glowing shards, he hurried out of the room leaving Ari staring after him, full of misgivings.

When he didn't return, Ari slunk out of the laboratory, prickling with unease.

• • •

A few hours later, the Riftmaster returned home.

Bailey was pleased to see him, but, as Bailey had suspected, his mentor didn't seem to have had a stellar day. In fact, the young man noted, he seemed awfully prickly.

"Ollie thinks he's the dogs bollocks, the way he talks to the other researchers. But he's going about it all wrong! He might *say* he's trying to look at the bigger picture, but the things he wants are barely related," the Riftmaster muttered, hardly glancing up at Bailey as he dumped his satchel and shed the cloak from his shoulders.

"Really?" Bailey asked quizzically, looking up from his notes for a second. "I wonder why."

"Because he's no real researcher, of course! Just because you can talk to people doesn't mean you can pick apart the universe! Can you believe it? Rather than having me analyse my findings and turn it into a breakthrough, he just took my research and left it at that," the Riftmaster snorted. "He didn't come back, so I just left him with my mess to worry about instead."

Bailey chuckled, at that. "I'm glad you got to throw a little shade on Oliver, at least. What did you say you were studying again?"

Bailey was unnerved by the odd sparkle in the Riftmaster's eye as he withdrew a small, black shard of crystal from his satchel, scarcely bigger than an inch. Bailey looked at it, slightly narrowing his eyes.

"I'm in the crystal division. They're meant to be studying how we can use these crystals from the planet's crust to bend the Rift to our will," the Riftmaster said proudly.

"I thought as much... may I ask where you got that?"

"I stole it," Ari said, without even the slightest trace of regret. "I thought I'd do a little homework whilst I'm at it."

Bailey stared at him. "Of course you did. Go on?"

"It's in... well... it's in the early stages, and as you know, it mostly focuses on keeping the Rift away. But I've made a couple more discoveries when it comes to reversing the current through the crystals." The Riftmaster sniffed with disdain, closing his fingers around the crystal and putting it away. "Doing that has the ability to create Rifts, Bailey. Can you believe it? I never would have thought it possible."

Bailey's eyes lit up. "So you can *control* it?"

"Well, I..." The Riftmaster floundered slightly. "Not quite. Even if we were to use it to leap from planet to planet, we still wouldn't know where it'd send us."

"But you're gonna find out, right?"

"I'm sorry, Bailey. It almost always breaks them, so Oliver made me stop. He said he'll be putting me on some other task."

Bailey's expression fell.

"...but this could be an opportunity. Even just choosing

when we rift is a huge step forward, even if we can't decide *where.* I know you were hoping for more, but…"

Ari trailed off.

Bailey watched him for a moment. Sensing the need for a change in subject, he loudly cleared his throat.

"I've made a fair amount of progress on translating the journal," he said, with a little more enthusiasm.

Ari looked up with renewed interest. "And?"

"There's this one chapter on Riftworlds, but so far it's mostly just repeating the things that we already know."

"Ah, I see. Keep at it!"

Bailey nodded with a smile. He'd just settled back down to continue studying when he felt a soft vibration begin in the earth, and hastily closed the book. "Heads up, Riftmaster."

This one was a particularly violent one, and sent both humans ducking outside, fabric and equipment falling off shelves with violent clatters. An innocuous-looking stone fell from a top shelf and shattered, revealing it was hollow, and filled with clusters of glittering white crystal.

As the tremors quieted, the two humans exchanged glances.

"I'm beginning to get a bad feeling about these quakes," Bailey said.

"Me too."

As they entered their shelter again, Bailey stooped down to scoop up the sharp fragments of geode. Absorbed in this task, he was only vaguely aware of the small creature that came slinking back in.

"It's about time you came back."

Flora's quills stiffened, and she shrank down.

• • •

Despite all their misgivings and former hatred towards Oliver, Ari found themself less able to be angry at him the following day. Perhaps it was the more amicable words they'd exchanged, or that moment when they'd been able to see past his tough facade and look at him in the same light they always had.

He was, after all, just a man who was lost, confused, and scared, far away from the world and culture he had once known. And more than that, he was the same person that Ari had taken under their wing all those years ago.

And despite all that had happened since, he hadn't changed at all.

Ari tried to ignore that tiny part of them that *wanted* to see him again, after everything he'd done.

Despite having left work suddenly the day before, Ari decided to set out for the lab once again, see what Oliver had to say for himself, and see what new 'tasks' their ex had for them since 'failing' the other. Privately, Ari still thought of the other experiment as a success. They had successfully managed, with that flash of light, to create a Rift, and store it in those crystals.

Now, if only it could be *used*.

And that was something that, in all their years prior, they would never have imagined possible.

To their immense surprise, Oliver was once again waiting for them when they arrived. They felt their stomach clench for a moment as they approached, but they waltzed up to him with the guise of cool confidence.

"Waiting to send me home?" they asked smoothly. "I wouldn't be surprised, after that mess I left you to clean up yesterday."

"Of course not, I'm just waiting for my... favourite *apprentice*."

Ari laughed through gritted teeth.

"Don't push your luck, Oliver."

• • •

The next morning started the same, and ended uneventfully. As did the next, and the next. Ari wished they could grow used to the peaceful monotony, their studies only broken by increasingly frequent and violent quakes.

But the Riftmaster was soon situated quite comfortably at the laboratory, contributing what they could, and felt like they were learning a lot. It helped, at least, having something more to focus on than simply being bossed around by Oliver, which he was clearly enjoying.

They mostly just ignored him as they worked and soon Oliver appeared to take the hint. He gradually drifted away, leaving Ari mostly to their own devices.

They decided, at this point, to make themself busy by reading the other researchers' notes. As Oliver had mentioned, they were mostly written in Renohaiin scripture, one of the languages that Ari was the most familiar with, so it was easy to translate.

There were a lot of them; the researchers, over the decades, had managed to fill a great number of books carefully crafted out of a strange, mottled blue parchment.

Ari had picked up one of the earliest, as well as a couple of the more recent ones.

They noticed, as they read, some interesting trends. The earlier books showed a much wider range not only of languages, but of results. It seemed there had been more experiments at some point; scientific doodles showed different sorts of machines to those present today, different wire arrangements for the machines Ari knew, and even different cuts of crystals seemingly utilised for a wide array of different machines.

Ari read one passage in a language they vaguely knew, but not fluently. It had been years since they had last seen it, let alone used it. But Ari felt themself drawn to it, mostly by the passages they could understand.

"...After crystals shatter, a residual energy signature is left." Ari muttered out loud, squinting as they translated with some difficulty. "The same signature can be found in the wake of Rift-walkers as they leap."

So we leave a trail? Huh...

"The strongest signature of all can be found on a Rifter's homeworld, where they left."

I have to speak to Bailey.

Ari flicked forward a few pages until they reached the next passage, desperately looking for more.

"Further tests inconclusive."

Ari's brow furrowed.

The next page was mostly Renohaiin scripture. They skimmed it but found nothing useful. They turned the page again. Here, standard notes began to transition into lists of numbers and stats.

Finally, they landed upon one final passage with familiar handwriting. "It's no use. I can feel it in the air, but the Rift will not carry me. Need more power."

And though Ari searched, that was all they could find.

After that, the same results repeated hundreds, if not thousands of times over. Ari was wondering yet again what the aim was, of all this, when they heard footsteps approaching from behind them.

Ari glanced up, offered Oliver a nod, then closed the older book, deftly sliding it behind the newer results.

"Oliver," they greeted, somewhat absently.

"Ar – I mean, Riftmaster," Oliver answered.

Although somewhat perturbed, Ari relaxed. While they had their suspicions that it was only to get them to cooperate, they were glad that Oliver had finally swallowed his pride enough to call them by title.

Their former apprentice was silent until Ari gave him a dip of their head, signifying that they were satisfied.

"Keeping busy?" Oliver asked.

"Mmm-hm," Ari said, pretending to be engrossed. "Just familiarising myself with everything we know."

Oliver nodded. "Good."

He fell silent, but much to their annoyance, didn't leave.

Ari paused for a moment, skimming although never quite absorbing, gently rapping their nails against the pages as they pondered what to say. With Oliver hanging over them, reading over their shoulder, it was difficult to properly focus on what they had been doing.

Clearly he wanted to make some kind of conversation, but was uncertain of how to begin it. Perhaps he wanted to ask them a question, or turn their focus onto a new task.

But, he simply remained silent as Ari uncomfortably pondered what to say.

"Bailey loves old books," Ari said eventually.

Oliver looked up in surprise, seemingly confused. "Oh, does he?"

"But to him, 'old' means from our era. His favourite is from the 1940s... 80 years old. Can you imagine that?"

Despite Ari's question being left open for an answer, Oliver simply huffed an acknowledgement. The Riftmaster suspected he was jealous.

They fell silent once more, casting one last glance over the book still spread out before them before closing it. They'd seen enough.

They stole a glance up at Oliver, and noticed curiously that his shoulders relaxed.

Strange.

Ari reconsidered the pages they'd read, none of it out of place given what they'd already known. Enlightening, it was true, but definitely not unusual.

"Oliver, can I ask you a question?" Ari asked after a while.

"Of... of course. What is it?"

"How long have you been here? On this Riftworld?"

Oliver paused, thinking back, considering. "I'd say... probably thirty years now. I've been a researcher for twenty-five, probably. And... head researcher for five years or so, after my research partner, the former head, got Rifted."

Ari nodded, slowly. It all seemed to add up. Ari was certain that the change in language from 'anything goes' to 'strictly Renohaiin' had happened five years ago, when Oliver took charge, but the change to more formulaic results was far more recent.

"Was that before people stopped leaving?"

"Er, yes. Yes it was."

"I see. Thank you."

Ari fell silent once again, running a hand over the etched writing on the front cover that roughly translated to; 'Riftworld research 89, Star-cycle 57'. There was a lot still bothering Ari; a lot that felt as though it didn't add up.

They felt Oliver's eyes still burning into their cheek, even as they considered. Finally they turned towards him, blinking expectantly.

"What is it?"

Their eyes met, but a moment later, Oliver looked away.

"It's just... I always thought you looked beautiful with longer hair. Now you look like a man. Sound like it, too."

Ari blinked. They weren't shocked, just confused. "Is that supposed to sound like a problem?"

"Well, it's just... don't you feel like you're lying to yourself? To Bailey?"

"I'm lying to no-one – especially Bailey. Nothing like that matters to me, Oliver, especially now that you're out of my hair. I want people... Rifters, humans, whatever – to see me for what I'm capable of. Not what they think I should be."

Ari's voice was even, yet firm.

"Okay, okay... I understand. There's no need to get worked up about it."

Ari's brows creased. They looked at him pointedly. "I'm not." They fell into a momentary silence before standing and tucking the research notes under their arm. Ari didn't look at Oliver as they made their way over to the books' respective piles and deposited them in their appropriate places.

"I've been out here, what? ...Five-thousand years?" Ari spoke slowly, and then paused, to let their words sink in. "I've met Rifters from all walks of life, from all sorts of planets. And of all the peoples I've met... You're the only one who's ever cared. Even our *children* knew what to prioritise."

They felt Oliver watching them, studying their movements, following them with his gaze.

"...You made a good mother, you know."

Ari winced. Pausing, they slowly looked up at Oliver, wondering where this was going. *Why,* exactly, was he bringing it up? And of all times, why *now*?

Couldn't he see they were busy?

"They never called me that."

"True. I always wished they had. You could use a more... feminine touch. Especially now."

Oliver's gaze trailed steadily down over them. They caught a touch of disdain creeping into his tone.

A realisation hit them, then, and their eyes narrowed.

"Is... that why it's easier for you to call me by my title, now? Because I look like a man?"

Oliver opened his mouth as though he was about to protest, only to close it again.

And then, he nodded.

Ari clenched their jaw.

"This is why we should never have been a couple," they said drily. "You're just so hung up on meaningless Earth traditions that are useless out here."

"Because we're different things, Aria!" Oliver's gaze hardened. He moved towards them, and even though his motions showed no ill-intent, with every step closer Ari felt themself tensing up. "You can pretend all you want, but you're different to me."

Ari didn't back away. They simply lowered their right hand towards their outer thigh, and said nothing.

"You're smaller, for one. You're more emotional, and softer, too. You have to be, so that you can–"

Oliver was cut off with a startled squeak, almost walking into the silver knife that was suddenly pointed directly at his throat.

The sharpened blade glistened wickedly, although it was somehow less frightening than the sudden coldness in Ari's eyes.

"Call me *soft* one more time, Oliver. I dare you," Ari hissed. "I've not survived thousands of years on my own to be told I'm *soft*. Who was it who mentored you, Oliver, when you were starving and parched, after just two weeks in the Rift? Who was it who raised *your* family because you were so convinced you had to be the provider that you forgot how to protect them? When you tried to do the right thing, who was it who suffered? Who is it, Oliver, that you're afraid of in this very moment?"

The Riftmaster allowed their questions to linger for just a little bit longer even as Oliver remained where he was, frozen. For a moment, they revelled in his expression, a fierce satisfaction rising in their gut... but that satisfaction, they knew, would be short-lived because in all their years Oliver had never, and would never, change.

No matter what Ari had done for him, how incredible the things they had accomplished, the body they were born with would always restrict his respect for them.

There was nothing left they could do for Oliver except pity him.

They turned away, and tried to hide the disgust in their expression as they began to leave.

"Consider this my resignation," Ari said, sheathing their knife. "If you really respect me that little, then I have better places to be."

"You... You're right," they heard Oliver say.

Ari paused, one last time. Their resolve, for the slightest moment, shook.

"About what?"

"E-everything. Maybe I was a pretty bad dad. Maybe you're not soft. And... Maybe I *was* looking for a second chance. From the moment I saw your face in the laboratory I hoped maybe we could... you know... go back to the way things were. Just you and me, and… maybe one day, a new family."

Ari's stomach dropped. Their throat closed up, but still they didn't turn to look at him. Only listened as though in a trance, as Oliver continued.

"Listen, I… I might not… understand, yet, but maybe you could… help me, understand. You could come with me. We could travel together between worlds again, just like old times. You were so special to me, Aria…"

…And in the moment he said their old name, their trance shattered. The illusion broke. Ari knew, then, that they would never go crawling back. Oliver would never see them for what they were now; only for what he wanted them to be.

"Special to you, maybe. But never on equal grounds."

"Aria…–"

"It's Ari. *Riftmaster* Ari. I'm not the same person that you knew back then."

And with that, Ari left Oliver behind where he stood, and didn't look back.

• • •

Bailey felt, now, that the answer was on the very tip of his tongue. The passage on Riftworlds was very nearly complete.

The sinking feeling in his gut was almost at breaking point. Bailey felt his efforts growing more fervent.

The planet waited for an answer with bated breath.

Riftworlds are small planets, with a thick outer layer of crystal that makes up their crust. All are formed from the same basic elements.

Nutrient-rich soil forms from mineral-rich water that bubbles to the surface of the planet in the form of small ponds, and means that they can evolve and support their own plant life.

Riftworlds are hollow on the inside, with an ocean in its core.

Unlike other planets, Riftworlds need not harbour indigenous life to draw Rifters to it.

Bailey read the words he'd translated over and over again, grinding his teeth in frustration. He heard the scampering of tiny paws, and saw Flora running towards him with something clasped in her jaws.

She'd brought him a fragment of geode; crystals glittering beautifully on one side. Sighing, Bailey examined it, turning the object over in his hand.

It was the third fragment she'd brought him today; a few others were piled up next to his bed. And her odd offerings seemed to be growing more frequent by the day.

"Just what are you trying to tell me, hm?" Bailey murmured, absentmindedly stroking her scales and receiving a small nip for his troubles.

Bailey was vaguely aware of the door opening just as he set up to begin studying again. "You're home early," Bailey said without glancing up from his notes.

"Tell me about it," growled the answer.

Bailey looked up, to see his mentor even more bedraggled than usual. His hair stuck out at every angle, his cheeks red. He hid his face as he passed, then lay down on his own bed of hides with his back facing Bailey.

The student raised himself upright.

"What happened?"

The Riftmaster let out a choked snort.

"Nothing. I'm fine."

"You don't look very fine to me," Bailey pushed doubtfully.

"Well then take a wild guess."

Bailey didn't think he wanted to.

"...Oliver?"

"...Yeah," the Riftmaster's voice was small, his voice breaking. "He tried to rope me in again, just like last time... Said things. Made me feel things."

Ari's tone darkened.

"But it's not going to work."

Bailey felt his stomach tighten with guilt. After all, *he* was the reason the Riftmaster had taken Oliver's offer. But Bailey quickly reminded himself that it was the best option. It gave him the chance to work, and the Riftmaster the chance to learn about the Rift in a way that no-one had before. Even with no scientific knowledge, 5000 years lent you a *lot* of experience.

"Well... maybe you could reschedule. Try and make sure you never come into contact with each other?"

"It's a little late for that," the Riftmaster's voice lowered, and he chuckled drily. "I... I quit."

Bailey's blood ran cold and for a moment, he was speechless.

"Why?"

"Because it's not working, Bailey! I'm going there to learn, but the moment I start experimenting with the wrong things, he's onto me like a spoiled child. It's always about what *he* wants to learn, and sometimes he won't even let me do that!"

"Maybe he's just trying to reconnect," Bailey guessed. "Through things you're both passionate about. Science is all about proving people wrong, right? And you... seem to enjoy that."

"Well I don't *want* to reconnect. He knows that, but he keeps badgering me. 'Oh, Aria, you'd look so much better with long hair!' ...well, he can bog off. I can't just *talk* to him, because he thinks he's so much better than me."

Ari sat himself down with a deep sigh.

"And today... Today he took a step too far."

Ari crossed his legs and with a sigh, rested his chin on a hand. He fixed Bailey with a long, appraising look. "So I quit."

"So... that's it then?" Bailey asked in disbelief.

"Yeah. Done."

"Don't you want to find out what he's up to?"

"I do, but... to do that I'll need time to clear my head. I just need to take a step back – I... I can't keep being near him. It's driving me insane. Plus I... might have threatened him with a knife..."

Bailey opened his mouth.

"You *what*!?"

But any further words caught in his throat. The earth had begun, once again, to judder and shake, with more ferocity than any quake they'd seen yet. Marbles shattered against the ground, equipment tumbling to the floor and the very foundations of the cabin began to groan.

Flora shrieked, and shot into Bailey's satchel. He shoved his notes and the journal in there alongside her.

Floundering in horror, Bailey felt the Riftmaster yank him to his feet and together they shoved their way outside into the meadow, stumbling as the earth shook. Both humans fell to their knees and hugged the ground as it continued to shake... and Bailey heard an enormous crack, a creak and a groan.

The cabin behind them collapsed in on itself, crumbling into mossy ruins.

Bailey looked up to see that a huge chasm had opened in the earth, almost cutting the Rifthoppers' district in two.

A distinct pain drew Bailey's attention down to his hand, where he realised that he was still holding Flora's geode fragment. The sharp crystals were cutting into his palm, but still glistened beautifully.

And suddenly it hit him like a brick to the face, crushing the air out of his lungs.

The answer.

The head researcher had been toying, spinning Ari's emotions into pointless circles and redirecting his focus onto things less important. Ari was convinced it was *him* that Oliver wanted – and perhaps he did, in part – but it was also a distraction, all to keep Ari's attention away from the real threat. What else could it be?

After all, Oliver was probably the only one in the universe who could keep the Riftmaster's eyes off the bigger picture. And he knew it.

Bailey turned to his mentor, expression quickly changing from bewilderment to horror... and suddenly Oliver was the least of his worries.

"Riftmaster, we have to go. Now."

Ari's tear-streaked face looked up at him curiously.

"Is there a... is there any space travel? Have they managed to use the Rift yet? Have they managed to control it? Do they have spaceships?" Bailey asked, voice high with panic.

"No, but... Oliver is the head of space travel. He's trying to study how to get to far-off solar systems using the Rift, and..."

"Has he managed it?"

The look on Ari's face told him that no, he hadn't. "Rifthopper, what's going on?"

"We have to get to the lab. This... this all makes sense now. Everything I've been translating. Flora has been trying to tell us all along. Riftmaster, this isn't a planet..."

Bailey almost laughed, even though he wanted to cry with despair. He felt suddenly dizzy with fear, and sick to the stomach.

"...It's an egg."

Chapter 20
The Escape

There was no time to lose.

Scarcely a minute later, they were running.

"We have to get everyone to evacuate, somehow," Ari heard Bailey gasp as he followed close behind at their heels, as the duo gunned for the town at close to a sprint.

Ari didn't answer as they ran, giving the growing chasm a wide berth. If Bailey was smart, he'd save his breath, too; Ari's endurance was second to none, and he needed to keep up.

Ari saw Bailey's friend, the ever-unlucky Cheek-pouches, staring into the hole, and they realised with a pang of pity that the creature's home must have fallen into it.

With eyes that were beady and sad, it watched them go, then began to lumber off into the woods to rebuild, as though nothing more was amiss.

"The Rifters – we have to get them out of here!" Bailey tried again, voice laced with despair.

"There's no time," Ari gasped back, finally slowing to a quick jog. "We have to save ourselves first."

The tremors had, for now, subsided, but Ari could still feel the remnants thrumming up through their feet.

"But what about everyone else?"

"They'll either die or Rift – there's no other way. If they're lucky, when that thing hatches it'll unleash a huge amount of power and… I think this… thing beneath us. It might be – no, it must be – what… causes the Rift."

The planet's crust... no... its shell... was made up of crystals that could both neutralise the Rift and enhance its energy, and the surface of the planet was populated wholly by Rifters. What else could it be?

"So there's a chance for them?"

"A slim chance, but a chance."

Ari fell silent, knowing that it wouldn't be enough for Bailey. It was never enough. The young man was too optimistic, too kind, too... human. But even he had to know that even if some Rifters survived, many more would not.

Ari could see the question lingering in Bailey's pained expression: *Surely there's more we can do?*

But Ari had proven to him, time and time again, that humanity meant nothing out here. If Bailey wanted to survive, he couldn't spare a thought for those he left behind. Even though Bailey didn't know these people, couldn't even talk to them, Ari knew he still felt for them.

He needed to learn that there were no heroes, out here.

Only survivors.

As they reached the town, the duo slowed to navigate the crowds, weaving and pushing their way through the throng of Rifters who panicked and milled around together. Many were moving the same way that they did, people of every planet flowing like a river to fill the laboratory courtyard, where researchers soothed or tried to push them back. Beyond the wall of researchers, Ari could see Rifters breaking past and making a sprint for it. Larger creatures struggled to push their way through, but the burliest of the researchers managed to push them back.

Occasionally a smaller escapee went sailing overhead as it was caught and hurled back into the crowd.

Ari caught scraps of conversation, but there were too many voices, too many languages, and they were unable to hold onto any threads of conversation for long.

"What's going on?" Bailey asked.

"We're not the only ones to notice something's off. They think the researchers will be able to help, somehow."

"Will they?"

Ari didn't answer.

They kept on pushing their way through to the front and soon, shouldered through the front line of researchers with a few short words in varying tongues. Bailey followed, only to be stopped at the very front.

The alien who'd stopped him – the same curly-haired creature that had let them through the last time – whistled something in the same tongue that Ari had conversed with it in before. Ari saw Bailey's expression change to a look of despair as he failed to understand, but strained to listen anyway.

But the language it spoke in was not one Ari had taught him yet.

Ari began to move back towards the creature, aiming to explain the situation so it would let him through. The guards here didn't need to know they'd quit, and they doubted Oliver had had time to spread the word.

Finally, Bailey spoke.

"S-sorry…" he struggled out, in what little he knew of the Renohaiin tongue.

And here, Ari paused.

The otherworldly beast tipped its head, eye flickering down at him. It continued speaking, but changed tones, rumbling instead in a low and gravelly growl. Bailey listened, panic, then relief in his expression.

"Research only. Will not pass," Ari heard it say. Bailey looked past it towards Ari, who offered an encouraging nod.

"Me… Rift-walker's student. With them," he struggled.

The researcher's four ears perked up in evident surprise. Here, Ari moved forward, gently taking a hold of Bailey's arm to lead him through. *"Yes,"* agreed the Riftmaster, in the same tongue. *"Researcher-in-training."*

"Apologies," rasped the researcher, with a bow of its longhaired head. *"Go through."*

They hurried on, sneaking a sideways glance at his apprentice, and saw a sparkle in his eye despite the direness of the situation.

And, even with the pain of loss and everything that had happened since still raw, Ari suddenly realised how far he had come.

The Riftmaster's heart swelled with pride.

Over their time together, Bailey had managed to fill a space in their heart that they didn't even know they'd had.

Bailey had grown from the boy who'd collapsed, shivering, to his knees in the snow before them, into a truly talented

Rifter. With Bailey's help, Ari had learned of things that they could never have imagined, overcome feelings that they'd never wished to face, and found renewed wonder in the infinite worlds of the Rift.

They hadn't felt this way in centuries, not since...

Bailey glanced their way, meeting their gaze. Ari caught panic in his eyes, but knew their own expression was quite calm – that there was a twinkle in their eye, even.

"What?" Bailey asked breathlessly.

"Nothing," Ari answered, hastily turning their gaze away.

The crushing realisation hit them that it could all be about to end.

But they weren't going to let that happen.

Ari turned their attention back to the route ahead. Truthfully, they had little idea of where, exactly, to go. Now that they were here, what could they do...?

Luckily for them, aside from the occasional researcher who hurried past them under a false sense of security, the halls were mostly empty.

"Why do you think they're stopping everyone getting in?" Bailey asked abruptly, breaking the silence.

Ari shrugged. "Any number of reasons. False hope, loyalty, promises that won't be kept..." the Riftmaster's voice lowered. "Most of them seem to think that so long as the research is protected, they'll be able to... I don't know. Perhaps stop the earthquakes, perhaps find a way off the planet. The research is the only hope they have."

Bailey paled. "Do you... get the feeling that someone has been preparing for this?"

"I do. It's nigh impossible to organise a thousand researchers of a thousand different languages in a time of disaster. They've been trained for this. Someone knows."

"...But who?"

"I have a few theories," the Riftmaster grunted, falling silent as they hurried on.

Ari's first thought was to use the crystals to try and create a Rift that would send them to the next planet, where their journey would continue as normal. The Riftmaster led Bailey between all the labs they knew, peering inside – but mysteriously, all the crystals, arranged so carefully on the tables just hours before, had gone. Perhaps other Rifters had already had the same idea.

Bailey followed, and for a while all that could be heard was their footsteps. The silence closed in, the tension all-consuming.

Ari heard the distant sound of shattering glass, and sprinted after it. A bright light streamed out of a doorway ahead of them, but by the time they reached it, the room was empty. All that remained was a sparking machine, a knot of wires and a few shards of what used to be an orb of glass.

In frustration, Ari turned their back and carried on.

"So… ah. What if we run into Oliver?" Bailey asked after a while. "I know you were having some… er… trouble with him. But he might be our only hope."

"In a situation like this, emotions don't seem so important," the Riftmaster panted back, with a visible wince. "If we want to survive, I can't waste energy on feeling bad. I've… got along without him before, and I will again."

Bailey grunted, perhaps doubtfully. But Ari got the feeling that he understood.

As they pressed deeper, Ari heard Bailey cry out, and turned to see Flora wriggle her way out of his satchel and drop to the floor.

"Flora! Not now!" Bailey panicked, obviously fearing that she was going to run away from them. After all, she knew where they were. But to both of their surprise, the little creature ran out in front of them, and hopped around, spinning in a quick circle before fixing a long look at them.

Ari blinked, then glanced up at Bailey. He knew the little creature better than they did, after all.

"She wants us to follow her," he said, with certainty.

So they did. The little creature took a narrow side passage, winding their way through labyrinthine curves and sharp turns until Ari had long since lost track of where they were. The laboratory's disorienting structure was good at messing with their sense of direction. Designed for it, even.

Finally, Flora stopped in front of a rectangular plate made of meteorite metal, embedded in the otherwise crystalline wall. "I think it's a door," Bailey said. Flora, pacing back and forth in front of it, appeared to confirm that theory.

With no better ideas, the duo tried to force it open, to no avail.

"Look at that," Ari said after they'd stepped back to consider it. They gestured to a small, crystal orb at eye level next to the door, and approached, pressing their hands against it, again to no avail.

So, it wasn't a button.

Ari heard a low rattle, as the building began to shake. Bailey sank to his knees as Ari still tried desperately to prise it open, and they heard him let out a panicked gasp of "Oh god, we're gonna be screwed over by a *door*."

As the quake subsided, Flora drew their attention with a shrill squeal.

Her skin flushed and swirled with colours, and with the tip of her tail she pointed at the orb, pawing at the highest point of wall that she could reach. Bailey hesitated, then scooped up the little weasel-like creature. To Ari's immense surprise, she didn't protest, so he held her up to it.

They saw her skin change colour, her texture sweeping into a flesh-coloured tone. A few moments later, the crystal flashed with a white light and the door before them slid open. In pure bewilderment, Bailey turned the little creature towards him and almost dropped her in disgust. Ari flinched with surprise, eyes wide with fascination. For there, on her chest, was an eye – and on her belly, was an intricately formed half a face.

Half of Oliver's face, no less.

Bailey stared as her skin flushed back to its normal green hue, the face disappearing as though it was never there.

"It must have been an eye scanner," Ari said with amazement. "Let's go."

Finally they entered the room. Ari's heart swelled with hope, for before them was a small, and sleek spaceship. Like the observatory, it was angular and faceted, glistening sharply in what little light was shed by the crystals illuminating the laboratory. Ahead of the spaceship was another closed door. But with no sensors or locks to speak of, it must have been opened remotely.

The door hissed shut behind them.

No going back now.

"It's... it's tiny," Bailey said, unable to hide his disappointment.

It *was* tiny. Just about big enough for two people, but no more.

He must have still been harbouring a sliver of hope that he could save someone.

"That's because it's an escape pod."

Boxes of decent-sized crystals were scattered around it.

But what had caught Ari's eye was not the spaceship, but the person loading it. And Oliver's gaze was, in turn, not on them, but on Flora... the tiny creature hissing and spitting at their feet.

"*You*... you came back," Oliver said, in surprise more than anger. "Not that it matters now."

Flora arched her spine, curled her tail, and finally shot up Bailey's leg and back into his satchel. Oliver ignored them, and continued climbing into the escape pod.

"You know Flora?" Bailey asked.

As if that was the most important thing right now.

"Bailey, now isn't the time," they snapped.

A moment later, Ari was sprinting towards the pod, and as Oliver made to close its door after him, pressed themself against it to hold it open. They gestured to Bailey, and despite their ex's struggles, the two of them managed to yank him back out into the open.

"What are you doing? I have to go – it's a... scheduled test flight," Oliver excused limply, staggering back to his feet. Neither Bailey nor Ari even came close to how tall Oliver was, and with his hair wild and eyes feral with desperation, Ari found their heart pounding. He cut quite the intimidating figure. But he was outnumbered, three... well... 2.5 to one.

"Cut the crap, this planet is about to fall apart," Ari snapped. "Whatever's in there's gonna break out soon."

"You... You know?! How?!"

"Whilst you were distracting me, my apprentice here's been hard at work." Ari exchanged a glance with Bailey. "You underestimated him, Oliver."

"And you," Bailey said. "How long have you been preparing this?"

"My research partner... he saw another Riftworld's collapse, a few thousand years ago." Oliver's jaw quivered. "When Rifters stopped leaving this planet, he told me that we had to start trying to harness the Rift, or we would both die."

Bailey's heart grew cold, his stomach dropping. "What happened to him?"

Oliver's eyes met his, and in that moment Bailey knew.

"He tricked me and tried to escape, taking my research with him…"

Oliver trailed off, but Ari was quite certain they knew the rest. *He failed.* He disappeared, leaving it all behind to Oliver. And it didn't take a genius to know just *how* he had disappeared.

"…But his apprentice escaped, and I never found it. That thing was always good at hiding."

Flora hissed as Oliver looked her way.

Ari broke in, their voice gentle. "Don't worry, Oliver. I don't blame *you.* We're all stuck in the same situation. But I need you to tell us where to find more pods."

"There *are* no more. This one is barely past the prototype stage. It shouldn't even be flying yet. It's never been tested," Oliver panted, face full of genuine terror. "I'd hoped to be able to produce more when it was finished, but… It's too late now, and we haven't the resources."

"Then we'll… just have to take this one," Ari said. "Is there room for us?"

"There's only room for two," Oliver pleaded. "The crystals don't provide enough energy to lift it off otherwise."

"Then we'll just have to make it happen. We can all get out of here," Ari snapped, looking up and down their former lover's tall, and muscular form. They clenched their fists. "All of us."

"No, Aria…" Oliver protested. "It's *us*, or just me. I'm the only one who can fly it, and…"

He turned a scathing look towards Bailey.

"I'd rather it be *her*."

That was enough for Ari. They nodded towards Bailey. "It's both of us, or *neither* of us, Oliver."

"Then please…" Oliver begged. "You have to get out of here. Find somewhere safe… after the planet breaks you might still Rift. That's how my partner survived. There's still a chance… But you'd have to go *now*."

"*Nowhere* is safe, Oliver. I'm done with chances… we're making our own luck," Ari said, their voice a low, dangerous growl. "Now please… move aside. If you won't let us in, then we're taking the pod."

They heard a sound like glass splintering, the earth

juddered beneath them, and all three stumbled.

A falling panel of crystal shattered against the ground, missing Ari and Oliver by inches.

They needed to get a move on; but Oliver's gaze remained fixed on Ari.

"You'd leave me here? After everything we've done…?"

Oliver's gaze slowly shifted to Bailey, who stared back evenly despite his obvious terror.

Ari's jaw tightened, their eyes narrowed. "Was I not clear? We're over, Oliver. We have been for a thousand years."

The Riftmaster sucked in a deep breath. "I have to look out for myself, now. Myself, and him." Despite everything, Ari felt their eyes well up with bitter tears. "I'm sure you'd understand, Oliver… giving up everything for the sake of someone you love." They paused, and took a deep breath. "…Even if the chance of survival is slim."

Realisation appeared to dawn on Oliver, and in that moment, he knew that he was fighting a losing battle. But he wasn't about to stop. His very life depended on it.

"But… you wouldn't even know how to drive it! Wouldn't you rather I… the one you *loved* survive, than you two – you three – all die?" Oliver paused, and turned his gaze away. "…Believe me, if I could save you, then I would."

The Riftmaster paused, releasing another breath.

"Maybe once I would have, but I can't cling to the past any more. I need this as much as you do."

Ari glanced sideways towards their apprentice.

"I'm not… I'm not letting you just take it. I can't," Oliver said.

The Riftmaster looked up, meeting Oliver's gaze for a second, and shared a moment of quiet acknowledgement. "I suppose we'll just have to fight for it, then," they said, drily.

"I suppose we will."

Ari began to move towards him, feeling as though their feet were dipped in lead.

They could see the tears in Oliver's eyes. "I still love you, you know," he said. "Even after everything you said."

Ari felt their heart stop. Their stomach dropped. And for a moment, they regretted everything. It would be so easy to simply give in, to leave Bailey behind and return to the way it had been, just them and Oliver. Wasn't it something they had longed for, for hundreds of years?

But no.

They weren't falling for that one again.

"I know," Ari said, voice hoarse.

Oliver's face fell.

And then an idea hit them, a realisation. A terrible, terrible idea that made their blood run cold, and their skin prickle with goosebumps.

It was their only option, the easiest, and the kindest. They couldn't just leave Oliver here to die, either in the collapsing laboratory or the cold abyss of space.

They didn't want to. But they had to.

They both knew full well that if the two of them *truly* fought, Ari would lose.

Ari felt a tear run down their cheek as they made their decision.

But in the end, it all hinged on him. His trust in them. His heart. His unbelievable stubbornness, and unwillingness to change.

"How about one last kiss, before the end? And then we'll fight it out... for the chance to survive."

"Of... of course," Oliver croaked.

...And so his fate was sealed.

Ari walked forward, step by painful step. It felt as though their heart was already breaking, but they kept their expression even. They extended their palms, and took Oliver's hands into their own.

Oliver took Ari into his arms. They took in every detail of his age-worn face, from the scattering of grey hairs to the contours of his nose, and tightly set jawline. They could see his eyes shimmering with tears.

"I missed you, in those thousand years apart," Oliver murmured, for only them to hear. "I'm glad that I got to see you again, one last time."

The words came through faint, muffled by the rushing of blood in their ears. Ari hesitated before returning the embrace, wrapping one arm tightly around Oliver's chest.

"You too," Ari murmured. "You really have no idea."

Ari looked up, gazing deeply into Oliver's trusting eyes.

And they wanted desperately for that moment to last forever.

They felt the ground began to tremble as another earthquake began to brew. They were taking too long.

It was time to let go.

Oliver's eyes flickered shut. Ari's eyes streamed with tears as they followed suit… but only for a moment.

They lifted their head, and pressed their lips to his. Ari took it all in; his musky smell, his familiar taste, the bristly feel of his stubbly cheeks against theirs. Seconds later, their eyes blinked open, gaze flickering.

His eyes were still closed, his lips still pressed to theirs.

Seconds blurred together. It was as though the body that moved then was not their own as the Riftmaster silently drew their knife. They ran a hand up his neck and through his hair, the other sneaking around his waist to rest against his back.

A moment later, Oliver screamed in pain. In that lingering moment of serenity, Ari had taken their chance.

The blade that Oliver had kept hidden up his sleeve clattered to the floor.

So maybe he *had* known, after all.

Ari's gaze trailed down towards the bloodied tip of the knife protruding from his collarbone. Nausea rose in their gut as a dark stain began to spread out around it, seeping through his clothes. Quietly, they removed the knife from his back.

Vaguely, they were aware of Bailey's face twisting into a look of silent horror.

They gently lowered their love onto the floor, tears streaming down their face like rivers.

"I… guess you win," Oliver choked.

Bailey looked away, silent, stunned.

"I'm sorry," Ari said quietly.

"I… I couldn't do it," Oliver gurgled, blood bubbling at the corner of his mouth. "I knew… I knew what you… but I thought…"

"I know," Ari murmured, gently, and with a touch of morbid humour. "You always were the sentimental one."

They ran a hand through his hair. It wasn't as soft as they remembered.

Oliver's jaw trembled, his tears following the creases around his eyes. Physically Oliver looked as young as the day they'd met, but somehow the age had crept into his hollow eyes. "Good luck… Riftmaster."

"Goodbye, old friend."

As the last, rattling breath passed from Oliver's lungs, Ari bent to plant one final kiss on his bloodied lips. They wound their fingers with his, tracing his golden ring as they laid his hands to rest on his silent chest.

Then, businesslike despite the tear tracks down their face, they turned towards Bailey, expression blank and unreadable. "Get in the pod," they barked. "Just cram yourself in there. We're getting out of here."

The Riftmaster picked up Oliver's knife from the ground as they passed, shoving it quickly into their satchel before flicking the blood off their own. Bailey squeezed into the escape pod, pressing himself up against the opposite window. He pushed his satchel into a small compartment behind the seat, and Ari did the same. Before they climbed into the escape pod, Ari spared one final glance back towards the body, and felt their vision spin.

Then they ducked inside, slamming the door behind.

Although there was enough room for two, it still felt like a tight squeeze. They and Bailey huddled close together as they tried to figure out the controls.

The research facility was shaking once again, and Ari's stomach turned with nausea. He heard a rumble from outside along with a distant creaking and groaning.

"Did you drive on Earth?" Ari asked Bailey urgently.

"I... I was learning, but I don't think it'll help. You?" Bailey answered.

Ari shook their head. "Even if I had, that was five thousand years ago."

So they were completely in the dark, then.

There were levers and buttons and switches galore, and it took a great deal of fumbling before the metal doors to the outside slid open a few metres ahead of them, revealing scattered Rifters trying to find their way in and the lines of researchers trying and failing to keep them away. Beyond that, the lilac sky and stars loomed. Hardly noticing the Rifters that were beginning to enter through the open doorway and make for the pod in desperation, Bailey and the Riftmaster turned their attention to the larger levers.

Ari flicked several switches in turn, then Bailey pulled a lever.

There was a booming sound as the engine roared into life, and the pod jumped forward a little as the thrusters activated, spitting plumes of fire.

Ari heard clatters as stray rocks and crystals bounced off the roof of the pod. If they didn't go now, then the laboratory would come down on top of them.

"I think this is the one," Ari gasped, preparing to pull down one last lever.

A small, feline alien began to scrabble at the side of the pod, mewling pathetically. Ari saw Bailey's eyes watering as he tried desperately to ignore it.

"Try these first!" panicked Bailey, flipping down a few more switches.

"I've already done those!"

The engine roared louder. Flora shrieked in terror, and finally Bailey clamped his eyes tightly shut. They both felt themselves thrown backwards as the pod began to move, lurching forward.

"We're gonna die here!"

"No, wait, I think I've got it!"

"You do!?"

"Y-yeah, this is just to steer! And that means…"

Bailey slammed his fist down on one final button. Both humans' breaths caught in their throats as not only were they lurching forwards, but upwards as well. They soared out of the open archway and over the desperate crowd watching their only hope fly away. Wobbling in the air, they left the ground in a wide arc that allowed them to cast a glance down at the world they'd just left behind. Bailey saw the crowds gathered around the laboratory, the meteorite town dropping away – and the Rifthoppers' district, with its homes and creatures flecked across the meadow like insects.

Ari soon turned their attention back to the controls, tilting the escape pod away from the planet until it grew smaller, and smaller, and…

"Look," Bailey breathed, leaning in close to Ari so that he could be heard. The Riftmaster looked up from where they wrestled with the steering.

They saw great crevasses that cut deep into the planet's crust, winding their way across the forests, and they could see dark crystal exposed beneath the surface. As their tiny ship soared off into the vast abyss, Ari could soon see that the entire planet was covered in cracks, some shards already beginning to peel away and float off into space.

Through the gaps, Ari could see faint white light emerging from the planet's core...

And then, before their very eyes, slowly but surely as they drifted further and further away, the planet began to split. Ari watched with morbid fascination.

They both stared. The planet's crust was pushed into two distinct and jagged halves, as the newborn creature nestled inside gave one final push, and awoke. From this far away, they saw it moving – saw the cracks widen, and finally a great, long head emerged. Then a long, thick, and streamlined body with massive scaled plates. Huge, flat, almost winglike flukes lined the sides of its body – more and more of them as the creature shed its shell – shook themselves free, somehow steering it as it soared through space. A pale white light emerged from the gaps between its scales.

In all their years, Ari had never seen anything quite like it; it was amazing, and yet terrifying, all at once. It reminded them almost of a great, planet-sized whale.

Curiously, it had no eyes that they could see.

The remains of its egg scattered as, with a push of great fins, the whale finally freed itself, sending what remained of the Riftworld spinning through space. Tendrils of light licked from beneath its scales at flecks of debris clinging to the broken pieces of its eggshell.

As Ari watched, it circled the remains of the Riftworld, its scales reverberating with trembling flashes of light, and it let out a call that rattled through the hull of their escape pod.

Ari realised then that they'd heard this same booming song once before; back when they'd entered the Rift for the very first time. And they saw from Bailey's expression that he recognised it too, and that the thought chilled them to the very core.

"What is it doing?" Bailey breathed.

"It's... creating Rifts..." Ari answered.

Ari realised with a shiver that each and every one of those flecks was an individual Rifter; the survivors that were still clinging to what remained of the Riftworld. Like shooting stars, they disappeared into space carried on tendrils of plasma extending towards the nearest star systems and beyond.

Ari could see the trails they left behind for an instant before, they too, disappeared.

"Why?" Bailey asked, mouth dry.

"I… I think it's searching for something. It must use the Rift to navigate."

In a few great sweeps of its tail flukes, the great whale was alongside and overtaking them, and appeared to have decided on a direction to go. Ari watched its great scales passing beneath them, its head rising up many miles ahead. They both felt it begin to sing again, this time in a low and mournful tone. It glowed brighter than ever before, and Bailey and Ari struggled to look away as the brightness burned into their eyes.

"O-oh no, it's gonna…!"

Ari heard a low boom as the great whale's fins pushed off nothingness. It blazed with light as though it were its own sun and the escape pod, too, was engulfed in bright whiteness. Ari and Bailey were pressed back against their seats as the pod was yanked into the Rift alongside it, and the infinite cosmos blitzed by just out of sight.

When the light had faded, they were facing a dark and empty sky. Only one thing could be seen in an infinite void of nothingness – a thousand shapes that danced and played, rippling with white lights in the emptiness. With one final flick of its winged flukes, the newborn sent their humble little ship spinning as it went to join its own kind.

With great difficulty, Ari took to the controls, managing after some time to stop the spinning and right themselves.

They shut off the power – and suddenly even that comforting rumble was gone.

When the dizziness faded, Ari pressed themself up against the window and looked out. To the left, they could see a sky filled with newborn stars and nebulas. But to the right, there was nothing – only empty abyss, as far as the eye could see.

Even though they'd escaped the Riftworld, Ari knew that this was the end; the whale had brought them to the very edge of the universe.

Chapter 21
The Edge of the Universe

"So... now what?" Bailey asked, after what seemed like forever.

Bailey could still see the wet tracks down Ari's cheeks, rapidly drying out into salt crystals. A bloodstain lingered at the side of his mouth from his final kiss. "There's nothing we *can* do. We're light-years away from anything that could possibly help."

Ari looked at him, hollow-eyed, and his lower jaw trembled.

They were close enough together that Bailey could smell the lingering residue of a thousand worlds on Ari's skin, overpowered in part by the stench of blood that clung to him like a tainted ichor.

Bailey's head spun with the thought that he was now sitting next to a murderer.

Flora pushed her way out of Bailey's satchel and climbed up onto the back of their seat, clinging to his shoulders to keep herself from floating away.

Even she was silent as she stared out into space, her ears flicking back against her head as all colour drained from her form, leaving her a pale and ghostly grey. It was a colour that could only signify pure hopelessness.

"All we can do is shut down our systems, kill our engines, and hope that the Rift comes for us before death does."

Bailey sank down in his half of the seat, letting

hopelessness fade into sheer and agonising emptiness.

"Will it even come for us out here?"

Ari didn't answer, seemingly deep in thought.

Bailey, meanwhile, looked out into space, back the way they'd come. The Riftworld was already light-years away; barely a fleck of light in the infinite cosmos.

Most of the Rifters there would already have died. But *they* had survived. Against all odds, and against everything that his heart told him was morally right, they'd escaped.

But that hardly mattered now.

Bailey's gaze shifted to darkness. The newborn whale had reached its pod – their many shapes coming together into one massive array of lights, a beautiful living constellation, welcomingly spinning around their newest star. Out here in the abyss at the edge of spacetime, they were the only things resembling stars for miles – flecks of light in the darkness. And soon, they too would be gone.

"So they... they're the cause of all this," Bailey said. "Have you ever seen them before?"

Ari shook his head. When he finally spoke, it was with careful consideration, but Bailey could tell his heart wasn't in it. Ari, like Bailey, was afraid.

"They must live at the very edge of the universe... Their eggs must incubate for hundreds of thousands of years... long enough to evolve their own plant life. They create the Rift to navigate space and find their own kind... or maybe a good place to lay their eggs.

"Maybe the Rift is like a series of threads that they can sense. It... could be a living starmap based on life-bearing planets. And folks like us... well. We're all caught in the crossfire. We're the pins on their maps. We're like *atoms* to them." Ari gathered up his knees, though Bailey knew he must already be aching in the cramped space. "Or maybe... We're their food, and... the Rift filters energy from living things... "

He paused, shook his head, and gradually the look of horror on his face became one of weariness.

"Not that any of it matters now."

Bailey didn't reply, simply stared off into space just the same as Ari and Flora. There was nothing else they could do. They had no food, so they couldn't eat... they had no space, so they couldn't move… but most agonisingly of all, they had nowhere to go.

They would soon run out of water.

And then, they would run out of air, too.

That is, if they didn't succumb to the cold, first.

"…It's beautiful, isn't it?" Ari asked, unexpectedly. Bailey looked at him – shared a fleeting glance with his bleak, sad eyes before following his gaze. He looked out at the void of blackness where the distant whales winked their lights, and then towards the entire universe that was laid out before them. "Just think…" Ari went on. "We're the only ones in the universe to ever see this, Rifter or no. And we probably always will be."

Bailey nodded. "Pretty amazing."

Another few minutes of silence passed between them. Finally, Ari let out a sigh. Bailey turned to see that the Riftmaster was looking his way again. "You can… you know. Borrow my knife, if you want. It'll be a long wait if you don't."

Bailey's blood ran cold as he understood, and he sat upright, turning towards Ari in horror. "So… that's it, then? You're giving up?"

Ari bowed his head. "Not much else we can do."

"No," Bailey said, shaking his head. He felt his stomach turn over as despair began to leak its way into his heart. "It's not hopeless. It can't be! You've spent 5000 years in the Rift! Surely you can think of something!? You're the Riftmaster. You can survive anything!"

"You said it yourself, Bailey; I'm self-proclaimed. I'm not a master of anything. I'm just… I'm just a human who's as lost as everyone else out here… And… I'm barely even that anymore." He cast his gaze down towards his hand, still stained with Oliver's blood. A moment later, he clenched it into a fist, and held it against his chest – as though to treasure the only thing that still remained of his love.

"You've probably overcome worse," Bailey encouraged. "What about that one time you–"

"No, Rifthopper, I haven't. Funnily enough, this is a first for me." The Riftmaster's voice shook, and his expression was sour. He turned himself away, as best he could in the cramped space. "I think it's time to give up, Rifthopper.

We're out of options. The end will be a lot easier to accept when you do."

Bailey sighed, staring again out into nothingness.

A while later, Ari spoke again.

"I... killed the love of my life for this chance. I killed him, and... look where it got us."

There was very little Bailey could say that would even come close to comforting his mentor, and so when he opened his mouth to respond, nothing came out. He released his breath instead in a sigh. "But... he let you. Didn't he? His love for you was stronger than his will to survive. He hesitated, and it cost him his life. Intentionally or not, he gave you this chance. Why waste it?" Bailey paused. "...Even if we fail, at least you'll have tried. It's... better to think about what you did do, than die worrying about what you didn't. And you did what you had to do."

Ari sniffed, but didn't respond.

Feeling the silence suffocating, Bailey thought about what else he could say. It was a while before he spoke again, this time changing the subject. If they were going to die anyway, might as well make use of the air they had left.

"How was it that you survived after leaving Earth? Did you have a mentor?"

The Riftmaster shook his head without looking at him.

"I was alone pretty much until I met Oliver – except for the other Rifters I met on my travels, that is. It was mostly by chance that I managed to survive at first. I found myself on a Riftworld quite early on, and managed to trade for a few of the basic necessities with trinkets that I'd picked up on other planets. That's where I managed to find the herbs I use for testing toxins, and my knife. Even so, I walked a fine line... I was always just a stone's throw away from dying, mostly through food poisoning."

"How did you... get over losing your family?" Bailey paused, glancing away. "Your... Earth one, I mean."

"Well... to tell you the truth, we'd been arguing on and off for years. I entered the Rift in the wake of a particularly bitter one."

Bailey watched the Riftmaster's expression as his gaze wandered out over the starscape outside. He saw sadness flickering across his mentor's face.

"We'd argued a thousand times before, but that one was... the breaking point."

"What happened?"

"We just... well, we wanted different things; my family wanted me to find a man, settle down, and have kids, but... I wanted to go out and find my own way. I wanted to travel the world, see things that no-one else had seen, do things that no-one else had done.

"In the end, they gave me an ultimatum: to agree to a future as an unhappy housewife, or to strike out on my own, just to prove that I could. I... didn't think it was fair that my life had been laid out for me before I'd even taken my first breath. I told my father that if being a woman meant living a miserable life, then I didn't want to be one anymore. Unfortunately, that wasn't an option. So that night, I packed my bags with a week's worth of food and some camping supplies, then left."

"You... ran away?"

"Well... yeah. Looking back, I don't think they meant it like that. They knew I had nowhere to go, no house or job. Those things take time."

"Where did you go?"

"Up Latrigg. I wanted to take one last look at the town where I'd grown up before leaving it for good. I reached the summit, looking out over the valley and the lake reflecting the stars... and I think I knew in that moment, that things were going to be different. That *I* was going to be different. I didn't have a word for it back then, and I still don't, not really. I sat atop that hill for hours, wondering what I had become as I waited for the sunrise."

Bailey felt a lump rise in his throat; he could picture the scene in his mind's eye.

"I never saw the dawn, though. Instead, there was a bright white light and burning pain. Looking back now, I suppose the Rift was... almost exactly what I'd asked for. But for the first few years, I always secretly hoped I'd return. Everyone does. At times, I was this close to simply lying down and giving up." He held up his hand to show Bailey; the finger and thumb almost touching, but not quite.

"What makes now any different?" Bailey asked.

The Riftmaster stared out into space, and let out a huff. But Bailey could almost hear the cogs turning in his brain as he began to think. He at least didn't look quite so defeated any more. "...A lot of things make this time different. For one, no-one's ever been to the edge of the universe before."

Bailey paused, then spoke once again.

"What about now? If you could reverse it all and go back, would you?"

The Riftmaster opened his mouth to respond, then closed it again. His brows creased, and then relaxed. "Maybe once upon a time I would have. But I've been gone too long to say for certain."

He let out a sigh, his brows furrowing again.

"...Reverse it all..."

Suddenly, the Riftmaster bent forward and began to look around beneath the controls. After some fumbling, he removed an obsidian panel by their feet. Behind it was a contraption made out of crystals taken from the Riftworld's crust, all of them shimmering with a soft white light and wrapped in coils of wire. It must have been the escape pod's power source. With a swift and unexpected motion, Ari drew his knife, and began to break the orbs of glass holding them.

"What are you doing!?" Bailey panicked. Had he finally lost it? Was he going to try and end their suffering prematurely by having the entire ship blow up?

"They're using the Rift to power this ship."

"What?!"

"...Bailey, we have one last chance at this. Do you trust me?"

Bailey met his old, world-weary eyes and saw that, for the first time since they'd met, they looked young and full of fire.

Those were eyes that had seen and learned so much. Eyes that had seen the births and deaths of empires. They were eyes that had been blinded by rage and blurred with tears. They'd seen through snow and rain and fire, and they'd been filled with understanding and curiosity both.

These were the eyes of someone who'd seen a thousand worlds, who'd created life and taken it away.

These were the eyes of someone who was neither a man or a woman.

But they *were* the eyes of a human.

Bailey's breath caught in his throat; he felt he had no other choice but to nod.

"What's the plan?" Bailey asked.

"I'm going to reposition the crystals in their wires. I'm no whiz at technology, but I was studying the effects of electricity on these... Let's see here... Usually, when you charge them, they produce an energy that counteracts the Rift, but... I found that if you reverse the flow of the currents through them, that energy begins to get backed up!" Ari's voice was fervent, and he worked with frantic quickness.

Bailey stared in fascination, and pressed himself against the window to offer the Riftmaster as much room as he could to work. The Riftmaster had just finished repositioning the crystals, their surfaces smeared with blood from stray glass shards that had pierced his skin.

Flora's pale hide began to blossom with little freckles of pink. She raised her head.

"Sooner or later, the crystal will begin to crack with the strain to ease some of the pressure... But we're not gonna let that happen."

The Riftmaster straightened up and twisted around, digging their satchels out from behind their seats so that they could be worn again. "We're gonna trigger all of the systems, all at once. Usually the crystals will prevent us Rifting... but we're gonna pour everything we have into those crystals until they release all of their energy into a single explosion. If it works, then the sudden influx of power will have the reverse effect, and trigger a Rift instead."

Bailey stared with wide eyes, horrified. "Where will we go? The Rift seeks life, right? So what if we just end up chasing them?"

Bailey glanced back towards the whales that swam through the distant abyss.

"Rifters leave energy traces on the planets they've been... So we hope the energy surge is enough for the Rift to take us back the way we came."

"How do you know it'll work?"

"I don't. And if it doesn't, our systems will shut down, and it might have punched a hole in the ship that means we'll be dead in minutes. We won't have to suffer long." Ari looked up. "So, are you ready?"

Bailey panicked.

"No!" he sputtered. He removed his own knife from his

belt, and cut a strip of material from the mountain-crawler cloak still draped around his shoulders. He tied it around Flora's middle, meeting her gaze as she gave him a small nod. Finally he sheathed his knife, and turned towards the Riftmaster with a wild grin. Whatever happened, this would be over in minutes; for better, or for worse.

"Okay, now I'm ready."

The Riftmaster grinned back.

"Okay. Start flipping those switches!"

Bailey nodded, and obeyed. Lights came on, exposed wires sparked and flashed. The crystals began to creak with the strain, threatening to shatter prematurely. They had to be fast.

Bailey looked at the Riftmaster – there was only one more button left to press.

They exchanged a small nod. Flora crawled down Bailey's arm and hid in his satchel. "Let's go," Bailey said.

Ari pressed the button, and the engine roared into life, powering them forward. He heard the sound of shattering glass as the crystals burst under the strain.

Then Bailey's vision filled with a white light, his skin searing with white-hot pain so sudden and intense that he cried out. The escape pod's walls disappeared around him, and there was only empty space.

And then suddenly, he felt himself falling – but he wasn't alone this time. The Riftmaster, his face full of relief and joy, was falling through the whiteness beside him. The pain faded, to be replaced by the sensation of a warm and powerful wind throwing them forward.

Bailey and the Riftmaster exchanged a look of pure ecstasy, and both reached out to one another as they fell. Mentor and apprentice took a hold of one another's hands. No matter where in the universe they ended up now, at least they'd be going there together.

Bailey saw the Riftmaster's lips move, and although the words were lost somewhere out there in space, he knew what he was saying.

'We did it.'

Pure and unfiltered joy at being alive coursed through Bailey's veins, and he laughed out loud.

For the first time, Bailey felt pure excitement at what they might find on the other side. For the first time, he was ready for whatever the universe might throw at him.

He almost didn't want to hit the ground, but he let go of the Riftmaster as he collided face-first with it, rolling over on his back and clutching at his stomach, winded.

Opening his eyes, the young man looked up and saw above him a beautiful blue sky, with white and fluffy clouds floating by. He felt grass... wiry grass that shimmered with frost, prickling at his hands and the back of his head. A chilly breeze played with the strands of black hair falling over his brow, and he felt the spring sunshine falling on his face.

Breathing in a deep breath, Bailey sucked in the scent of freshly-fallen rain.

Epilogue
A Farewell

The Rift had dropped them on a high hilltop plateau, with green mountaintops framing the sky in every direction that Bailey looked. The sun shone bright and high in a cold winter sky.

Climbing out of his satchel, Flora spun and danced in the sheer joy that came with being free and alive – she rolled in the grasses at their feet, and twittered excitedly. Bailey could only imagine it was something to do with the fact that they were alive and free.

But Bailey had his own reasons to celebrate.

They were home.

Suddenly nothing else seemed to matter, as Bailey shot to his feet, skipped, whooped, and punched the air with joy.

"You did it! You actually did it! You brought us back!" Bailey's only answer was the sound of the wind. "...Riftmaster?"

Ari was already standing. He had had perched himself at the very edge of the plateau, beside an old, worn park bench. He stood, quiet, alone, and serene, and didn't even turn as Bailey approached.

"Did you plan this?"

Ari looked up. "I... I knew there was a possibility, but..." He trailed off, and returned his gaze to the valley beneath them. "I didn't think that it'd... that we'd..."

"Huh?"

"We're on Latrigg. The very summit. This is where I was the day that the Rift came for me," he said, as Bailey came to stand beside him. "Meaning… that is…"

The Riftmaster gazed down at the valley that dropped away below them. Bailey could see the small town of Keswick sprawling far below, its houses tiny like children's toys, and beyond that, the sunlight glistened off a lake that shone deep blue in the sunlight. Tiny ferries trundled slowly across its surface, and cars whizzed their way to and fro along country roads and narrow streets.

"I didn't expect…"

Bailey gave him a nudge. "You should go and see if your family still lives there," he said, gently. "Tie up loose ends, y'know?"

The Riftmaster looked at him with a hollow expression, before looking back down towards the town. Bailey didn't think he'd ever see his homeworld again and – even after everything he'd seen – Bailey knew that this, here, was the most beautiful sight he'd ever beheld.

Lost for words, Bailey felt his eyes welling up with tears, and put an arm around Ari's shoulders.

"I'll come with you. I want to go home to London whilst I have the chance, but I can spare an hour or two."

Ari smiled gratefully his way, but said nothing as he led the way down into the valley, with Flora hopping along at their heels in a blitz of vibrant colours, batting at every flower and chasing every butterfly.

• • •

Bailey hung back as they approached Ari's family home, which turned out to be no more than a tiny cottage on the outskirts of town. Strangely, the door was ajar. Even now, coils of smoke drifted up from the chimney, and Bailey watched as his mentor raised his hand to give a few firm knocks.

Then they waited.

They didn't need to wait long as someone came to the door. It was a plump, short woman with tired eyes and a wrinkled face who looked to be in her late fifties. Her hair was mid-transition from auburn to grey.

She took a moment to process the sight of the stranger at her door, blinking long and hard.

"You're... you're the girl from the photographs," she said in wonder.

"I was... wondering if my mum and dad still lived here. Josephine and Robert Jameson?"

A bewildered, then pained expression slowly crossed her face.

"You don't know?" she asked.

Ari shook his head.

"They were my great aunt and uncle. Robert passed away just two weeks ago, but Josephine has been dead for almost forty-three years now. We're just clearing out the last of their things."

A look of dismay crossed Ari's face.

Bailey kept his distance as Ari was ushered inside with the offer of a warm cup of tea, but as the lady beckoned to Bailey, too, the student shook his head and held up his hands to politely decline. While he waited for Ari to return, he went off to explore the small town of Keswick, and figure out how to get back to London.

• • •

As they entered the old, snug cottage, Ari was hit by a wave of nostalgia.

Everything brought back memories, from the grubby, floral-patterned carpet to the faded books on the well-worn bookcase. There were some unfamiliar things; but it had been so long that their hazy sense of nostalgia clung to just about everything like an old, and lingering fog.

Their nostrils drew in the fading old-folks smell, and the musk of old books.

Ari's eyes welled up as they gazed around at the place that they had lived for so short a time, and missed for so unbelievably long.

They felt suddenly and violently out of place against the drab mix of browns, reds and creams in their bright-pink mountain-dweller cloak and boots. The rest of their garb was, as usual, a mix of lilac fabric and iridescent scales.

It was yet another reminder of just how much had changed.

After thousands of years, they'd thought that they would be prepared. They had thought the memories of Earth would have grown foggier with time. But after all the years, time hit Ari harder than it ever had.

"Tea?"

Ari glanced up at the small, plump woman – a distant cousin, Ari supposed – who had spoken through bleary eyes. It took a moment for the question to register.

"Oh, um. Yes, please," they finally said.

"How would you like it?"

"Hot, please."

The lady gave them an odd look. "…Milk and sugar?"

Ari froze as though they'd been stung. And then, before they could stop themself, they let out a nervous laugh. "Er, y-yes please. I'm sorry, it's been a while."

As she waddled off into the kitchen, Ari's gaze returned to the room. Their gaze trailed slowly over the old bookshelves and display cases with intricate floral patterns. The old, old statues of otters and birds, little decorated plates painted with woodland scenes, many of them already taken down or loaded into cardboard boxes sitting on the old, yellowed sofas.

Ari walked, the floorboards creaking under their feet.

Finally, they came to a dusty display full of photo frames. Raising a hand, they cautiously opened the ornate glass door, and removed the first one they saw. It was an old, brownish photograph of two young parents, and a young girl in a frilly dress. They were just as Ari remembered them.

Abruptly, their legs weakened, their chest grew tight.

They were distracted, however, as the kitchen door creaked, and the distant cousin re-entered once more, with a plastic tray and a small china tea set. Ari hastily set down the photograph back where it had come from.

"I'm sorry, I'd use bigger mugs if we had any," the lady said, and Ari was struck by how apologetic she sounded, as though it was really a problem.

"That's okay," Ari said after a moment's consideration, if only to hide the fleeting embarrassment that they didn't remember what a 'mug' was.

"I've brought some biscuits too. I hope you like custard creams," she continued as she set down the tray onto a small table, nudging a little plate of cream-filled biscuits over to Ari.

Ari's expression brightened for a moment. They nodded, and gratefully leaned forward to pick one up. Ari watched the steam rising from the teapot's spout and then as she poured it, entranced. They engulfed the biscuit in a single bite, and could have wept as they chewed and swallowed. It had been so long since they'd tasted something made by human hands.

By the time their cousin had finished pouring the tea, Ari was already reaching for another.

"You can sit down, you know," she said, with a bemused expression.

Ari's freckled face reddened. A moment later, they were sinking down into a well-worn sofa, feeling the threadbare fabric beneath their weight as they adjusted their position for a moment more. They heard a creak as the plump woman did the same.

"So, you're... a Jameson, right?" she asked, when they were both settled, and Ari had been situated with the saucer on their lap.

Ari tensed. "That's right! Er, you can call me Ari," they said.

"Ari as in... Aria?" the woman pushed.

Ari shifted uncomfortably. They paused, hesitating, as they looked up at the woman, apologetically. "Er, that's right... should I know you? I'm sorry, I don't–"

"Oh no, of course not. Robert was a distant relative, at best. My parents didn't see him or Josephine much after their daughter ran away, so I never knew them well. I'm Carol. You'd be my cousin, I think. Distant cousin."

"Well, it's nice to meet you, Carol."

Other than that, Ari found themself at a loss. After finding out that their father was already gone, Ari had nothing left here. There were no loose ends, no-one they knew. The world had moved on.

Ari's gaze flitted over the boxes, packed ready to be taken away, of all the things that Ari's parents – or, their father at least – had come to own and love over his long lifetime.

"I saw you looking at those old photographs," Carol said, abruptly. "There are a lot that look just like you. But that wouldn't make any sense."

Ari let out a small huff, glancing up at her for an instant with teary-eyed humour. "Believe me, even if you knew the truth, it still wouldn't make any sense."

"So you... are Aria, then? The missing girl?"

"The one and only."

"Where have you been all these years?" Her tone was filled with wonder, as much as with accusation. "*Did* you run away?"

Ari paused. Initially, yes. But they didn't know if they would have stayed away for so long had they remained on Earth.

"I... er... sort-of."

"...Were you kidnapped?"

Ari let out a breath. Now, there was something they could work with. "In a sense, I suppose."

"Who by?"

"Something terrible," Ari said simply. "Something... uncontrollable. I'm... afraid that's all I can say. I probably... won't be here for very long."

Ari looked at their reflection in the teacup on their lap before taking a sip. The taste was different from how they'd romanticised it, over the years. Plainer, somehow, than they were expecting. And yet, still infinitely better. They'd have to ask if they could take a few teabags, for the road ahead.

"Do you want me to call the police?"

Ari looked up, blinking in surprise.

"The police?" they took a few moments to consider, then chuckled. "Not at all. It's not something that you need to worry about."

Carol still looked uncertain; she grunted and eyed them as she took another sip of her tea. Ari supposed that they *had* made their explanation slightly melodramatic. They were good at that. Subtlety had never come easily to them.

Ari supposed it would be helpful to encourage an intelligent species like humanity to begin research on the Rift whilst they could, though. Whilst they were here, Bailey and Ari could help kickstart that. But that didn't need to involve everyone, least of all people that had no need to ever fear the Rift. Ari and Bailey were, after all, two in a million.

"If you're sure," Carol finally said after a long pause. Nonetheless, Ari didn't think she believed them. "I just...

don't know what I'd do if my boys suddenly disappeared one day, without trace."

Ari paused mid-gulp of tea, lowering the teacup a moment later. They didn't respond for a while, but their expression sank and softened, all at once.

"Me too, Carol."

It had only been recently that Ari themself had remembered how it had felt. To be completely cut off from someone, to never know what became of them was worse, infinitely worse, than simply losing someone.

When Ari had killed Oliver, there had been a sense of closure. Grief, perhaps, but closure. When they had gone back to the desert planet, they had found what remained of their children, and now all these years later Ari could finally mourn.

But Robert and Josephine had lived what remained of their lives in fruitless hope, never knowing what had become of their child. And after such a bitter goodbye, Ari knew that they would have always, in some sense, blamed themselves.

But not everyone had to live like that. Some lives could be reclaimed. Some stories could still be told.

Bailey was here, and bound to Ari. Soon, their journey would continue, and he would have to leave it all behind once again. He'd say goodbye to his parents, his grandparents, and everything he'd ever known, quite possibly for good this time.

But maybe… just maybe… there was another option.

Without speaking, Ari gently rested their empty teacup on the table.

They slid a hand into their satchel, and brought out a small and carefully wrapped wad of fabric. They unfurled it to reveal a tiny shard of black crystal, dully gleaming and powerless, the one that they'd stolen from the laboratory.

As they looked at it, turning the gleaming object over in their hands, Ari felt a lump rise in their throat.

With this, it could all be over, and Ari knew they weren't ready for that, nor would they ever be. Leaving so many people and so many worlds behind had made an armoured heart a necessity. And yet, nothing had ever been let go willingly.

Perhaps it was time to make that choice.

As a mentor, and a friend… but most importantly, as a parent.

After all, making that same choice all those years ago would have saved them many years of woe.

As they sat back in their chair, examining it, they cast a sideways glance at the display cabinet full of old photographs, then back towards Carol, who was watching them, full of concern.

"What's gonna be happening to them?"

"Bin, probably. I don't think there's anyone left in the world who'd want them."

"Do you mind if I…?"

"Of course. Take as many as you need."

Ari stood up, and made their way back towards the oak display cabinet. They lifted the photograph that they'd been looking at before, and blew off some of the dust. They looked back towards Carol with blurry eyes.

"Thank you."

• • •

Although Bailey swore he'd been in the Rift for almost a year, it was only late February… just over a month since he'd been first taken away. And as it turned out, they'd missed Ari's parents, but his father's funeral happened to fall on the very next day.

Although Bailey's heart despaired to return to his parents, and his university, to say his goodbyes whilst he still had the chance, Ari begged him to stay for just one more night. The Riftmaster traded in the last of his diamonds for enough money to book a hotel room, and the next morning, set off for the nearby Crosthwaite Church.

Bailey watched him go, trudging out alone into the quiet and frosty morning.

He couldn't imagine how Ari's family would react to seeing him there, especially not dressed like he was. It was hardly appropriate to go to a funeral in lilac clothes and a bright pink cloak and boots; but Bailey said nothing. He could hardly judge someone else's sense of formality.

That being said… it wasn't like either of them had anything better. The few remaining scraps of his Earth clothes had already been put to use elsewhere, to bind wounds, and he needed to save the rest of their money to return home.

Even so, Bailey didn't even want to imagine how he looked to the townspeople… and smelled, for that matter.

The otherworldly musk still clung to his body even after he'd showered the morning away.

Whilst Ari was gone, Bailey called a taxi to pick him up in Keswick and drop him off at the nearest train station. It would arrive at 4pm that day, which gave him just enough time to find the Riftmaster after the funeral.

As he set off, grey skies gave way to a soaking drizzle which clung to his skin and made him shiver. Flora hid in his satchel, where it was warm.

Bailey immediately picked out the Riftmster's silhouette as he walked up the path towards the church. He was standing by himself, and aside from Bailey, was the only figure that could be seen amongst the headstones.

"Hey," Bailey said as he drew near.

Ari looked towards him in surprise. "Hey."

"How did it go?" Bailey asked.

"It was… fine. It was nice seeing my cousins again, even if they weren't sure it was really me. I got to meet their kids, and grandkids. It's… strange to see them so old and grey." The Riftmaster didn't look up at Bailey, his gaze fixed instead on the three tombstones before them, belonging to Robert, Josephine and Aria Jameson. "They said it was amazing to see how little I've changed. They even showed me my own memorial."

He gestured to the one belonging to Aria, by far the most weathered. "It's strange, you know, seeing your own grave."

"I can imagine," Bailey breathed, considering for a moment. It seemed an inappropriate time to make a joke, but… the mood here could use a little brightening. "In a way, though, it's not wrong."

After all, the Aria that his parents had known was long, long gone.

The Riftmaster chuckled at that. "Yeah," he said. "I was thinking the same thing."

"Did they ask where you'd been?"

Ari nodded. "Yeah. I told them I've been travelling the world. I said I'd discovered the secret to immortality in the

Amazon rainforest, and spent the last 60 years protecting it. …I don't think they bought it, but they didn't question it too much. After all… It's not every day someone disappears for 60 years and returns just as young as when they left. If only they knew, eh?"

"Mmm-hm," Bailey chuckled.

They stood in silence for a moment, the only sound the soft pattering of the rain.

"I suppose you'll be wanting to go soon, then?" the Riftmaster asked after a while.

Bailey nodded. "My taxi will be here at 4. Are you coming?"

The Riftmaster shook his head. "Nah. Let's keep things short. I suck at long goodbyes."

"…Goodbyes?" Bailey said in surprise. "But we'll see each other again soon, when we Rift. Right?"

The Riftmaster didn't answer, but he saw the glisten of tears in his mentor's eyes. He smiled, though, a shaky smile. "Naw. I've been thinking, Rifthopper. You've come so far, and learned so much. I think it's high time you spread your wings without this old fart dragging you down. Besides… If I take this, there's less chance of you Rifting before you're finished here on Earth."

The Riftmaster reached out to hold the jewel resting against Bailey's chest, polishing it with his thumb. Bailey's vision grew blurred.

"I suppose so," he wavered. "Thank you, Rif–"

"Please… Call me Ari. You've earned that much."

Bailey nodded. "Thank you, Ari. For everything. Do you really think I'll have what it takes to survive out there? Alone?"

Ari gave a small nod. "I think you always have."

Bailey spread out his arms, and mentor and apprentice exchanged a goodbye hug.

"I'm proud of you, Rifthopper," Ari said, as he held Bailey close.

Bailey felt a lump rise in his throat.

He wondered if he'd ever see the Riftmaster again out there; whether they'd ever end up travelling together again. Whatever the case, it certainly wouldn't be in a single human lifetime. When they finally broke apart, Ari held Bailey at arm's length, and looked into his eyes.

"Just promise me that you'll learn from my mistakes."

Bailey nodded, afraid to speak in case his throat closed up.

Ari finally let go. As Bailey untied the necklace that bound him to his mentor, the Riftmaster withdrew a small leather pouch from his satchel, and held it out to Bailey. "Trade?"

"What's this?" Bailey asked, taking it, and giving his mentor back the jewel.

"My cousins wanted to make sure I got something from my dad's will… not that I have any use for it. If you want, give it to your family. I'm sure they'll appreciate it. Or just trade it for gold… then you can take it into the Rift with you."

Bailey took the pouch, and was about to pull it open when Ari stopped him by placing a hand upon his. "Save it for the journey home," Ari said with a tearful smile.

"Alright then," Bailey said.

He glanced up as the church bells began to toll a mournful tune, marking his time to go.

"Speaking of… the taxi will be here soon, so… I'd better go." He looked reluctantly towards the churchyard's gates, but because of the rain, couldn't tell if anyone was waiting outside. "I'm gonna miss you, Ari."

The Riftmaster nodded, and smiled as they met one another's eyes for the last time.

"I'm gonna miss you too. Take good care of your little friend." He winked down at Flora, who had popped her head out to look up at him from Bailey's satchel. Bailey turned to leave, but a moment later, he hesitated and turned back.

"I… I'll see you round?"

"Maybe… We'll see. Good luck, Bailey."

Bailey looked back only one more time as he left the churchyard, and when he did, the Riftmaster hadn't moved from where he was standing, alone.

By the time he'd climbed into the taxi, and slammed the car door shut behind him, the rain was pouring in icy cold sheets, and he couldn't help but worry for Ari, out there in the cold. But as the taxi pulled away, there was a boom like thunder, and a flash of light from the churchyard.

He heard Flora rattle softly from where she was curled up inside his bag, so Bailey reached out a hand to gently stroke her scales.

"Looks like we're getting a thunderstorm," the taxi driver said, as they began to drive away.

"Yeah, seems like it," Bailey answered. But he knew better.

Once they were on the road, Bailey finally took the time to open the small leather pouch that Ari had given him on their parting. Inside, he found a thick wad of cash, and a tightly folded piece of paper. Bailey rustled around to see if there was anything more, looking for some kind of memento. A tooth, perhaps, or a scrap of fabric. Or perhaps one of the diamonds that Ari had so loved to boast about. But there was nothing… that is, until he unfurled the paper to reveal an old and faded photograph of a girl with a familiar face. When he unravelled it further, a small shard of crystal fell out onto his lap.

Bailey's eyes widened. His breath caught in his throat. He picked up and held the purplish crystal in the palm of his hand and turned it to the light.

Turning the photograph over revealed a note, poorly scrawled and difficult to read, with old-fashioned handwriting.

He felt his eyes well up with tears as he bent his head to read.

Bailey.

My time on Earth has long passed. but that doesn't mean you can't treasure yours. Charge this crystal. and keep it close. Watch your family grow. And then. when your time here is finished. re-enter the Rift.

I'm sure we'll meet again one day.

Good luck. young Riftmaster.

Love. Ari Jameson.

Bailey's hand closed tightly around the crystal, so dark and beautiful even without the power that would hold off the Rift. He turned over the note to look at the girl in the photograph who smiled back at him. Her hair fell to shoulder-length, carefully curled, and her cheeks were lightly freckled. She wore an old-fashioned dress with a floral pattern, which might have been yellow in person but was here, a washed-out grey.

Bailey's gaze was finally drawn to her eyes, which were young and fiery.

...And although Bailey had never known *her,* he knew for certain that he was the only one on Earth to know what became of her.

The End

Acknowledgements

So, here you are, at the very end. The book that began as a simple daydream all the way back in my childhood has is finally made its debut out in the real world. It's been quite the ride, and I hope you enjoyed following Ari and Bailey's journey as much as I did.

Before we go, I'd like to take a moment now to offer my heartfelt gratitude to all the friends, family and loved ones who helped out along the way and brought the book you hold in your hands to life.

First off, to those who read the book back when it was a cluttered disaster of thoughts and words. To the family and friends, parents and grandparents who offered feedback, and questions, and criticisms. To everyone who tore it down so I could put it back together, stronger.

Without those first few voices, *Riftmaster* wouldn't be what it is today. You all know who you are. So, with all my heart, thank you.

I'd also like to express my deepest gratitude to my best man, Taylor, who went through the book, beginning to end, with an editor's eye. They brought their own unique experience and perspective to my book at a time when I needed it the most. And to Alice as well, who asked the questions I never even thought to answer. And finally, a very special thanks to my younger sister Abbie, who was the very first person on earth to follow Bailey's story from beginning to tearful end. I can only hope that there are other readers in the world who love it as much as she does.

Thank you as well to my publisher, Elsewhen Press, for seeing the potential in this humble little book. It's been a lot of fun making it the best it can be! Pete and Sofia listened diligently to all of my crazy ideas and worked with me every step of the way to bring it all to life.

I want to also extend my deepest gratitude to my husband. Chris has been with me from the very beginning. He watched me grow from girl to man, and supported me every step of the way. He has been there since this story was nothing more than an itch at the back of my brain, and has watched it grow from the first word on the page. He's helped me more than he can ever know, talking through ideas and offering honest feedback from beginning to end. Without Chris, *Riftmaster* might not have even existed at all. He always knew it would make its debut one day, and has been waiting patiently since the day I started querying for the day he could hold it in his hands.

Now all he has to do is read it!

Chris... I know you'll make it here eventually, and I can picture the smile on your face when you do. The same smile you gave me when you read this exact same message after you finished the Forge and the Flow.

That's the one!

Finally, thank you to you, the reader, for sticking with me this far. I hope it made you laugh, and cry, and perhaps even question the things you know. But most importantly, I hope you fell in love with it as much as I have.

Thank you so much for reading *Riftmaster*, and I hope to see you again one day!

Miles Nelson
February 2021